CHILD OF MINE

a nostalgic romantic comedy

Boston Classics
Book 4

KAREN GREY

Published by HOME COOKED BOOKS

A division of Jasper Productions, LLC

Cover art and design by Lana Pecherczyk

Subjects: | BISAC: FICTION / Romance / Romantic Comedy.|

FICTION / Romance / Historical / American.|

First edition, December 2021

Content guidance for this book can be found at www.karengrey.com/contentguidance

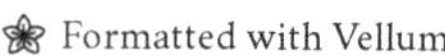 Formatted with Vellum

---

Content Guidance

The content notes below are meant to give readers a generalized view of potentially triggering subjects within this novel.

- Use of expletives: frequent but not mean-spirited
- Sex/Nudity: several sex scenes
- Violence: none
- Death: main character's parent
- Drugs and alcohol use: main character (in the past)

If you'd like a more detailed list of content warnings (which may include spoilers) they are available at:

https://www.karengrey.com/contentguidance

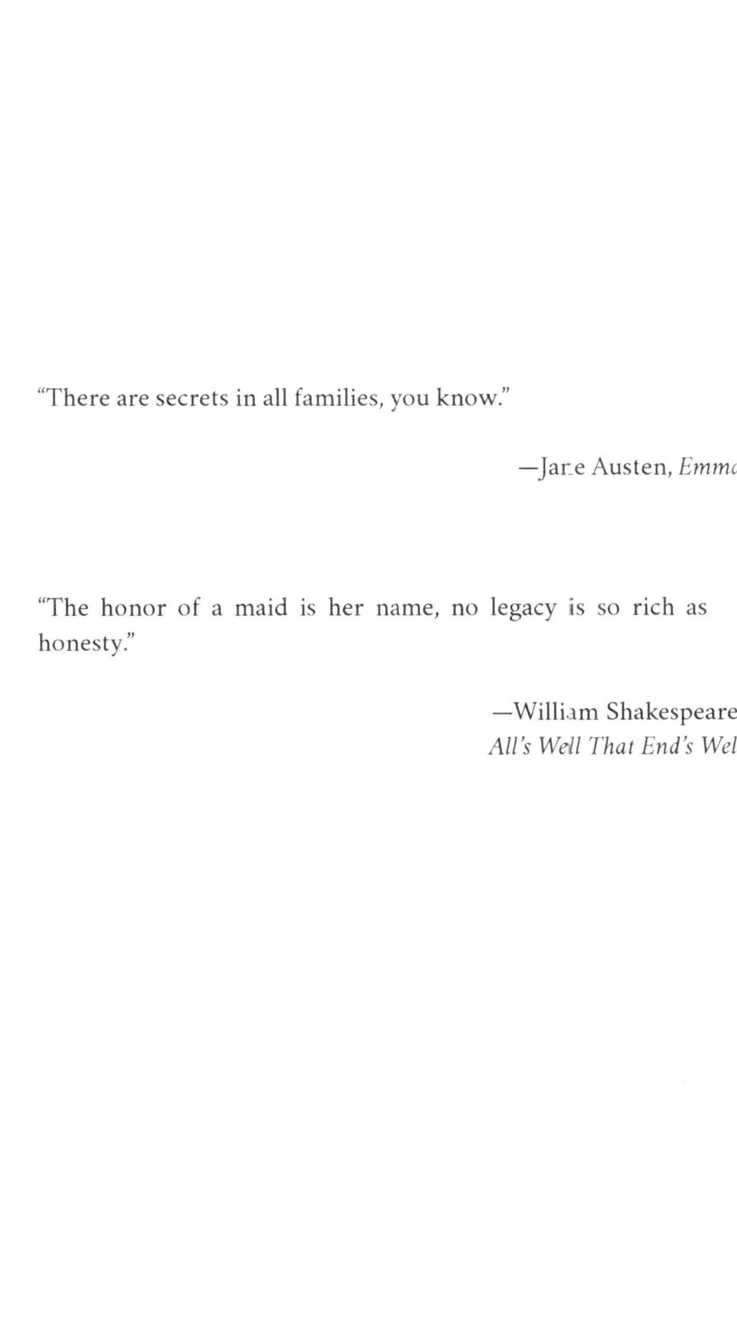

"There are secrets in all families, you know."

—Jane Austen, *Emma*

"The honor of a maid is her name, no legacy is so rich as honesty."

—William Shakespeare,
All's Well That End's Well

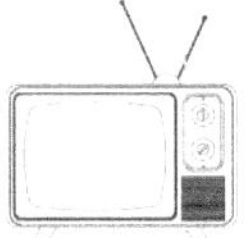

Prologue

1982

"SERIAL UPDATES: Actress Isabelle York had a nice run on *As the Earth Revolves*. In fact, she found herself to be quite popular as the incorrigible villainess Quinn Carter. She won't say why she's leaving the show, just that she looks forward to some projects she's keeping under her hat for now. She did confess to me that "If I couldn't act, I couldn't live!" We wish her well in her promising future…" *Daytime TV News*, November 1982

BELLA

I've put off cleaning out this dressing room for a couple of reasons. One, it's been my home away from home for the past nine years. Two, I'm kind of afraid of what I'll find.

I'm not worried about dust bunnies or mildewed makeup sponges lurking in the corners—the TV network's cleaning staff is too thorough to leave anything like that behind. It's the tokens of past selves that might be tucked beneath fan mail in drawers, between shoeboxes on the shelves, or behind the boxes of wigs. My villainous character Quinn donned a variety of disguises when she snuck around trying to poison, kidnap, entrap, or you-name-it other characters in the soap-opera town of Elmwood.

Surprisingly, though, the process is somewhat therapeutic. When I come across an old marketing photo from my days on the kids' show *Boom*, it's hard to believe the girl in the photo is me. Izzy, the name I went by back then, was thirteen when she wowed the cameras on *Boom*'s very first season and had girls across the country working on their back walkovers.

She—that is, me—was an innocent. A free spirit. Fun.

Loveable.

All things this twenty-three-year-old hasn't felt for a long time. My public persona, Isabelle York, may be wrapping up a successful soap opera career with what my agent calls good prospects for a leap to prime-time TV, but my heart is as selfish and self-destructive as Quinn Carter's. Being in the public eye during one's formative years will do that to a girl.

I consider hanging onto the Izzy memento for about three seconds before balling it up and tossing it into the garbage. Angry letters to Quinn I thought were funny when I first got them go in there, too. I'm ready to trash both identities because neither has served me terribly well. Izzy—too optimistic. Quinn—too hedonistic.

"Isabelle" is the name on my résumé, but the name I adopted last year feels more me. Initially, I used it to keep my presence in rehab a secret, but since my return to the real world a few months ago, I've been wondering if "Bella" is the name I could be a grown-up with. I've been a party girl since I was fifteen, even while working full-time. Maybe it's time to be responsible. Reliable.

Boring!

The voice in my head that cuts off my own thoughts? That's Quinn talking. I guess she's not quite ready to be packed away with all these pretty clothes.

As I drag a hand over the rack of outfits sheathed in plastic, I have to admit that I'll miss network-funded shopping trips to the private room at Saks Fifth Avenue, but maybe the next job will offer me something even more glamorous. Before I gear up for pilot season in LA, though, I have amends to make. My mom is at the top of the list, so I've promised to spend the time between Thanksgiving and New Year's helping her at the family bookstore. Away from the prying eyes of the gossip rags, I certainly won't need heels and sequins.

Once I've dragged the bags of trash out to the hallway, I take a quick shower, do my hair and makeup—all by myself for a change—and don a simple green dress. Long-sleeved, but with a flattering neckline and a stretchy fabric that hugs minimal curves.

Daytime TV News blast: "Isabelle York is still too skinny! Give that girl a milkshake."

Thinking how refreshing it'll be to have a break from the constant attention from the gossip pages, I take a last scan of the room, tuck my bag away, and gear up to make an appearance at the network's annual anniversary party. It not only kicks off the holiday season, it's the only time we actors have access to the writers. Get one drunk enough and she'll reveal upcoming character twists. Or be susceptible to a suggestion or two. I'm pretty sure that's how Quinn ended up switching the paternity test results of her baby's with her sister's.

The fallout of that escapade was a lot more fun than I'd like to admit.

However, playing a villain is one thing. Acting the villain in real life—well, I'm lucky I made it out alive. With that little reminder, I lock my past and the door behind me.

What I'm still not quite ready for? Getting through a work party without a drink. Or a pill. Or a line. I've only been back from rehab for a few months, after all. But I'm an actress. Maybe I'll pretend to be drunk. Or maybe I'll play the role of a confident young woman ready for the next chapter in her life. Pull up some of that Izzy energy, that girl the camera loved enough to rocket her from after-school-kid-show phenom to soap opera stardom.

Life's an adventure is what long-lost Izzy would say.

Life's a bitch and then you die would be Quinn's line.

Whatever you want to call it—an adventure or a bitch—it's all a game. As I stride into the sea of humanity that is a major network shebang, I channel both Izzy's goodwill and Quinn's nerve. I'm leaving chin high, no tail between my legs. They didn't fire me. I'm just ready for something new.

Nodding and smiling, dodging the waiters and their trays of champagne, I make it through exactly seven and a half meaningless conversations. After squelching the memory of my first unchaperoned network party at age sixteen—of being handed cocktails and getting just drunk enough to make it something I wanted to do again—I decide I deserve a break.

Instead of fighting my way back through the overheated room, I head for the little hidden balcony where I can literally chill out for a few minutes. But after I slip through the door—a No Exit sign has never been a barrier for a rule breaker like me—I have to stifle a gasp of surprise. Someone else has found my escape hatch, and he's using it to do what looks like an extremely silly victory dance.

HENRY

I know this party isn't for me, but it sure feels like it.

Who'd've thought a Carolina boy with a state-school degree could beat out not one, not two, but *three* other guys—all of whom have Park Avenue parents and Ivy League educations—for the highly coveted spot of assistant producer on the hottest investigative news program in the biggest of the big apples?

Not an assistant *to* a producer, mind you. *That* I've slogged away at for the past half of a year. *That* was several steps up from my first job as a page. Now, I'll be running down my own stories. And before you know it, I'll be producing my own segments.

Creating my own shows.

Running my own damn network.

Right now, though? I'm about to burst. I've nodded and smiled and accepted congratulations from so many people I need to take a run around the block. I also need to call home and tell my parents about the promotion. My dad never understood why I'd want to leave a perfectly good city like Raleigh, why I didn't join the family landscaping empire like my siblings have. I can't wait to tell him that despite his lack of faith, despite his opinion that—how did he put it?

You're just spinning your wheels up there, wasting time and money.

Before I tell him just how wrong he was, I need a moment to myself to sit with the news, and I know just the spot. There's a hidden balcony off this ballroom where I've escaped multiple times over the past two years. I swear the architect added it as a joke. Tucked between a stairwell and a garbage chute lies a gem of a spot with a view any exec would die for.

After dropping off a half-finished glass of bubbly on a server's tray, I slip out the secret door. With all of New York spread out in front of me, I can't help it. Fist in the air, I let out a "Yes!" and kick up my heels like I just ran the length of the football field to score a touchdown, dodging the other team's defense the entire way.

Life is just too good not to celebrate.

■

BELLA

I really should go back inside, say a few goodbyes, and finally get out of this place. The fact that someone else has found my sanctuary is probably a sign that I really am done here. Instead, I'm spellbound watching this nut dance.

I could join him, throw my body around in that goofy, herky-jerky way too. But I'm always afraid now. Afraid of losing hard-won control. Afraid of calling attention to myself and having whatever embarrassing thing I've done spread across the pages of *Soap Chat* or *TV Tattler*.

Will I ever be able to let go of these fears? Will moving on to prime-time TV or movies just make it worse?

"Hey! Look at that! A beautiful woman on my secret balcony!"

His drawl is charming, but he's obviously been drinking, so I give him a polite wave and beat it for the door.

"Nooo. No, don't leave. I just—agh!"

His entreaty is cut off by a thud behind me. *Just keep going,* I tell myself.

But he's so sexy, Quinn's voice sighs. *And what if he fell off the roof? Wouldn't you feel terrible?*

Quinn can be a master manipulator, so I probably shouldn't turn around. But I do, just to make sure he's okay.

After brushing off the seat of his pants, his grin is sheepish. "Oops."

I'd kiss that mug, Quinn says.

Squashing that dangerous thought, I keep my voice politely distant. "Are you okay? Can I get you some help?"

Hands on his hips, he just grins. "Nah, I'm fine. My buddies inside poured me a few shots and I came out here to escape and"—he sweeps an arm through the air—"can you believe this view? It's like I'm in my own movie. I just got the job of my dreams, and New York before the holidays is like a fairy land and—Hey! Dance with me!"

With Quinn shouting *Hell yeah* in my ear, I have to make myself take a step back. "I'm good, thanks."

Despite my tone and the frown I'm wearing to match it, he takes another step closer. When the light falls across the planes of his face, I'm treated to quite a view, like somebody mixed Kurt Russell with Leif Garrett and served up a perfect blend of both. High cheekbones and a strong jaw delineated by an amber-tinted beard, hair that curls over his temple in an effortlessly sexy way, and eyes that match them both. Desire flares for an instant, but then his expression shifts from delight to recognition.

Shit. He's a fan. Alone with a Quinn admirer on a hidden balcony? Not good.

"Oh. My. God," he whispers.

The reverence in his voice has me stepping back faster, right into a large planter. Brushing branches out of my way, I step to the side to get around it, but he grabs my hand. When I snatch it away from him, his go up in surrender. "I'm sorry. I just can't believe it. You're *Izzy*."

My childhood nickname on his lips stirs to life the girl who wouldn't hesitate to dance on a rooftop in the moonlight.

"You were my first crush. Ever." When he takes a step back and raises a single brow, the smile that takes over his face could talk me into anything. "Dance with me?"

I don't remember saying yes or no. He holds out a hand, I float into his arms, and we're dancing. Waltzing. I can practically hear a Viennese orchestra. Adding to the magic of the moment: I've never been held like this. Respectfully. *Gentlemanly*. No grabbing or groping. Sure contact at my waist and a gentle palm guiding me through the small space.

It's sexy as hell.

Before I can say a word, he stops, steps back, and bows. Like it's 1782 instead of 1982. When he meets my gaze, his eyes are clear. "Thank you. For a perfect end to a perfect day.

I just stand there, muted by surprise. He's almost to the door by the time I manage a "Wait!"

And then Quinn takes over. "Wanna fool around, big guy?"

HENRY

Hey, I'm not one to look a gift horse in the mouth, so I nod and let this gorgeous wisp of a woman grab my hand—hers small in mine but surprisingly strong—and tug me toward a door I hadn't noticed before.

"Where are you taking me?"

Her eyebrows waggle, making her more Goldie Hawn than Cheryl Tiegs for a moment. "Wouldn't you like to know?" She presses a finger to my lips, setting off an electric buzz that zings directly south.

You'd think six months as a page giving tours of this iconic New York building would mean that I knew all her secrets, but Izzy—I still can't believe that it's her, the girl that literally gave me my first wet dream—leads me through hallways I didn't know existed. We're sparingly lit by the bare bulbs, so our shadows are long on the stained concrete. "How did you know about this back route?"

She slips me a secret smile. "I've worked here a long time."

"Right out of school, huh?" If she's my age, a long time can only be a couple years.

"Pretty much." Her eyes shutter briefly, but she grips my hand more firmly. "Almost there."

A metal door leads us to a loading bay, which opens into the scene shop. Now I know where we are. She picks up the pace as we cross the enormous space. When we reach the other side, she bites her lip and tries a door that I know leads to the costume shop. "Damn. I thought maybe we could cut through. We'll have to go another way."

"If you tell me where we're headed, maybe I can help. I used to be a page."

"You were?" She narrows her eyes at me. "I never saw you."

"Where do you work, anyway?"

"Never mind." Tugging on my hand again, she pulls me toward the door that leads back into the public realm. In the small reception area outside the shops, we run into a security guard. He flicks a questioning gaze at me. "Everything all right, miss?"

The smile she flashes the older man is respectful but familiar. "All good, Charlie. I'm just picking up a couple things."

He purses his lips as he gives me another assessing look. "You take care of yourself, sweetheart."

"Always."

He doesn't say a word as she marches through the doorway to the dressing rooms—forbidden territory for tours. There's a dummy dressing room that we'd show off, but I've never seen the real ones. Stars need their privacy.

"Are you on a show here?" I'm in the news division, and I rarely watch the other daytime or primetime fare the station churns out.

Her step falters, but she responds with a "Pfft. Just because I was on *Boom* for a season? Nah, I'm a—Hang on." She opens the door to an office and reaches under the cushion of a chair. "People are creatures of habit. This is where Nancy always hides her… Ah, got 'em." She holds up a ring heavy with keys. "For a script supervisor who's supposed to be on top of all the details, she's super lax."

"Are we breaking and entering?"

"It's not breaking and entering if you have the key, is it?"

Moments later, she's unlocking a dressing room door that, unlike the others we passed, isn't labelled with an actor's name. She flicks on a lamp instead of the overhead lights, tosses the keys on the counter, pulls me all the way inside, reaches around me to lock the deadbolt, and then crowds me up against the door until there's nothing between us but fabric.

"You are something," I say with what little air is left in my lungs, her touch amplifying the feeling that anything is possible.

"Shhh." When she presses her index finger to my lips, I can only lean in to her touch. "I happen to know that this actress is leaving," she whispers with a conspiratorial grin. "She's all packed up and out of here, so let's take advantage of that. As much advantage as humanly possible."

This day just keeps getting better.

·

BELLA

Just once, just once let me have my way with a guy in real life, Quinn whispers.

At least, I think it's her. Something about this guy has resuscitated parts of me that I thought my drug-filled days and nights buried six feet under. But I'm aware of every inch of my skin, of heat building in my core, of the need to be touched. Simply being held by—"Wait. What's your name?"

He grins. "I wondered if you were ever going to ask. Hal. Hal—"

I stop his lips with mine before pulling back to say, "Let's just keep it to first names."

He frowns, so I add a brow waggle. "More fun that way."

That's what I want—no deserve—right now. Pure fun. Simple desire. To enjoy the physical pleasures of sex while completely sober.

Which would be a first, Quinn notes.

Banishing that thought—and all thought for that matter—I unbutton his coat and press my breasts against hard pecs. Strong hands glide down my back. When they stop inches above my ass, I grind my hips into his.

Before he can ask or say anything that might break this spell, I cover his mouth with mine again. This time, slightly chapped lips open to give me room to roam. Tug. Devour. Then, finally, he gives as good as he gets.

When he breaks the kiss, panting, his light brown irises are almost entirely eclipsed by black-as-night pupils. Grasping both sides of his face, I whisper, "I want more of... whatever that was on the roof. Just touch me how you touched me when we were dancing. But with our clothes off. Can we just do that? No talking?"

I give him a few seconds before taking his silence as permission, then shove the sport coat off broad shoulders. He wriggles out of it while I unbutton his shirt, but before I get to the bottom, he stops my shaking fingers.

"Wait, how old *are* you?"

I can't help but roll my eyes. "I'm in my twenties."

"Oh, same as me." Thankfully, he finishes taking off the dress shirt. "I guess since I saw you on *Boom,* I think of you as younger..."

"I'm getting older by the minute, mister." After pointing at the undershirt and pants he's still wearing, I lower the side zipper of my dress and ease my arms out of its sleeves. "One request, though. Don't talk about this. To anyone, ever. Okay? If you do, I will find you and... do something bad to you."

Saluting me, he grins before taking off his T-shirt. "I never kiss and tell."

"I want more than kissing," I say as I shimmy the clingy fabric down my torso and past my hips. "But absolutely no telling."

He stares wordlessly at the skimpy bits of lace covering my non-existent butt and boobs. Not sure what he thinks of what he sees, but I'm loving my own view. I've been up close and personal with the naked chests of some of the hottest young studs of daytime TV, but this one beats them all. Golden skin with a dusting of tawny curls. Tight pecs and ridged abs. My fingers ache to appreciate the contrast of soft skin and hard muscle, but he stops them mid-reach. "I would like to get to know you a little before going further, if that's okay."

I shake my head. "You know the best version of me: that girl you watched on TV every weekday afternoon. My body may have changed since I was thirteen, and I may have learned a few tricks since then, but believe me, the rest of me isn't worth getting to know."

"I'm sure that's not true."

"Believe me, it is." When both your parents leave you in the lurch before you turn sixteen, you know better than to believe in fairy tales.

His grip on my shoulders is firm, but his eyes still carry uncertainty. "I just want you to be comfortable."

Turning in his arms, I capture his hands to press one over a breast, the other atop the lace barely covering my heated center. Leaning back, arching my neck so that I can nip at his jaw, I whisper, "I just want you to blow my mind."

Chapter 1

"Our two actresses tied for Best Actress in *Soap Chat*'s annual poll are good friends and enjoy each other's company off-camera as well as on the set of *One Way to Live*. Each was delighted to share the trophy and will celebrate with a picnic together!" *Soap Chat*, May 1989

BELLA

The Sunday of Memorial Day weekend, as my daughter and I drive to a suburb west of Boston, the sun warming the car is a welcome reassurance that winter's truly over. After we locate the blocked-off street and park nearby, Lilah helps me find the right house. She then insists on ringing the doorbell herself. After a few moments, a freckle-faced redhead with a toddler on her hip opens the door.

"Hey, you must be Bella and Delilah. I'm Penny, Cal's sister. We're so glad you guys could come!" Ushering us inside, she gestures at a living room where every surface is covered with toys. "You can set your stuff in here before you head out to the street. There are tons of kids at the block party already." Squatting so that she's eye to eye with Lilah, she adds, "Don't worry. I know a big girl like you doesn't want to play with a baby like Danny here. He has cousins that are older, and there are all ages in the neighborhood. Do you want me to introduce you to some of them?"

"No, thank you," Lilah says politely. "I'm gregarious."

Straightening, Penny shoots a brows-up look at me before addressing my little word sponge. "Um, I think that means you're not shy?"

"That is correct. Also, I prefer Lilah." Lilah nods solemnly. The way she does everything.

Penny's monologue seems to have run out, so I steer Lilah toward the living room. "Let's find a spot for your bag, and then you'll know where to find it in case you want to take a break and read."

"How old is she?" Penny mutters under her breath.

"I'm five and three quarters," Lilah says over her shoulder. After handing her plaid backpack to me—no toy themes for this girl—she turns back to Penny. "I grew up in a bookstore, so I like to read."

"Good for you." Penny nods. "Maybe you can teach Danny here."

When the toddler pulls his thumb from his mouth and slaps his mother on the cheek, Lilah winces. "Maybe."

Bouncing Danny, Penny walks us to the front door. "I was just about to put him down for an N-A-P, but Cal and Jess are out there somewhere. If I know Cal, he's probably monitoring the waterslide to make sure the kids are being safe. Did you bring a suit, Lilah?"

"I have it on already." Lilah lifts her T-shirt to reveal her one-piece. "Also, as soon as he learns to read, you won't be able to hide things from him by spelling."

"That is an excellent point." Penny points a finger at her. "I will keep him ignorant as long as possible."

Taking my daughter's hand, I start down the front steps of Penny's house. "Thanks for letting us stow our stuff here, Penny."

"Anytime," she calls over a loud yowl from Danny.

After Penny shuts the door and we head toward the crowd of people down the block, Lilah squeezes my hand. "Don't worry, Mommy. It'll be fun."

I make a pooh-pooh gesture so over-the-top I'd never get away with it onstage. "Who's worried?"

Her expression makes it clear she's not buying it.

"Okay, okay, you're right. I wish I were as outgoing as you." I put an arm around her and hug her into my side. "But I'll be fine."

What my daughter doesn't know is that when I was a kid, I was even more of an extrovert than she is. Driven by an unquenchable need for the next high—achieved at first through novel experiences, then risk-taking, and finally, sex, drugs, and alcohol—only rock 'n roll was left off the list of my adventures.

These days, I pretend to be an introvert. Makes it easier to keep temptation at bay and to hide from the consequences of past poor choices. Just like on stage, it's more comfortable for me to play a role than myself.

For instance, today I'll play the role of laid-back but responsible single mom. I'll keep an eagle eye on my daughter while pretending not to. The waterslide is at the other end of the block, so I smile and nod at the people who look up as we pass. In this suburban neighborhood outside of Boston, every single family seems to consist of a mom and a dad and at least two children. Probably a dog and a cat and a canary, to boot.

Lilah has been excited about coming to this block party ever since Cal invited us. She not only has a huge crush on him, she's adopted his girlfriend Jess as her auntie. Cal's family is just like the one she's always wanted—like the families she's read about in books, with uncles and aunts and grandparents and cousins. And fathers.

None of which my little girl has ever had.

Briefly, an image of her father flashes in my mind. What if he hadn't disappeared without a goodbye? Would he be walking down this street at my side, helping me watch out for our little girl, his palm on my hip a promise of things we might do later?

As lovely as all that sounds, that's not my reality, so I pack it away. If I've learned one thing in this life so far, it's that there's only one person I can truly rely on, and that's me.

Besides, what Lilah doesn't know can't hurt her.

"MOMMY, THERE THEY ARE!" Dropping my hand, Lilah sprints away from me to tackle Tami and Abby. Jess's nieces are a couple of years older than my daughter and treat her more like a doll than a friend, but Lilah seems to love the attention.

"Hey, everything okay?" Jess interrupts my thoughts as I approach the group.

Shaking my head and pasting on a smile, I say, "I'm fine. Just being a worrywart." I tip my chin at the clutch of girls jumping up and down in excitement. "I'm still not sure the sleepover tonight is a good idea. She's never had one before, and I'd hate for your nieces to get tired of Lilah just as she's falling for them."

Jess gives me a side hug. "My sister's a pro, treats kids at her practice all day and still never loses it with those two."

"And your nieces are such nice girls. I'm sure I'm just having jitters. Not ready for my baby to leave the nest."

"I thought you'd be more worried about the dog-and-pony show we have to put on at the fundraiser tonight."

"Ugh. Thanks for reminding me."

"You know our scene and our delightful personalities will charm the money right out of those Shakespeare Boston donor pockets." She links arms with me. "Have I told you how much I love playing your sister? It's much more fun squabbling onstage with you than fighting with my real-life one."

Like daughter, like mother, I guess, because I find myself wishing Jess *were* my sister. She's become the next best thing: my closest friend. I wonder, though, would she like me so much if she knew everything there is to know about me? The things that didn't make it into the gossip pages, as well as the ones that did?

"Hey, how's my second-favorite Boston actress?"

After this greeting, I'm enveloped in a warm hug from Cal Alonso. Even though I've spent a lot of time with him since he and Jess got together, it still throws me every time the voice and the body come together. It's not the scars that cover the left side of his body. It's that I listened to him on the radio for years before meeting him in person, and I'm still a little starstruck… the way some soap opera fans feel about me, I suppose. It's been a few years since someone recognized me at the grocery store, but between my time on the PBS show *Boom* and the soap, I was on TV and in the public eye for ten years. Ten long years.

"You ladies should eat, fuel up for tonight," Cal says, steering us toward the food tables.

It's a relief that he and Jess aren't drinking. Jess wouldn't since we have to perform tonight, but I really appreciate that Cal isn't popping a beer either since he's the one driving the girls back to Boston.

With one eye on Lilah, now running toward the waterslide— *where did she leave her clothes and can we find them again?*—I fill my plate. "Cal, you should've told me it was a potluck. I would've brought something."

"Penny says there's always way too much food at this shindig. Don't worry about it."

We settle on some folding chairs and watch the kids on the slide. A couple of dads are supervising, making sure everything's safe, so I let myself relax. "Man, I don't remember the last time I had fried chicken. This is so good."

"Same here," Jess says. "Literally finger-lickin' good."

"Any of that for me?" Cal asks.

She swats him away. "Get your own!"

When he makes a pouty face, she groans before giving him a wing. "He's got me trained better than his damn dog." After finishing her own, she wipes her hands on a napkin. "I'm ready for dessert, anyway. If you two are lucky, maybe I'll bring you some."

Cal shoots a smile at me. We're both glad to see that Jess has gained some weight back. Her time in therapy seems to be paying off. The look on his face as he watches her skip away is a testament to the work they've both put into the relationship. They might've had a rocky start, but it's clear they're good for each other. I can't imagine letting a guy into my complicated life, but I'm glad it's working for them.

"I have a confession to make," Cal says.

When he doesn't continue, I intone, "'How many days since your last confession?' Is that what I'm supposed to say next?"

He laughs. "Don't tell my mom, but it's been so long since I went to mass I've forgotten the script."

"Your secret's safe with me." I circle a hand in the air between us. "Go on, get it off your chest. I'm sure I've done worse."

"I don't know if you noticed, but when we first met, I was probably a bit cold to you."

Furrowing my brow, I try to remember. "Maybe. I figured you were probably just shy."

He shrugs. "I am still working on letting go of self-consciousness about my scars, you know, not assuming that it's the only thing a person sees when they meet me."

"Well, I was probably awkward too. Every time you open your mouth, I expect to hear music."

He laughs. "Guess I should carry a boombox with me."

A squeal from Lilah has me rising out of my chair, but when I find her face in the crowd and see that she's laughing, I sit back down again. "Sorry. What was it you wanted to confess?"

The right side of his mouth lifts in a lopsided, sheepish grin. "When I saw you for the first time, all I could see was Quinn."

"You watched *As the Earth Revolves*?" I do a quick calculation. "Wouldn't you have been in school when it was on?"

"I missed a lot of school recovering from surgeries. It was my mom's favorite soap. We both hated you." He leans in close to whisper, "I actually had nightmares about you."

I wince. "I'm sorry. I promise I'll never reveal that you slept with my sister."

"Or kidnap me?"

"Or force you to rob a bank with me."

"Or convince everyone that I'm possessed by the devil?"

All I can do is shake my head at the memories. "Man, the older I got, the more outlandish Quinn's capers were."

"It's probably a compliment to you that they thought you could carry it off."

I shrug, my cheeks heating at the praise. "I don't know about that."

He folds up his paper plate and the remains of his meal. "Anyway, the first few times we met, I really had to convince myself that you're not like her."

Adopting Quinn's blunt tone, I ask, "How do you know I'm not?"

After a theatrical shudder, he points at Jess, engaged in chat with another guest. "Because that one loves you." Nodding at my daughter, now running around with a bunch of kids shooting each other with water guns, he adds, "And you made that one."

"Maybe I've got you all fooled." When I let loose with Quinn's signature cackle, he crosses his forearms over his face.

"No, no! Not the laugh!"

We're both howling with genuine laughter by the time Jess sits down, balancing a towering selection of desserts on her lap. "I don't even want to know," she says. "All I want is this chocolate cake."

She only takes a bite before drawing a line in the air between us with her fork. "Okay, I lied. What were you two laughing at?" She twists in her chair. "Do I have a sign on my back or toilet paper stuck to my shoe or something?"

"Nah, sweetheart." Cal rubs her shoulder, and she relaxes into his touch, practically purring like a cat. "Bella was just torturing me with her Quinn laugh."

"You brought it up!" I protest.

Jess offers up her plate of goodies for sharing, and after I take a cookie she says, "I don't think I ever saw you on the soap, but I loved *Boom*. It was so cool to see kids like me doing skits and singing songs that other kids sent in. I wanted to audition, but the shooting times conflicted with dance and Hebrew."

After taking another bite of cake, she tips her head to the side. "You know, I never told you this before, but I didn't even know that was you. Izzy, I mean. I knew you were on the soap because Becky told me when you auditioned for the company the first time. But I wouldn't have recognized you otherwise."

It's not easy to keep the corners of my mouth turned up. "I was a lot younger then."

"It's not just your age." Jess shakes her head. "You have a completely different energy. Izzy was so…"

"Innocent?" I finish when she doesn't.

"Mm, maybe. More carefree, I guess."

"Being a mom kind of piles the cares on." No need to mention the choices I made that snuffed out that Izzy energy in me.

Cal leans in. "I'm just glad she's not as scheming and evil as Quinn."

"How evil was she?" Jess asks.

As Cal details Quinn's sensational schemes, I egg him on. Better than talking about my real-life problems. By the time he's finished, the pile of sweets on Jess's plate has disappeared and I've relaxed again. Mostly. Quinn may have been a villain but playing her was fun. Until it wasn't anymore.

After scanning the crowd to make sure Lilah's okay, I flop back into the webbing of my folding chair. "Ugh. Now I'm stuffed."

Everyone goes quiet for a few minutes, and I sit back to enjoy the warm sun on my face. The background hum of people chatting, punctuated by the occasional shout from a kid going down the slide, calms any remaining agitation.

My mood is as tranquil as the setting when Cal asks, "So, are you guys excited for tonight? Nervous?"

"Both," Jess says.

"Yep," I agree with a groan.

"I'm more nervous performing in rep than doing our scene tonight," Jess adds. "You're lucky you're only doing one show, Bella."

When my mom talked me into auditioning for Shakespeare Boston last summer, I told them I could only do one play a season. Not only do I want to be around for Lilah, but I help out at my mom's bookshop.

"I've never rotated between two shows like you do in repertory," Jess continues. "I keep having nightmares that I go onstage in *The Tempest* wearing my *Comedy of Errors* costume."

Even though they fight like cats and dogs most of the time, directors Nick and Mira managed to convince the company powers-that-be to try out a repertory schedule this summer, arguing that tourists will get a chance to see both shows if they're playing every other night.

"At least you don't have to worry about the lines," I point out. Jess's memory is like a steel trap. She only has to do a scene once and she's got her lines down pat. "I swear, the older I get, the harder it is for me to hang onto my words. I don't think my brain could handle learning two shows at once."

"You might be relieved of your excuse sooner than you think." Jess tips her head toward the slide. "My nieces look like they're ready to adopt her."

My gaze follows Jess's pointed finger. The three girls pose for a photo, which has me instantly on alert. So far, I've managed to keep Lilah out of the public eye, but anybody can sell a photo to the tabloids. When I see that it's Penny taking the picture, my heart slows.

It is a sweet shot. My little fair-skinned, blue-eyed girl is flanked by Abby and Tami, who, like their aunt, have golden-brown skin and jet-black hair. Tami's face is rounder, framed by corkscrews as wild as Jesse's. Abby's hair is long and straight, and she's tall enough that she has to bend down to get in the frame.

"My sister's a pretty good photographer," Cal says. "Since they always give you double prints these days, I'll get you a copy."

Moment captured, the girls are off again, this time to the food table. I do my best to convince myself that Lilah is safe at this party full of strangers, but the fear that my daughter will someday have to pay for the sins of her mother is a hard one to let go of.

So far, Lilah's the one thing I haven't screwed up.

■

JESS CATCHES a ride with me back to Boston and the gala since Cal is driving the girls back to Esther's house. When I ask her how therapy is going, I'm awed by how brave she is. Not only is she facing her inner demons, but she freely shares her struggles with me. She's talking a mile a minute while my own thoughts crowd her words, but one phrase snags my complete attention.

"Wait, what did you just say? About the voice in your head? Sorry, I think I was zoning out."

She laughs. "I totally geek out when I talk about this stuff."

"No judgement here. I'm just curious. Have you ever named the voices in your head?"

She tips her head to the side as she considers. "I don't name them. But I do have a picture for the one I'm wrestling with now. She looks like this ballerina doll I had as a kid. Perfect body, perfect bun, always on point. She's super mean. My therapist is helping me figure out how to listen to her without getting hurt or angry."

"What does she say?"

"Mostly stuff about women's bodies. Like I'll be behind someone in the grocery checkout, and she'll tick off everything wrong with the poor woman's body—saggy butt, fat rolls around the bra straps—"

"Damn. Remind me never to stand in front of you in line."

She sighs. "First of all, you have pretty much the ideal body in her book. Second of all, she's harsher with me. I'm not sure if it's worse if I see a woman she thinks is perfect or someone she thinks is a mess. For the one, she picks me apart and tells me how I'll never be perfect. For the other, she tries to convince me that I'm headed in that direction."

"Wow. I thought mine were bad."

"What do yours say?"

Why did you bring this up? one of the voices in my head asks.

Who cares what she thinks? the other counters.

I glance over at my friend. I've never really had a girlfriend like Jess. The actresses I worked with in New York felt more like rivals. Later, after I had Lilah, my efforts to make mommy friends met with little success. I'd reach out to moms who came into our shop or who I saw at the park, but I always felt like I didn't quite fit in, like the groups formed at some previous stage I missed. They were all married and knew each other from church or their other kids' schools. They'd pepper me with questions about working on TV, which made me uncomfortable. Or they'd make backhanded comments about Lilah not having a dad.

So I gave up.

But Jess has found her way into my heart. She's trusted me with her secrets. Maybe I can trust her with mine.

"You still with me?" Jess asks.

I shake my head to clear it. "Sorry, I get lost inside my head sometimes."

With an easy laugh, she says, "Tell me about it."

Swallowing past the panic that rises whenever I crack open the door I slammed shut after I had Lilah—the only way I could figure out how to protect her from my past—I make myself say, "I've always been fascinated by how other people's brains work. Wondering if anyone's is at all like mine."

"Me too. It's one of the things I love about acting," she says. "Like you get to try out being in a different brain. A different set of thought patterns, different emotional habits."

"True," I agree, deciding to just jump in the deep end. "So, when I was on the soap, I was a bit of a party girl."

Ha! That's putting it mildly, the party girl herself says.

"Surrounded by hot guys, I can imagine," Jess says.

"Yep. That and a lot of other temptations."

You can't tell her about the addictions, the good girl warns. *You're not allowed.*

She's right, but I think I can skate over the details and still get Jess's opinion. "I was also pretty much unsupervised after I hit sixteen, and I had a hard time figuring out what was right and what was wrong. At some point, it was like my conscience split in two."

"Like an angel and devil in the old cartoons?"

"Kind of like that, yeah. One didn't want me to do anything risky, and the other wanted to take *all* the risks. I ended up kind of reeling from one extreme to the other—staying out all night and then feeling bad about it and working really hard to be good."

"That must've been a little crazy-making." Jess's voice is full of compassion.

Unlike the mom group, she's not pressing me for sordid details, which makes me want to tell her more. "You could say that. At some point..."

In rehab, a voice sing-songs.

But she can't say that, the other cuts in.

"I, uh, named them," I confess.

"Oh, that's an excellent idea," Jess says. "I should name mine. What do you call them?"

"I call the virtuous one Izzy."

"Like you when you were a teenager?" She nods slowly. "I can see that."

"Yeah? It sounds kind of crazy when I say it out loud."

"Uh-uh." Eyes on the road, I catch a firm headshake in my peripheral vision. "I think my therapist would say it's healthy. What about the other one? The naughty one."

"She's Quinn. I mean, half the people I partied with called me that anyway. It was easier not to correct them."

"Wow. That's perfect. So, your preadolescent self and the character you played for... how many years?"

"Nine."

"That's a long time to live in a character's head." She faces me, tucking her left leg under her. "You must've given her some sort of backstory, right? To motivate all that bad behavior?"

That's right, Quinn sniffs. *I'm not just a mean girl. I'm a risk taker. It's good to take risks sometimes.*

I took risks too, Izzy insists.

Quinn rolls her eyes. *In gymnastics.*

Ignoring their bickering, I focus on Jess's question. "The writers wrote some in, but I did make up more. It was mostly about her father. She craved his attention, but no matter what she did, he never gave it to her for long."

Sounds like someone else I know, Quinn mutters.

Jess sits back in her seat. "I can't imagine playing a character for that long. I mean, at some point, it would have to affect your personality." She pats my thigh. "Not that I think you're a mean girl, but I can see how you'd have to organize those inner thoughts."

She doesn't press for more details. Instead, she enlists my help in naming her own inner mean girl. Someday I'll tell her how grateful I am for her friendship, but for now, I'm just going to enjoy the feeling of trusting another person with one of my many secrets.

A FEW HOURS LATER, as I steer myself through the crowd of faithful Shakespeare Boston supporters, smiling and nodding and making small talk, my grip on sobriety is shakier than usual. Working in the bookstore and parenting Lilah, I can pretty easily avoid situations where people are drinking. Since returning to the theater last summer, it's been a bit more challenging. I've only entered a bar one time in the past seven years. After the closing of *Two Gentlemen of Verona,* a few of us took Ben for drinks before dropping him at the airport for a flight to Los Angeles. I felt so guilty about how my big mouth had messed things up between him and his girlfriend Lucy that I rallied the gang to make sure he knew we all loved him.

Thankfully, those two worked things out, and Ben's an East Coaster now. Now that I think about it, nobody at Shakespeare Boston has ever questioned my excuses for avoiding alcohol at the handful of parties I've attended. I suppose they either think it's because I'm a mom or they just don't care.

Anyway, today's afternoon barbecue and this evening's gala are different from the never-ending partying I did in New York. As I take a sip of sparkling water with lime, I remind myself that I'm lucky to be here. I'm lucky to have Jess and real friends in my life. Friends that don't feel like they might stab me in the back if the situation warranted it. Just as I'm wondering what has made the difference, I hear my childhood nickname.

"Izzy?"

I steel myself for a *Boom* fan. Since I shifted to Bella when I moved back to Boston, I can tell what kind of encounter it'll be by the name a stranger uses. If they call me Quinn, it'll be a negative reaction, like Cal's. If Bella, it's usually a Shakespeare buff or a book person. But when it's Izzy, they'll want to tell me how we did a play they wrote or a game they made up. The show's premise was "for kids, by kids," so if a viewer sent in a suggestion that the producers thought would be fun, it went on the shooting schedule to be performed with little rehearsal or skill, but a lot of enthusiasm.

Instead of a stranger, I find a familiar face. "Oh my goodness, Carol. You look exactly the same."

The slim, well-dressed woman laughs. "You're too kind. I feel like it's been thirty years instead of fifteen since I saw you last—in person, at least. You're all grown up."

It's my turn to laugh. "Yeah, I think I'm still working on that."

"Me too. Working with kids will do that to you."

"Are you still at WGBH?"

She nods. "I am now the head of children's programming."

"Congratulations. I love that." Carol was an associate producer on *Boom*. There was a director that called the shots—literally, he was in charge of the cameras and how the segments were filmed—but APs like Carol were the ones that coached us kids through bringing viewer letters to life.

We spend a few minutes catching up—we both *have* kids now. Unlike me, she's married. She compliments my work in the scenes we performed earlier in the evening and says she's sorry she missed seeing me in any of last season's shows.

"It's funny that I saw you tonight, though," she says, tapping a finger on her chin. "We're gearing up to shoot a reboot of *Boom*."

"In the summer? Not during the school year?"

"Yes," she says. "For better or worse, the shop is union now, so we can't work kids at night after they've been in school all day."

"Makes sense. I mean, adrenaline got me through it all, but I do remember being pretty exhausted the day after taping."

"I think it'll be good in the long run. We'll have the kids five days a week and get the season wrapped in a shorter period of time. It's less disruptive for them."

"Maybe it'll cut down on the bullying too." It wasn't too bad for me, but some cast members were teased mercilessly in school after episodes began airing. More than once, we had to bolster a fellow castmate's confidence before we could get to work.

Carol nods. "This will give them a little distance from their regular life. We're also going to do team building to help create a cast dynamic." She makes a face I remember so well. The one where she's got an idea but is worried it might be too out in left field.

Laughing, I say, "Just spit it out. I know that expression."

She laughs. "You always were so perceptive... and so interested in how things worked." Tipping her head to the side, she adds, "I remember you hanging out in the control room with the adults rather than playing charades or board games in the green room with the other kids."

"Huh, I forgot about that." Picturing that now, I remember how welcoming the crew was. They put me on headset and even asked my opinion about things on occasion. Not that they used many of my ideas.

"So, what's your commitment to the theater this summer?" Carol asks. "Any chance you'd have time to play associate producer as well? We just had an AP have to take an early maternity leave to go on bed rest, and we're scrambling to find someone to step in."

This is not where I thought this conversation was going. I figured she was working up to ask me to help with a fund drive or something. "Wow. That sounds fun, but I'd have to see. I'm a single parent."

A man sidles up next to Carol. After she introduces me to her husband, he puts his arm around her and gives her shoulders a squeeze. "Speaking of children, we told the babysitter we'd be back by ten."

Carol checks her watch. "I didn't realize it was so late." She searches her clutch for a few moments before blowing out an exasperated breath. "I don't have any cards with me, but you can just call the station and ask for me." She grasps my arm. "Could you come in next week so we can talk about it? I'd love to have you on the team, and I'm sure we could work things out schedule-wise."

"Um, sure. I'll call."

She gives me a hug before her husband hustles her away.

I think I just got a job offer. Problem is, I already have two jobs on top of my responsibilities as a mom. And going back to television? Just the thought has my mind and my heart racing.

And I'm not sure if it's in fear… or anticipation.

Chapter 2

"TV FOR TOTS: Producers of the recently syndicated children's show *Cowboy Clem* are pleased to announce that their western-clad star has charmed his way into more lineups across the country, expanding the franchise into thirty new locations. It just goes to show that captains and clowns aren't the only authority figures kids will cuddle up to!" *TV Today,* May 1989

HENRY

It's my last day at work at the Raleigh affiliate. The place I thought would be a way station for a year. Two tops.

It's been seven.

When I first took a job here, I told my just-widowed mother that I needed the break from the hustle of New York, that I wasn't ready for the big promotion I turned down after an aneurysm took my dad from us. I told myself that I was staying here for my family.

The truth? I was so weighed down by guilt, I could barely make it out of the house in the morning.

My dad was my hero. He was the one who got me my first Super 8 camera at the age of ten. He'd watch the crappy little movies I made as a teen and critique them like I was Martin Scorsese. He encouraged me to take the first job in the big city, even helped me pay the bills until I got myself situated. Family was the most important thing to him, but he knew that I wanted to change the world by making TV that was thought-provoking as well as entertaining.

But the last time I saw him, his face was red, and he hurled insults that I lobbed right back at him. Losing him without being able to make peace had me questioning every choice I'd ever made. So I threw myself into reconnecting with the family I still had—my mom, three siblings, and too many cousins and aunts and uncles to count.

No matter how hard I tried, though, I still never felt like I quite fit in. I was useless at the family landscaping business—grouchy with customers, killing plants left and right—and every time I tried to babysit my younger second cousins, I somehow made somebody cry.

So I got the best job I could find in this one-horse town: running a camera at a local affiliate TV station. I kept busy there. Moved up quickly. I've tried to be satisfied with life here, with the career I've patched together.

Truth be told, I probably acquired more knowledge about the actual workings of a television show than I would have had I climbed the producer ladder in New York. I was willing to do anything, so I've operated cameras, navigated the editing suite, and assisted directors and producers on every locally produced show from the news to *Romper Room*. It was my idea to develop our own kids' show when *Bozo* got too expensive. Now our franchise, *Cowboy Clem*, is nipping at the clown's heels around the country.

And I'm leaving it all behind.

Ralph—the station's weatherman and my closest friend since high school—still doesn't get why I'd leave one provincial city for another one. Especially one where it actually gets cold in the winter.

As we take a table in the cafeteria, he shakes his head. "I still can't believe you're going to move a thousand miles away just to dodge Christine. What's up with that? You break up with your sister's best friend, you have to leave town?"

"I may be afraid of my sister, but I'm not that afraid."

"It's one thing to leave. But why would you choose Boston over Los Angeles? I just don't get it." He pokes at his salad. Since his work is in front of the camera, there's more pressure to stay trim, which is not as easy at thirty as it was in our teen years when we played every school sport there was. "I mean, I'm sure there are pretty girls in Boston, but the girls in LA..." He sighs, obviously picturing girls like the Malibu Barbie my twin sister had.

"Not everyone lets his dick make all his decisions, Ralph." I'm not ready to admit that I don't have the guts to conquer a major market anymore, even to my best bud. Or that I'm worried that I may have missed my chance. I've got another argument instead. "If I took that operator gig in LA, I'd make more money, but I'd be a cameraman forever. There's no crossover. In Boston the public station is more like it is here in that everybody does a bit of everything."

"You could stay here. You've still got your looks. Why don't you go for my weatherman slot when I move up to the desk? Or sports?"

I almost choke on my RC Cola. "Are you kidding me? Wear makeup and smile and make stupid jokes?"

Ralph drops his fork. "You think that's all I do?"

"Nah, I'm talking about the sports guys." I shake my head, picturing his easygoing patter as he reads the teleprompter and gestures in front of the green screen. "I don't get the weather."

He shrugs. "I just read the script."

"I'd still have to perform."

When I aim my best smirk at him, he rubs a hand in the air between us. "Oooh, I take it back. That smile is scary."

We finish lunch in companionable silence. I will miss this guy. After we toss our trash, we exit the cafeteria together. He pauses in front of my office, where my stuff is in boxes. "Seriously, though. What's so great about Boston?"

Leaning against the doorjamb, a heady cocktail of nerves and anticipation dances through my veins. "That station makes some of the most interesting shows on TV right now, and they've promised that once we get *Boom* rebooted, I can pitch my own ideas. You know I've wanted to make documentaries since I was in junior high."

Ralph nods slowly. "I'll never forget that one you did on Reggie Jackson. It was super cool how you used footage of newspapers and that music for the background. I learned something, and it didn't even hurt." After treating me to his smile—one that the camera loves—he heads down the hall to his own office. Walking backward, he calls, "Do they know kids are scared of you?"

"Kids aren't scared of me," I protest weakly. I don't mind them, but kids sure hate me.

"Henry. You're like the anti-Bozo."

I roll my eyes. "Just because I made that girl cry *one* time."

He grins. "It was a whole gaggle of girls. And at least five times… that I know of."

"She stole Cowboy Cam's hat!"

"They're only four years old, man."

"I didn't send her to juvie. I just made sure she understood that you don't touch station property."

With a salute, he saunters down the hall. "You're either going to kill it or you'll be back in six weeks."

THE DAY BEFORE I LEAVE, I stop by my twin sister's house to drop off some boxes she's storing for me. She greets me at the door with a hug, followed by a punch in the gut. "I still can't believe you broke up with Christine."

What ever made me think letting my sister run my love life was a good idea?

"I didn't break up with her. She broke up with me." Tucking my chin on the top box to keep them all from falling, I ask, "Where do you want these?"

She opens the door to the basement, flicks on the light, and gestures at the stairs. "After you gave her an ultimatum."

Groaning, I take the steps carefully since I can't really see where I'm going. "See, this is why it's probably best we ended it. Either she's delusional, or she's lying to you."

"Why are you being such a jerk?" She points to an empty space in the shelving that lines one wall. After I set my boxes on the shelf, Jill presses a button on her label maker, whips off the sticker, and presses it to the top box. It reads "O'Henry's Crap."

My sister has a truckload of nicknames for me, including the candy bar among others less family friendly.

"Jill, you can't micromanage my life the way you run your house and your husband and the Apex store. I love you, but it's my life."

Screwing her face up in a pout, she throws herself onto the over-stuffed couch that dominates my brother-in-law's hangout. "But it was going to be so perfect. We'd all live in the same neighborhood and our kids would grow up together and I'd be president of the PTA and Christine would be the vice-president."

Shoving my hands in my pockets, I grumble, "I'm sure that can all still happen. Just without me."

She kicks a beach ball in my direction. "But I'll miss you, you dummy."

"You don't even like me." After trapping the ball with a toe, I knock it back to her.

She swats it away. "Because you're a big grump."

"Which is why I shouldn't be anybody's dad." Flopping down next to her, I let the couch take the weight of my guilt as well as my muscles and bones. "Listen. I told her I was taking this job. I suggested that we could use the time apart to see if we really want to be together. If she heard that as an ultimatum…"

"What's she supposed to do? You didn't ask her to go with you, and you made it seem like she's not enough to keep you here."

"Well, she's not."

She kicks me. "That's mean."

"Ow!" I scoot away from her. "I'm sorry, but it's the truth. There are things I need to do with my career, and I can't do them here. Christine hates how much time I spend at work as it is. Moving with me somewhere that she doesn't know anybody wouldn't make her happy. You know it, and she knows it."

She sighs, starts to say something, but then stops herself.

"What?"

She sighs again. "It's not like you could've saved him."

"I missed a lot of time with him."

"Yet another reason to stay here. With your family." She bumps shoulders with me. "There are other women in Raleigh. It doesn't have to be Christine."

I'll never admit it, but my sister's right. Not about Christine, but about a lot of things. Still, something is telling me that I need to do this, that I'll lose a piece of myself if I don't at least try with this job.

"This is an opportunity I don't want to pass up. Public television stations like WGBH put out all kinds of shows that are entertaining and revolutionary and interesting. I don't want to work with a cowboy anymore."

"You're still working with kids," she pouts.

"But not whiny little kids. Teenagers. Or almost teenagers."

"They're worse. Don't you remember what an asshole you were at that age?"

"Was not."

"Were too."

"Not."

"Nuh-uh."

"Pfft. You weren't exactly a princess."

"I'm still a princess." She ends the argument with a regal sniff.

Kicking her gently, I whisper, "I am going to miss you, Jilly Billy."

She whispers back, "I'm gonna miss you too, Corny." And then she kicks me—hard enough to make me wince.

ON MY WAY out of town, I stop by my mom's house for a final goodbye. I wish I didn't feel compelled to make my own mark on the world, taking myself away from the people who love me despite the fact that I stick out like a sore thumb around them. I feel guilty leaving again, but I know I'll just make everyone around me unhappy if I stay. "I yam what I yam," as Popeye would say.

If I couldn't make my dad happy by being what he wanted me to be, I've got to at least take what might be my last shot to be what *I* want to be.

At least I'm leaving things in good shape. The family business is thriving. My siblings and my mom will do fine without me. Sometimes I wonder if they'll even miss me.

My mom's hug is comforting, but she pushes me away after just a few beats. Before I can open my mouth to say I'm sorry for leaving again, she pats me on the shoulder and practically pushes me down the front steps. "Henry, I love you and you've been my rock the past few years, but now you need to hightail it out of here and get yourself on the road. Lord, you'd think I wasn't a grown woman who can take care of herself."

"Mama, you know I don't think that."

"Well, it was true right after your father died. I did need help. I needed my babies around me, and I'll be forever grateful that you put your own life on hold to come back here."

Hanging on to the wrought-iron railing at the bottom of the front steps, I toe at a divot in one of the bricks. "I missed y'all too. It's not like I've hated living here."

"And we will be glad to have you back on every major holiday or" —she waves a hand in the air—"whenever you can get away. I know TV doesn't necessarily behave the way the rest of the world does. But you know how I am. I won't be able to relax until you get to Boston, so you'd best get on your way."

Following me to my car, she gives my dog a final scratch behind the ears before I hustle him into the passenger seat of my truck, and then we're off. Within minutes, the street I grew up on disappears from my rearview. Again. Ten years ago, I was fresh out of college and headed for a hard-won job in New York City. My dad stood next to my mom, waving as I drove down the block.

As I merge onto I-85 North, memories of that time pop up one after the other. The crappy two-bedroom apartment that I called home in Hoboken, shared by three other guys who were all as wet behind the ears as I was, each of us ready to conquer the big bad city in one way or another. The polyester uniform I wore for that first precious job as a page. The tourists who were as excited to see what happened behind the scenes of the headquarters of a television network as I was to share it.

Six months in, I got my first real job: running tape for reporters. I was over the moon, feeling like I was actually a part of getting the news from the street to the screen. My trip up the ladder was lightning quick after that until, before I knew it, before I'd even been in the city two years, I was celebrating a promotion to assistant producer in the investigative division of the prime-time news-magazine.

And then, the night that changed everything. The night I met the woman I thought I had a chance at making mine, and the night I found out my dad had died at the age of fifty-five.

I went home for the funeral and never went back to New York. Some other guy stepped into the job I'd worked so hard to get at the network. Some other guy probably has the girl I left behind the night I met her.

It's odd that I think about her more often than I do Christine. My sister's choice for me is a very nice, very pretty girl that I've known since the third grade. The other girl, the one I only know as Izzy, haunts my dreams. We were only together for a few hours, but every moment of that night is seared into my memory. Pale blue eyes that danced with amusement when she caught me celebrating on the rooftop. All I had to do was touch her hand and a bone-deep desire lit me up from the inside out. When the sides of her mouth lifted a fraction of an inch, I needed to feel that smile with my own. I've never had an encounter like it, before or since.

If we'd had the chance to get to know each other for real, would we have been able to sustain that passion? Probably not. But it might've mellowed into something else. Something equally special.

My parents had that kind of relationship. I don't know—and I don't want to know—about the passion, but they worked side by side for thirty-odd years and were always kind to each other, always making each other laugh. Every once in a while, my dad would stop in the middle of the house or the store or the greenhouse and just hold out his arms. Without a word, my mom would step into his embrace. They'd just stand there for a few moments, and then they'd go back to what they'd been doing.

It never occurred to me to do anything like that with Christine.

It's the truth that I'm not leaving because of her. I'm leaving because since my dad bought me a camera, I've been making stories with it. I'm addicted to the feeling I get when something I've made gets someone to see a subject in a new way. I need to make a difference with a camera one way or another, and that's not going to happen in little old Raleigh, North Carolina.

So, I'm leaving the nest again, headed to a different city in the Northeast and a different kind of job, but one that I hope will get me back on track.

I'll admit that a tiny part of me took the job because of its association with Izzy. She was in the original *Boom's* first season, so maybe there's a chance someone is still in touch with her. Maybe there's a chance that she's not married to someone else. Maybe there's a chance that we could find that spark again.

But first, "We have to get to Boston, right buddy?" I ask my faithful hound as I scratch him behind his silky ears.

Chapter 3

"Last week on *All His Children*: Michael disturbs Barbara by saying that you can't depend on a father's love. This disillusionment was created when he discovered his father at Janine's. Meanwhile, Rosa has an unsettling experience." *Soap Opera Land*, June 1989

BELLA

As I walk through WGBH's glass doors, I'm hit with a wave of nostalgia. The scent of the building is exactly the same as it was fifteen years ago: a mix of the lemony cleaning fluid they use on the floors, a musty smell I associate with the miles of cable snaking through the studios, and—I swear—an aroma of garlic that clings to the set of Julia Child's kitchen, still tucked away in a corner. Adrenaline courses through my veins, just as it did before every rehearsal and performance. Back then, once I put on the striped rugby shirt we all wore, I could focus that energy into my performance.

Too bad I don't have that armor today.

Or Izzy's fearlessness. My heart is filled with worry, but my head is equally full of determination. I don't know if I'm capable of stepping out of the carefully constructed blind I've built for myself, but something's urging me to take a few baby steps into the light. Since talking to Carol at the fundraiser and on the phone the next day, I haven't been able to stop a flow of ideas for how we could make *Boom* an even better show. Anticipation buzzing behind my solar plexus, I approach the receptionist and let her know I have an appointment.

When I was thirteen and a cast member, I thought everything about Carol Ferris was super cool: from the mod outfits to the long hair held back with brightly colored headbands to the neon lipstick that framed her wide smile.

I remember feeling safe with Carol too. Like I couldn't really screw things up. Some of the APs were a little more uptight and the director would sometimes lose patience if we messed up too many takes, but Carol always had a way of finding the good, even in a mistake.

Being on *Boom* kicked off my love affair with television. Even though that particular relationship ended badly, I do have many happy memories from this time in my life. Besides, it's not like I'd be in front of the camera if I were a producer.

So, once we get the small talk out of the way, I pull out my notebook. Before I get too far down my list of ideas, however, Carol laughs and holds up a hand. "I'm happy that you're raring to go, but let's save the brainstorming until the whole team's together." Hand over her heart, she explains, "I oversee all of our local programming, then James—do you remember James Wheeler?"

"Was that 'don't call me Jim' James?" The face of a gruff cameraman about Carol's age comes to mind.

"That's him," Carol says with a smile. "And he still prefers James. He'll be *Boom*'s new executive producer. We have a new hire from North Carolina coming in to direct. He's getting a tour of the facility now, which I didn't think you needed."

"Since I spent so many hours prowling around it?"

"Exactly. Anyway, I'm happy to hear your thoughts, but you'll be stepping onto a moving train. We have the cast in place. The next steps are narrowing down which audience suggestions we'll use and mapping out the shooting schedule."

I'm still not sure if this is a job interview or if she's offering me the position. "I'm probably being a little obtuse here, Carol, but are you talking to other people? For this job?"

Her smile is hopeful. "We are officially, but I'd really love to have you on board."

"Even though I don't really have experience?" Probably not the thing to emphasize, but I don't want to oversell myself.

"You have experience that the rest of us don't have."

I nod. "My mom said the same thing, that I might be a good advocate for the kids."

"I always thought Doris was a wise woman." She checks her watch. "I told James we'd meet them in reception about now, so let's head down there."

As we walk, she explains the funding situation for the show. The current political climate has meant tightening budgets across the board for public broadcasting, but Carol has doggedly pursued sponsorship from alternative sources and gotten grants to support the *Boom* reboot. "Or the Boomerang, as I like to call it. We're calling the cast members that too, unofficially."

"Nice." I nod, relaxing further. "So right now, there's funding for one season."

"Exactly, but I'll continue to solicit more. We've learned our lesson and no longer rely on a single source of support for any of our programs. But that's not to say that the funding doesn't come with strings attached."

She's explaining that the new sponsors all want more emphasis on math and science as I open the door to the reception area, but when the two men waiting there look up, what I see stops me in my tracks.

HENRY

June in Boston is nothing like June back home. In Raleigh, the cherry blossoms have come and gone already but here, they've barely started to bloom. I don't blame them because I haven't seen the sun since I got here, and the temperature has dipped down to the forties at night. Plus, the apartment I spent the long weekend getting settled into is overpriced and tiny.

But enough grumbling. I'm glad to finally be at the station, where I can focus on the reason why I'm here: working at a place that can give me opportunities I'd never have found back in Raleigh. And that's one of the first things my direct supervisor, James Wheeler, asks me.

"I can't imagine we were your only option. What made you choose Boston over New York or LA?"

"I get why you'd ask, but as I told Carol in my interview, I'm actually glad I had to leave New York before I got entrenched. The market's bigger, but that comes with constraints. From my research, GBH has the best track record in the country right now in terms of creating smart, innovative shows that go on to syndicate successfully."

"What about the Children's Television Workshop?"

"If I were only interested in kids' programming, CTW is where I'd want to be, sure. *Sesame Street* and *The Electric Company* are the gold standard. But I have ideas for a general audience that I'd like to pitch after I prove myself on *Boom.*"

He nods slowly, and I'm a bit worried that I've jumped the gun. But then he smiles. "I look forward to seeing how you shake things up."

Hand in the air, I qualify, "I have things to learn, and I can't imagine a better place to do that. I mean, *American Experience* is already winning awards, then you've got *Frontline* and *Nova*, in addition to the lifestyle shows."

James pauses in front of a door and peers in its narrow window.

"Speaking of which, they're cutting *This Old House* right now. Let's take a peek."

After a quick round of introductions, where I do my best to not fawn all over the man who created this show and *The French Chef*, I have to hide my disappointment at the equipment laid out in the suite. It's the same clunky CMX setup we had down in Raleigh. Sure, it allows you to do random-access editing, but the prep work takes forever.

Despite that disappointment, and despite the fact that I already miss my family and my friends at the old station, I know that my new colleagues will challenge and inspire me. And as director-producer, I'll have the best of both worlds. I'll get to have a say in the look and the pace and the content of the shows we create, like I would have if I'd been able to stay in New York. But my stint in Raleigh means that I have hard-won knowledge of what works and what doesn't.

In my interview for the position, I was promised that we weren't simply replicating the old formula, which is a good thing. I loved the old *Boom* as a kid, but now it'll have competition that moves faster and is more irreverent—not to mention the fact that there's a lot more of it. I may not be the best at working with kids, but I am pretty darn good at making calls about what keeps eyeballs on the screen.

At least there are no clowns or cowboys at this station. From what I can tell. Bonus points for that.

"We've got a production meeting after lunch where you'll get to meet the rest of the team, but I told Carol we'd meet her to interview a potential associate producer to replace the one we just lost to early maternity leave." James breaks into my thoughts as we head down yet another long corridor. "Carol ran into an old cast member last weekend and thinks she might be a good candidate."

"Someone who was on the show as a kid?"

"Yeah, she's involved with the Shakespeare company in town or something."

Probably not Izzy, then. No way she'd be here in Boston working for some local theater. Good thing because while I'd love to see her again, the nature of our one and only meeting would make it very awkward to try and work together.

James has steered us back to the reception area where oversized posters of the station's successes decorate the walls. *Masterpiece Theatre, Evening at Pops, Nova*—every single show is the best of its kind. Scanning the images of fresh-faced kids from the original *Boom*, my eyes immediately track to Izzy.

Staring at her photo, I wonder again what would've happened if my dad hadn't died. Would we have been a couple? Would we still be? My imagination goes crazy, painting pictures of a glamorous life in New York together. Big-time TV producer married to big-time TV star. A fabulous penthouse apartment on the Upper West Side where drivers pick us up to ferry us to early calls, leaving our brilliant, adorable kids behind with a reliable nanny. Someone very Mary Poppins-like.

Just as I'm decorating the weekend house we keep up in the Berkshires, James's voice echoes across the open room. "Ah, here they are. Carol, you remember Henry."

"Of course," says the woman who interviewed me for the job. As she steps forward, she gestures to another woman. "Bella York, meet another co-conspirator in bringing *Boom* back to the airwaves, Henry Smith."

"Hal?"

"Izzy?"

Fuck.

■

BELLA

I could be babbling nonsense, I could be answering their questions, I could be reciting lines from either of the shows Shakespeare Boston's putting up this summer. Unfortunately, this is no comedy of errors, and it's worse than any tempest the Bard could imagine.

Oh. My. God. It's him, Quinn's voice says. The voice I mimicked just a few days ago with Cal. Brassy, sexy, and always only out for herself.

Ohhh. Him. Her counterpoint echoes. The innocent voice, the one that doesn't know how harsh the world can be. Izzy.

The sexiest guy I've ever been with, Quinn whispers reverently.

Great. Not only do I have a moral dilemma the size of Manhattan to deal with, but I need to make a quick exit before any of the pieces of me says something I'll regret.

I'll just make an excuse, and once I'm safe at home, I'll call Carol and tell her thanks but no thanks.

There's no way I can take this job. If even one of the stupid mistakes I made as a young actress in the big city gets dredged up—secret addict runs away from it all to hide the baby she conceived in her dressing room with a guy she met once—PBS wouldn't want me within ten feet of *Boom.*

Not to mention what that kind of attention would do to Lilah.

Carol's hand on my shoulder brings me back to earth, but not quite all the way. I'm still hovering above it all, watching myself. "Bella, are you all right?"

"I'm not sure," I manage.

James gestures to a chair. "Do you want to sit for a minute? I'll get you some water."

"I'm so sorry; it's probably something I ate. I need to go."

Carol's brow furrows. "Are you alright to get home? Should I call you a cab?"

"No, I... I think I can make it." Just a glimpse in Hal's direction has my stomach roiling. I don't even have to pretend to be sick as I make myself say "Nice to meet you" before I sprint to the door.

HENRY

"Well, that was odd." James says as the doors close behind Izzy. Bella? I think that's what Carol said her name was. It was all so surreal. "It was like she saw a ghost."

Yeah, and I'm pretty sure that ghost was me.

What I don't get is why she'd run away. Our past encounter makes things awkward, but I'm the one who should be embarrassed. I left her in that dressing room without saying goodbye or explaining what happened. In my defense, all I knew about her was that she was Izzy from *Boom*. She was in her twenties and gorgeous, so I figured I was just another notch on her belt. I mean, in New York in the early eighties, anybody with a pulse was sleeping with anyone and everyone. And she was the one who came on to me.

I think. That night is a bit of a blur in my memory. Dreams came true, then turned into nightmares.

"Are you okay, Henry?" James's laugh is forced. "Maybe there's some sort of bug going around?"

I shake my head and paste on a smile. "No, I'm good. What's next?"

Following Carol and James to a conference room, I pack the memories away. Once I've found my bearings here, I'll find Izzy and apologize. Or Bella. Whatever she goes by now.

If I can. This time, she's the one who's done a disappearing act.

Chapter 4

AND NOW... A FEW WORDS FROM OUR READERS!!
Q: Can you tell me if the young woman who played Quinn on *ATER* will be returning to TV? I'd love to see her on my screen again. Thank you for all you do for us fans. Jane Whitley, Clearview, FL
A: We've checked with all of our sources, and unfortunately, it seems that Isabelle York is staying out of the spotlight for the time being. I'm sure you'll join us in wishing her the best. K.G. *TV Today*, June 1989

BELLA

After I stagger out of the station and unlock my car with shaking hands, I can't get out of the parking lot fast enough. Lilah's in full-day kindergarten and my mom doesn't expect me in the store because of this meeting, so I do what I do best.

Run away.

I may have protected Lilah from the notoriety of my party-girl days, but it seems I can't completely escape the fact that she's a product of my misbehavior. I buried Hal's existence so deep that I managed to convince myself he didn't exist. Like I was the Virgin

Mary—without the virgin part. Laughing a little hysterically, I gun the engine to merge onto the Mass Pike.

That's hilarious. You. A virgin, Quinn snickers.

That night was pretty surreal, Izzy says.

That man is all too real, Quinn sighs. *I'd really like to get naked with him again.*

After a quick gasp of shock, Izzy says, *You can't do that before telling him he has a daughter.*

Eh, he'll probably be relieved he's escaped paying child support all these years, Quinn says. *I mean, what hot single guy wants to be burdened with a kid?*

Maybe he's married, Izzy says. *How would his wife and kids feel about this?*

"Shut. Up. Both of you," I say. "I can't—we can't… I mean. Gah! I'm talking out loud to the voices in my head."

I'm also halfway to Worcester. If I'm going to make it to rehearsal on time, I've got to head back, so I take the next exit. After paying the toll, I find a drive-through and grab a late lunch. Focusing on the food and the road, I make it to the rehearsal hall without further comment from my own personal peanut gallery. However, I'm still so distracted by my real-life drama that I phone in my performance all evening. Thankfully, no one seems to notice.

Except the guy I'm in almost every scene with, my friend Will. On the first union-mandated break, he plops down next to me. "You okay? You've gone a little pale."

Nodding, adding a little grimace, I lie. Again. "I think I ate something off yesterday. I've been a bit queasy."

"'Unquiet meals make ill digestions'… or something like that?"

"Is that from this show?" Will can pull out a Shakespeare quote for any occasion, but this one sounds familiar.

"It is indeed." He pats my arm. "Anyway, you want a soda or something?"

"Thanks, that'd be nice."

You're such a good liar, Quinn says with true appreciation.

It isn't good, Izzy counters. *She's just digging herself in deeper.*

By the end of rehearsal, I'm completely exhausted. Squelching the voices in my head and pretending I'm sick—on top of the acting I'm supposed to be doing—takes its toll. When I park my car behind our house, all I want is to peek at the little girl I haven't seen all day and then collapse into bed. On my way, I discover my mom working in her office off the kitchen.

"Hey, Mom. What are you doing still up?"

The expression on her face matches one I glimpsed in the mirror earlier today. She's hiding something.

"Oh," she says, scrambling to gather papers into a pile. "Uh… what time is it?"

Pointing to the clock right over her head, I say, "After eleven."

When her face pales, worry punches me in the gut. "Is Lilah okay?"

"What?"

"Lilah? Your granddaughter? Is she sick or something?"

"No, no." She looks past me. "I don't think so."

"Mom, are *you* okay? You're being weird."

"Everything's fine." She tries to shield the last of the papers from my view, but I catch a glimpse of red.

"Mom." I cover her hands with mine to get her to stop shuffling papers. "You're a terrible actress."

After pulling her hands from under mine, she drops her forehead into them. "Dammit."

My hands are shaking, so I press them to my sides. "Are you sick?"

She just rocks her head from side to side. The movement draws my attention to the paperwork on the desk.

"What is it? You're scaring me."

Clasping shaking hands together, she whispers, "We're about to lose the store."

"What?" The chair by her desk catches my butt when my body suddenly gives up on the battle with gravity. "What do you mean?"

With a heavy sigh, she drags herself to the armchair where she usually sits to pore over advance reader copies and book catalogs. Then she meets my gaze.

"We've been operating at a loss for more than a year," she says, her voice ragged. "I took out a second mortgage, thinking that things would turn around, thinking that it was the financial crisis. But—" Her breath hitches and takes a moment to swallow before continuing. "Things just keep getting worse." Her hands flail in a circle. "Customers go to the mall to shop. I can't afford the rent there like the chain stores can. I can't offer the big discounts they can. Another author cancelled a signing."

"What? Are they cutting down on publicity tours or something?" The store gets a big uptick in sales when an author does an appearance, so I know that's not good news.

"I think they're just not coming to *my* store. I have a feeling I'll see something posted at the Waldenbooks at the mall."

"That sucks. You've always taken such good care of the authors. They love you."

She sags into the couch cushions. "It's not really the author's choice. It's the publicity people."

I do the day-to-day shelf stocking, but she orders and pays all the bills. I'm embarrassed to admit that I haven't noticed a change in sales. It does seem like fewer people come in than used to, now that I think about it. Scrambling for a solution I ask, "Well... what about my money?"

"Your money?"

"The savings set aside from the soap. The chunk that I couldn't access till my thirtieth birthday? I haven't touched it. I'll loan it to you if it makes you feel better."

The look on her face makes it clear that there's more bad news. "I didn't tell you at the time because you were already so mad at him, but..." Her hands make a helpless *What could I do?* gesture. "I had to help him."

She doesn't fill in any more blanks, but the conclusion isn't hard for me to find. "Are you fucking kidding me? Dad stole my money?"

"He didn't steal it." She shakes her head. "He got into a financial bind and let me know that he was borrowing from that fund to get out of it. But as far as I can tell, he hasn't paid it back."

"How long ago was that?"

"A couple of years."

Any response I could have to this news would wake up Lilah, so I swallow the words I'd like to scream. Instead I mutter, "Just when I thought he couldn't be any more of an asshole."

"Sweetheart, he has reasons. If you'd just talk to him—"

"After everything else he did, I'm supposed to be understanding about why he'd take the money that I earned? I can't believe you forgave him after what he put you through."

"I had nothing to forgive."

It pisses me off that she always says this. "Right, because you weren't there. You didn't get to come home after a long day at work to the apartment you paid for—at the ripe old age of seventeen—to find it full of a bunch of strange men, your dad high out of his mind, playing show tunes on the piano!"

I press my palms over my eye sockets to try and contain the rage that threatens to explode out of me.

When my mom takes my hands and pulls them away from my face, I resist until she says, "I'm sorry, Bella. I'm sorry for all of it. I should've told you. About the money, about the store, but I just"—her head drops with a heavy sigh—"I don't know how to do anything else, and I don't know how to fix this."

Anger at my father flares hotter before sputtering out. Yelling at my mother won't do anybody any good. Instead, I sit on the arm of her chair and rub her back, murmuring that it'll be okay, we'll figure something out.

When I came home pregnant and jobless, my mom treated me like the prodigal daughter, welcoming me back. She never asked about Lilah's dad.

You should tell her now, Izzy whispers.

Why? Quinn asks. *What good would that do?*

I guess it might be a burden she doesn't need right now, Izzy allows.

She should crawl back to the station, tail between her legs, and beg for that job, Quinn says.

So you *can take care of* her, Izzy says, brightening.

Things could get interesting with Hal, Quinn says with a smirk.

Oh, dear. Now I have no idea what the right thing to do is, Izzy whines. *If she goes back there, she risks losing Lilah to a total stranger. But if she doesn't, her mom will lose the store.*

Wow, Bella, Quinn cackles. *When you fuck things up, you don't mess around.*

THE NEXT MORNING, I go through the getting-Lilah-to-school and opening-the-store routines on autopilot, exhausted from spending half the night trying to figure out what to say to Carol. Letting my fingers do the walking seems safer than actually driving to the station, but when I'm put through to Carol and she asks if I'm feeling better, my hands are shaking so much that I drop the receiver.

"Bella? Are you there?" Carol asks.

"Yes, sorry." After crossing my fingers—like that'll cover the half-lie—I spit out a story. "But... well, I have a confession to make. Yesterday, I didn't have food poisoning. I had a reaction to seeing Hal. I mean, Henry."

There's a slight pause on the other end of the line before she asks, "A reaction? Did he do something inappropriate, or—?" She breaks off, like she's afraid to fill in the blank.

"No, nothing like that," I reassure her. "We... have a kind of a history."

"Oh." Another pause. "Will you have a problem working with him?"

"No, but—" I literally have to force the words past my lips. "You might have a problem working with me." Then I remember something Jess said recently—that she didn't even realize that Izzy and Bella were the same person when we first met. "Do you ever feel like you've changed so much that when you look back, the person that you used to be doesn't even seem like you?"

"I guess," she says, sounding a little confused. "Motherhood seems to rearrange the brain significantly. I definitely worry a lot more."

"Oh, yes. That's true for me to, but—" I'm momentarily distracted by the whiteness of my fingers before I realize that I've wound the phone cord around them so tightly that the circulation is cut off. Freeing them, I shake out my hands. "When I was on the soap, my behavior was... I was not the person I am today. Nor the little preteen you knew. I have a bit of a checkered past."

Ha, Quinn snorts. *That's rich.*

She wasn't as bad as you, Izzy defends me.

"When I was in New York, I was in the papers quite a bit. For being a party girl."

You think Carol knows what that means, exactly? Quinn asks.

"Go on," Carol says.

"Sorry. So, I, uh... I've worked hard to put that all behind me and to keep my daughter's life private. To do that, I've avoided doing anything that would put me in the public eye."

"But you're performing with Shakespeare Boston."

"I was worried about that at first, but the *Boston Globe* and *Soap Opera Land* don't exactly have the same audience," I say, my laugh only slightly hysterical.

"I think you could say the same of a PBS station like GBH," Carol ventures.

"Probably? I hope so. But to be sure, if I were to work on *Boom*, I'd like to stay completely behind the scenes. For the good of the show and my family."

"And how does Henry fit into this picture? Was he involved in that... partying?"

"No, no. At least not that I know of. We met on my very last day at the network." *Met* is obviously an understatement, but there's definitely no need to go into detail. "Seeing him was a shock and brought back a lot of memories. Not happy ones, I'm afraid."

I beg to differ. I've got some very happy memories from that meeting, Quinn says.

After a long pause, she says, "Will you be okay working with Henry? We are committed to him. He's moved here from Raleigh."

"Oh, no. I mean, yes." Shoving the fact that it will be quite awkward to the side, I repeat, "Like I said, it isn't him, per se, it was what he reminded me of. That time of my life. I thought I had it all packed away but seeing him… it all came rushing back. And I really don't want my baggage to bring down the show." *Or my daughter.* "What I'm saying is that I'd love to work on *Boom*, but I don't want be in the spotlight. Nor would you want me to be."

"I see." She clears her throat. "The publicity department may be disappointed that you won't be available for a more public role, but as an associate producer, your work would be behind the scenes. If you remember, the team of APs works with the executive producer and the director to choose ideas from the viewer letters we get. Then each AP takes on a segment or two each episode and works with the kids and the director to bring it to life."

"On the floor with us—like you, right? Explaining the game or the recipe, or casting the plays?"

"Exactly."

I can't help my smile. "Back then, I thought all I wanted was to be seen. By the camera, by the audience. But in my old age—"

"Careful there, missy. I'm ten years ahead of you."

"In this particular time of my life," I clarify with a smile, "I believe I can use what I learned over the years in front of the camera to make things work from the other side. And I'd be very excited to try it."

"Wonderful. Welcome to the team."

"That's it?"

"That's it. There will be a lot of forms to fill out. But I need you to jump in as soon as possible. In fact"—papers shuffle, and she hums as if she's scanning through them—"if you could start tomorrow, we have a production meeting first thing, after which, you can get to work sorting through the letters from kids."

"Wow. Okay. Awesome."

"Welcome back to *Boom*, Bella."

"Thank you. I'll... see you tomorrow."

After I place the receiver in its cradle, I'm flooded with relief. Telling a tiny part of the truth seems to have given me a chance to support my mom while she figures out what to do about the store.

Facing Henry again feels like jumping off a cliff, but whether I work with him or not, now that I've found him, I have to tell him about Lilah. It's the right thing to do.

Mind full, I need a walk before opening the shop. When I was locked away at rehab, I spent most of my time alone. Since everyone was there in secret, there was no group therapy, no sharing of stories. I'd meet with a therapist twice a day, but the rest of the time I spent walking and wrestling with the urges that had gotten me there.

I've always been stubborn. That was how I talked my parents into letting me audition for *Boom* and into moving to New York, how I succeeded as an actress. Rejection didn't slow me down. The word "no" just made me try harder.

But it also meant I didn't know how to put on the brakes when I needed to. So, on those long walks I decided I had to retire both Izzy's willfulness and Quinn's self-indulgence. I could keep Izzy's optimism and Quinn's savvy, but Bella needed to be much more discerning about who she would trust.

Which, after I found out I was pregnant, was essentially my mom and myself.

Even though deciding to keep and raise Lilah derailed my plans to go for a prime-time career, it was probably the best for my mental health in the long run. Who knows if rehab would've stuck if I'd dived right back into acting in a high-pressure situation? At Shakespeare Boston, I've been pleasantly surprised to find fellow actors that prioritize bringing the Bard's words to life over stirring up controversy in each other's personal lives. My circle of trusted friends has grown. I know that Jess, Ben, and Will love and respect me for myself and my talent, not for what I could do for them.

In the process, I buried my baser urges so deep that Quinn was bored to death. I really thought I'd killed her off. After all, a big thrill these days is stopping at Herrell's for ice cream after a long day of rehearsal.

But right now, those old personas won't shut up They've both got very strong opinions about whether, how, when, why, and where to tell Henry about Lilah.

You don't need to tell him anything, Quinn says. *He left.*

You can't deprive Lilah of her father, Izzy counters.

Hey, if you do tell him, you can get laid again! Quinn crows.

That is a huge presumption, Izzy says primly. *He may not be interested.*

And on they go, round and round, driving me crazy.

Or maybe I was nuts to begin with.

Whatever the status of my mental health, I am going to have to tell him. But I'm not going to sleep with him, even though little reels of the hours we spent worshiping every inch of each other's bodies keep flashing through my brain.

In Technicolor and stereo surround sound. I mean, it was the day I finally got why people get so worked up over sex.

It was the last time you had sex! Quinn shouts.

And look what happened! Izzy yells back.

"I got Lilah out of it!" I yell this so loudly, a woman stares at me from the driver's seat of a car stopped at a light.

Sending her a sheepish wave, I groan.

I can just see the *Soap Opera Land* headline: *Quinn's not dead, fan claims. "I saw her talking to herself on the sidewalk!"*

That's all I need. May as well add, *Soap Baddie Had Secret Baby! Details on page 3!*

Whatever I do, I'm screwed. If only the right thing didn't feel like such a bad idea.

My point exactly, Quinn says.

Chapter 5

"STARS AND THEIR PETS: While Don Walton (John Winston on *The Only World*) can't seem to find a girl he can set his heart on, sources tell us he's found the *dog* of his dreams. The daytime hunk was seen just last weekend walking the friendly pooch through Central Park. When asked about the pooch's breed, he joked, 'He ain't nothin' but a hound dog.' What a character!" *TV Tattler*, June 1989

HENRY

The past couple of days have been full of meetings, getting to know the crew, and filling out paperwork, but that hasn't stopped me from daydreaming about Izzy during every free moment. I haven't seen her again since she ran out two days ago, so I assume she turned down the job. Guess I'll have to add finding her to my to-do list.

Right now, I'm soaking up the last hours of precious sunshine after a long day inside. I could be flirting with any one of the young women who, like me, are hanging out watching their dogs play at the park near my apartment. House. Whatever it is. Boston isn't full of high-rises like New York. Instead, most of the residential streets in the city are lined with two- and three-story places split up into apartments. Which is nice, even if they're crammed way too close together from my suburb-of-Raleigh point of view. I mean, you could open your window and talk to your neighbor without even raising your voice. I am thankful the station found me a place close to GBH headquarters, and more important, one that lets me keep a dog.

My family always had a dog growing up. Or my dad did. After his last dog passed away—from grief, I swear—my mom didn't get another one. Said she didn't want to be tied down. When I argued that it'd be good company for her, she came right back with "*You* could get a dog."

"Like I could take care of a dog," I argued. "I can't even keep a plant alive."

She had no argument for that, so I didn't have to admit what really kept me from putting any kind of roots down in North Carolina. Getting a pet or buying a house or seriously dating anybody meant giving up on ever getting back to New York. On ever jumping back into the high-flying, competitive world of network news where I'd be working twenty-hour days and would never make it home to feed a dog, let alone take it for a leisurely walk. I just wasn't ready to let go of that dream. Not that I did anything to make it happen.

But then one day, I was driving to a friend's cabin up in Lake Lure to get away for the weekend when something ran out of the woods. Right at my car. Thankfully, I swerved before I hit it. When I got out of the car to see what it was, this scruffy bag of bones and fur greeted me like I was his long-lost buddy. Skinny as a rail and full of fleas, before I could say "boo," he'd jumped into my truck. Instead of continuing on to the lake, I drove back to the office of our old family vet.

He was just about to close for the day but let me in because he was a buddy of my dad's. As he checked him over, he asked, "Where'd you find him?"

"'Bout thirty miles west on 64."

"Mm-hmm. I 'spect he's a dog that won't hunt."

"You mean they starved him to get him to hunt better?"

"No, they dump a dog like that on the side of the road and shoot at him if he tries to follow 'em home."

He pointed to a spot on the dog's scabby skin. "Press your finger right there." After I did as instructed, he asked, "Feel that? That's buckshot. I bet if we did an X-ray, we'd see hundreds of 'em."

Half-starved and shot at, he was still sweet as could be. When his mouth curved in a doggy smile, I couldn't say no. To Ribsy. In that moment, I named him after the dog in my favorite Beverly Cleary books growing up, the ones where the main character shared my name and found a scrappy stray dog. After Doc finished a thorough exam, he sent us home with flea shampoo, meds for Ribsy's mange, and some special food to fatten him up.

That's the funny thing. These days, Ribsy is like me: we run to fat if we don't exercise every day and watch what we eat. Luckily, Boston has lots of parks, so we run together every morning and then come to this park in the evening so he can socialize with other dogs. He's a chick magnet, so it's no hardship.

Unfortunately, I haven't clicked enough with any of the lovely young ladies he's fetched so far for me ask them out—especially for the past two days, when daydreams of a fantasy life with Izzy have clogged my brainwaves. Interestingly, now they're set in Raleigh. Like, what if we'd been actually dating when my dad died? Since she seems to have left her New York acting career, she might've come with me to North Carolina. I could be providing the grandchildren my mom's always on about—something she seems to think you can never have enough of. Bella could act in local theater while I shoot to the top of the local TV scene. Maybe, with my own family to support, it would've been okay to direct and produce less-than-imaginative crap.

Then it occurs to me that there must be a reason Izzy moved to Boston. Maybe her own family needed her. I know that *Boom* kids had to be Boston locals, so she must be from here originally. And in the long run, pipe dreams aside, I should probably stay away from her if I want to keep this job and advance in the career that I've put before everything.

She's probably a cat person, anyway.

THE NEXT MORNING when I walk into the production meeting, I'm surprised to find Izzy, or I guess it's Bella now—got to get that straight—seated at the conference table. She doesn't see me because she's focused on a pile of paperwork, the same slew of stuff I had to pore over and sign two days ago.

Meaning they've hired her.

When I pull out a chair and it makes a scraping noise, she looks up. A pained expression crosses her face before she rearranges her expression and flashes me the smile that makes the camera love her. That drew me to her. When I was a kid and then a giddy, on-the-way-to-the-top television exec.

Which reminds me that I'm not that kid anymore. At thirty, I'm too old to waste time. In Raleigh, I had to fight every step of the way to advance my ideas and my career. I'm here for my career, not to chase other dreams, so I keep my smile professional and focus on the task at hand.

Unfortunately, when James calls the meeting to order, the first thing he says throws a monkey wrench in my plan to innovate. "A year ago, when we were throwing around ideas for a new kids' show, we couldn't come up with a single format or concept that was better than *Boom.*"

Do I risk offending my new bosses right off the bat? Or is it more of a risk to have my career pinned to a has-been show that gets revived, only to die again? I've never been known for prudence or patience, so I raise my hand. After James gives me a nod, I begin with, "There's a saying where I'm from"—amping up my hometown accent, I drawl—"if it ain't broke, don't fix it."

James nods. "My point exactly."

But before he can take another breath I add, "The problem with that, though? What's your definition of broke?" Pausing to let that sink in, I survey the table to see who might be with me. I've at least got everyone's attention, so I plow ahead. "For example, way before ad revenue dropped for a local gardening show, Nielsen told us that viewership was on a downward slide. The brass only cared about the income, but when you're losing eyeballs, eventually your advertisers are going to go elsewhere."

"We don't sell advertisements on public television," Carol points out, "as I'm sure you know."

"Of course." I sit up straighter and direct my focus to her. "But you can't completely ignore the data, right? I mean, there must've been some reason why the sponsor of the original *Boom* dropped out."

James and Carol share a quick glance before she answers. "It's complicated. As you've suggested, Burger World decided they could sell more fries by buying commercial time on network shows. We also faced a political climate that was less supportive of public television. Now, however, we have funding from foundations that are all about education. We will be adding more science and math to the show at their behest."

"I hope you'll consider making some other changes, too, like shooting outside the studio. The research I've done on the old *Boom* shows a big spike in interest when the short documentaries were added."

James nods. "We had considered that—"

Before he can add some backward-ass reason for why they can't possibly change anything so precious as the original *Boom*, I cut in. "That's great. I'd love to have some freedom with the pacing, too. Changing up the cut gave our cowboy show a much-needed facelift, which, as you know, led to a successful syndication." This not-so-subtle reminder having landed, I barrel on. "Our competition isn't just the networks this time around. Nickelodeon has some great shows, like *You Can't Do That on Television* and *Don't Just Sit There.* The soaps are even aiming for the after-school crowd"—I give Bella a nod, but she frowns at the suggestion, so I turn to a different staff member—"plus game shows and even video games. *Boom* may have been fast-paced when it debuted, but in today's field, it's slower than a herd of turtles."

At least I earn a few chuckles with that.

After a long pause, where no one seems to know what to say, Bella raises a hand. "Taking the kids away to do team-building is a huge change already. What if we shot some footage of that process? For documentation purposes, if nothing else."

"That's exactly the kind of thing I'm talking about," I say. "Kids won't sit through a bunch of scenes with the same old black background. We need the show to move."

The other associate producers chime in with their own ideas, making me feel like my point has been made, so I wrap up by throwing a bone back to Carol. "I remember you saying during my interview that the stuff viewers send in is more original than anything fifty adult writers in a room could come up with. I'm not suggesting we get rid of that. I just want it to feel current so we can keep up with the competition. Or even beat it."

BY THE END of the meeting, we seem to have taken two steps back for every one step forward. Frustrated and desperate for an ally, I jog to catch the person who seems like she might have the most sway over Carol. "Bella, can I talk to you for a minute?"

When she flinches at my touch, my hands go up in the air reflexively. "Sorry, I—"

"It's fine. You just startled me."

I shove my hands in my pockets so I'll be sure to keep them to myself. Despite whatever it is that draws me to her personally, I'm here to get us on a professional footing. "I really need to stretch my legs. Walk with me?"

She nods down the hall to the doorway where the other APs are gathering. "I need to join them, but I guess I can take a quick break first."

Since my time with her is limited, once we're outside, I cut right to the chase. "I feel like we need to clear the air. I always told myself that I was probably barely a blip on your radar, but the way you looked at me yesterday—"

She shakes her head. "It's fine, Hal. I mean, Henry."

"You can call me Hal."

"I think it's best if I call you Henry."

"Oh, well, okay. Anyway, it was a shock to see you, but—" Filing away the warm feeling I get when she calls me by my old nickname, I press on. "I just want to tell you what happened. I'm not the kind of guy to walk out like that."

Her expression is guarded, but she nods.

After blowing out a breath, I lead off with, "That day was a life changer."

Her face pales. "What do you mean?"

"I think I told you I was celebrating a promotion. Well, it was huge. It would've put me on the fast track to producing network news."

"Would have?"

I stop and face her in the shade of one of the trees lining the sidewalk. "When I left that dressing room to go back and find my overcoat, I ran into a coworker who'd been looking for me for an hour trying to get a message to me. My dad had collapsed at work and was in the hospital." Her expression shifts like lightning, from walls-up to shock to sympathy. The last has my throat clenching as tight as the fists in my pockets, but I keep going, the need for her to understand greater than the need to avoid the memories. "I went straight to the airport and got on the first flight home, but he'd had a brain aneurysm and they couldn't save him."

Her hand lands on my forearm. "Oh my god. I'm so sorry."

"Thanks." When she lets go, my arm feels bereft. "Um, anyway, that's why I disappeared. Do you forgive me?"

"Of course." She opens her mouth, seems suspended for a beat, then closes it. After shaking her head slightly, like she's erasing an

Etch-a-Sketch, she asks, "So, you didn't go back to the job in New York? You've been in Raleigh all this time?"

"Yeah, I needed my family, and they needed me. I ended up getting work as a cameraman at a local station and worked my way up. But I was off the fast track, and there was no way of getting back on."

"So why did you come to Boston?"

"Long story short: I've got some ideas, and I think this is the place to implement them."

"On *Boom*?"

I huff out a grunt. Since I'm baring my soul here, I may as well go all the way. "Honestly, this was the best job I could get with my résumé. I hope to pitch and produce my own shows before too long. Of course, that'll never happen if this show fails. I don't know about you, but I didn't come here to resuscitate a tired format of a show only to watch it die a slow death because it can't keep up with the competition."

"I don't know." She winces. "I'm really just here for the paycheck."

"That paycheck won't last long if the show gets canceled after just one season."

Sighing, she glances back at the building. "True."

Sensing that my time here is limited, I press on. 'But you're with me, right? We need to innovate more to get kids' attention these days."

She nods, but in that way where you're half shaking it *no*. "And to hold kids' attention, I guess."

"I mean, filming the boot camp or whatever this"—I make air quotes—"'retreat' is? That's a great idea."

"Well, we can't just shove cameras in their faces." Folding her arms over her chest, she looks back at the building again. "Bonding as a team should be the priority, but we could pitch it as a way to gradually get them used to being in front of the camera. It takes time. My group jelled as we created the opening sequence, but it took longer than those few sessions to let go of self-consciousness when that red light would go on." She glances back to me. "At least for me it did."

"It's too bad that the show's already cast. Shooting the auditions would've been great."

"Hm. I could see… Well, this might be dumb."

"What?"

She wrinkles her nose.

"Come on. There are no dumb ideas. Just ideas that might not work."

"I don't know about that but… Okay. What if, for the opening sequence, we literally show how they're a regular kid—just like the viewers—walking on a street or coming out of a school on their way to the studio?"

"I like it. We could show iconic parts of Boston. Harvard, the State House, Paul Revere stuff."

"Right. They could also wonder about things along the way, like, I don't know… What kind of horse did Paul Revere ride?" She points at me. "Which could set up taking things out of the studio."

At the possibility that I've finally won her over, my grin is wider than it's been since I got to this stuffy town. "So, how many letters have kids sent in so far?"

"I'm not sure. Speaking of which"—she tips her head to the side—"I do need to get in there." I fall into step with her as she heads back toward the building. "I heard it's only a trickle, though. Back in the day, the show got thousands a week. I think they did a push through local schools this spring, but so far there hasn't been a huge response."

"What if we shot a promo commercial? Show the new cast getting ready to be on the show, but they can't do anything without the ideas of the kids at home."

"We could show them taking on the challenges at boot camp…"

When she trails off, I finish her sentence. "And then just sitting in an empty studio with nothing to do. Plus, we can cut it in a way that'll show Carol and James the potential of more dynamic editing."

She opens her giant shoulder bag and paws through it. "Let me see if I have something to write this down. Snacks, Band-Aids… this mom purse is full of everything except a notebook," she mutters. "Aha! I have a magic marker and napkins. That'll have to do."

"You have your mom's purse?"

She gives me a look like I'm the one speaking nonsense. "Uh, no. *I'm* a mom."

I just nod. I should say something, but the only words filling my brain are *Who's the guy?* Even less appropriate: *Can I take him?*

Her tone is sharp when she cuts through the testosterone fog. "It won't interfere with my work, don't worry. I've already worked out the schedule with Carol."

Hands up again, I manage, "No, hey. No judgement here. You're lucky."

"I am," she says, before practically running toward the building. "I should get to work."

"Yeah. Me too."

■

AFTER THAT ROLLER coaster of a conversation, I force my brain to power through the many tasks waiting for me at my desk. Then I make some calls to production rental companies in town. After pricing out a package of lights and cameras we could take to New Hampshire, I write up a proposal and budget for documenting the week at camp.

I'm focused enough to get the work done, but a heavy feeling's dogging me, and I think it might be disappointment.

That Bella's not available.

I mean, she's even more attractive now than she was in her early twenties. Like her beauty has mellowed. Fewer sharp angles. The high cheekbones and wide-set eyes that'd make her a delight to light are still there, but everything is softer now. There's a guardedness, but I think that's all about the night we shared. Which is under-standable.

I'm glad she's on the team. I could brainstorm with her from dawn to dusk. It's probably a good thing that she's married and has a kid. Less temptation to get involved. Lower probability that I'd fuck things up between us, mucking up things here at work.

Unfortunately, the temptation is all too real. Memories of the few hours we spent together have been flashing through my mind for the past two days. Good memories that I thought I'd packed away with the bad ones from that day. If she weren't married, I could've convinced myself that it was worth the risk to relight the spark that bounced between us the moment she caught me dancing on that rooftop balcony.

But it's better this way. We'll have a fruitful professional relationship, and I'll bury those other ideas where they belong.

Not that I'd want to take on a woman with a kid even if Bella were available because, as was proven by my experience working on clown and cowboy shows, I'd be a terrible dad. I may have been accused of barking at the kids on the show in Raleigh. More than once. But come on. Those kids were brats, they outnumbered the adults, and somebody had to be the bad cop. And the baby-talk thing my brother does with his kids? Just the thought of it makes my gonads shrink.

Nope. With my Oscar the Grouch persona and my workaholic tendences, I am definitely not dad material.

That doesn't stop me from obsessing like a junior high school girl over the conversation with Bella for the rest of the day. So when I pick up my phone just before closing, it's ironic that the first words out of my best friend's mouth are "They figure out that you hate kids yet?"

"So nice to hear from you, Ralph. Thanks, I'm doing well. How about you?"

"Cut the bullshit, man."

"Yeah, yeah. Just trying to be an adult here." Leaning back in my chair, I relax for what feels like the first time in a week. "How's the weather in Raleigh? Sticky and hot yet?"

"Well, let's see here." He shuffles some papers and puts on his weatherman voice. "The relative humidity is a mere fifty-one percent, despite the above-average high temperatures in the low eighties. Light winds out of the northwest and an incoming low-pressure system will—"

"My eyes glazed over at 'relative humidity.'"

"The weather is an integral part of people's lives, man. Don't dump on the weather."

"You're right. What else would people have to talk about at boring dinner parties?"

"I notice you didn't answer my question."

"I haven't seen any kids yet, if that helps. And I've been on my best behavior."

"Pushy, impatient, stirring things up?"

"Pretty much." Hopping up and stretching the phone cord to its limit, I close the door to my office. No need to fuel gossip over something that was over before it started. "There was a potential hiccup my first day here, but that seems to have resolved itself."

"Hiccup? Is that code for they almost fired you? No worries, man. They're missing your hard-hitting ways around here already. I hear the girl they got in to replace you has no idea what to do in the editing suite. And the camera guys just ignore her."

"Poor thing. You tell Barney I'll tell everybody he uses hazelnut creamer if he's not nicer to her."

"It's Barney that uses up the good stuff? No way."

"Way." I nod, suddenly homesick for the crew I thought I was so sick of.

"So, what'd you do? Piss off the gaffer?"

Scrubbing a hand over my face, I tell myself that maybe Ralph will have a perspective on this I haven't thought of. "Nah, it was more personal. Did I ever tell you that I had a one-night thing in New York? With a childhood crush?"

"Like someone you went to elementary school with?"

"Nah, I worked my way through those in high school once I grew and put on some muscle."

"So modest."

"Just being honest."

"Who was the chick, and what does this have to do with your job?"

By the familiar creak of his office chair, I know he's leaning back and putting his feet on his desk to settle in for a chat, so I do the same. "Did you watch *Boom* growing up?"

"Sure, didn't everybody? I mean, what else was there to watch while you waited for your mom to burn dinner?"

"Remember Izzy?"

"The blond who did a back walkover? With the long pigtails and longer legs?"

"Her."

"Aww. You like her."

"I'm not fourteen, Ralph."

"So, what was the problem? You couldn't get it up?"

"That may be your problem, but never mine."

"Methinks the man may protest too much."

"The problem was," I continue, ignoring him, "we had an amazing few hours together—right before I found out my dad was in the hospital. I left town without letting her know."

"That's on you, but it was a long time ago. Plus, she's a little old to be on *Boom*, right?"

"She's an assistant producer on the new *Boom*. And you wouldn't believe the look on her face when she saw me."

"Like you owed her money?"

"Worse. Like I ruined her life or something."

"Sex with you is that bad, huh? Maybe she joined a nunnery afterwards."

"I don't think so, because she has a kid now."

"Well, that's some other poor bastard's problem."

"Yeah, I guess."

When I don't continue, he clears his throat and says, "You said 'hiccup,' so I take it you smoothed things over despite your lack of social graces?"

"I can be charming when I want to." What I don't say is *My charms may have worked on Izzy, but they're falling flat with Bella. Who is married anyway.*

"You keep telling yourself that. Speaking of which, I gotta go. Hot date."

"With a barstool at a sports bar?"

"With a living, breathing woman. You should try it sometime. Check you later." Always a bundle of energy, I hear the knock on his desk and shaking of keys before he says, "I miss you, you dipstick."

"Miss you too, man."

After I hang up I'm lonelier than when I picked up the phone. Time to head home and to the dog park. Maybe I'll pretend I'm Ralph and ask a living, breathing woman out on a date. No one may be as intriguing as the one working right down the hall, but I need to find some way to leave those feelings where they belong.

In the distant past.

Chapter 6

"Last week on *As the Earth Revolves*: Dena is furious with Phil for showing more affection and attention to the baby than he does to her. Later, she admits to Rona that she is jealous of the baby. Bob's deepest secret is nearly revealed." *Soap Opera Land*, June 1989

BELLA

A little over a week into my employment at WGBH, I get an odd assignment: Watch TV. Henry's argument seems to have swayed Carol and James enough that they've tasked me with researching our competition. Of course, we could just get the listings from the TV guide but watching them will give me a more complete picture of what we're dealing with.

Unfortunately, another reason I'm doing this is that we really don't have enough letters coming in with usable ideas. I think Henry's right on that score, too. A promo commercial might be just the thing.

I am glad Henry's too busy to do this with me, though. I've avoided him since I missed the opportunity to tell him about Lilah when he apologized. The moment was there, but I just couldn't do it. Now I don't know how to circle back.

Like, *Oh hey, remember when you told me what happened to you after we had sex that one time? Well, I forgot to tell you that my life changed in a major way too.*

I have no better ideas, so I focus on the job at hand, using the remote to click through the channels, thinking that even this little device makes a big difference. Back when I was on *Boom*, not only were there only four or five channels to choose from, but viewers had to actually get up out of their seats and walk over to the TV to change the channel. With the clicker, it's way too easy to move on to something else if a show drags.

It's *also* way too easy, I find, to get hooked on something you didn't intend to watch in the first place. When my old show flashes on the screen, I'm sucked back in before I know it. I haven't seen it for years, but people who were like family to me are right there, in rooms I practically grew up in. My sister on the show is a young mom, just like me. The father is a guy I had an affair with, on the show and in real life.

I can't believe she went back to him, Quinn huffs.

When the episode ends, I'm hunched forward and my heart's racing a mile a minute. After I turn off the TV, I pace around the room shaking out my hands and remind myself that I've left those dramas behind.

Not very far behind, Izzy says. *You have secrets in real life, you know.*

True, but no one's waiting outside the doors of WGBH hoping to get a photo of me. No one's offering me a bump or a hit or a tab to get me through the day. An ever-present bowl of candy is about as exciting as it gets at this network. Plus, at least for now, I get to go home at five o'clock instead of the wee hours of tomorrow. No wonder half the cast and crew were hooked on uppers and cocaine. We worked an inhuman schedule.

Going out afterward didn't help, Izzy says.

But it was fu-un, Quinn sing-songs. *Her life now is so bor-ring.*

Speaking of which, it's almost time to pick up my boring little girl and bring her back to our boring apartment above our boring shop.

Growing up above a bookstore might not have kept me from getting into trouble, but it did give me a lifelong love of reading, something Lilah shares. It'll be tough on her if we have to give it up. The groups of toddlers and moms at the story hour she leads love her, and the feeling is mutual.

As I pack up my things, Henry's comment about the soaps aiming for a younger audience crosses my mind. I hadn't believed him, but when I think back over what I just watched, there were more characters in their teens and early twenties—including a slew of hunky guys. The middle-aged regulars were mostly in the background. And lots of people record their favorite shows on the VCR, so more kids could be watching them even if they're at school when they air.

I flip through the TV Guide on my way down the hall toward the exit, noting that *ABC's Afternoon Special* is still running, unbelievably. Like most network programs it's in re-runs for the summer, but there are plenty of other options.

The UHF channels have old cartoons like *The Flintstones* and *The Jetsons*, or sitcoms like *Diff'rent Strokes* and *Punky Brewster*. The new cable channel called Nickelodeon seems to be our main competitor, but the sheer volume of programming creates our biggest challenge. How do parents even keep up with everything battling for their kids' attention, let alone figure out what's good for them or even appropriate?

Luckily, I know a parent of a couple of girls in our target age group, and I'm supposed to pick up my daughter from her house in fifteen minutes.

WHEN I GET to Tami and Abby's house, Esther isn't home.

"I'm sorry, Jess," I say when my friend opens the door. "I can't believe you're babysitting my kid."

"Don't worry about it," Jess says, pulling me inside. "We've been having a great time. Esther got stuck at work and asked me to come over." She checks the time. "I do have rehearsal soon, though, so if you could stay till Esther gets home, that'd be great. It's always a tricky time, that week or so between when the school year ends and camp begins."

"Being a working mom is tricky no matter how you slice it." Yet again, I'm reminded of how lucky I am to have my mom to watch Lilah. But it does get more complicated when Lilah wants to spend time with other kids, like Tami and Abby, who might not want to spend the whole day in a bookstore.

"As I am learning," I continue. "The rep schedule is actually better for me with this new job. I can even go with the cast and crew on the retreat next week up in New Hampshire."

"Lucky you, only one tech week to deal with. I have two in a row," Jess grumbles.

"Why don't you go ahead now? Take a few minutes to wind down before you have to wind up again for rehearsals."

"If you don't mind, that would be good. I need to eat dinner and grab my script from my place."

"I don't mind at all. I miss my baby." A chat alone with the girls might give me more intel than if Jess or Esther were here, anyway.

A few minutes later, I'm impressed at how little TV they watch, but I'm also disappointed. Esther's girls may not be a representative sampling of our audience after all.

"We're only allowed to watch one hour of TV a day, and it has to be educational," eight-year-old Tami tells me.

"But that doesn't include movie nights," Abby cuts in. "We have a lot of good videos."

"You watch Nickelodeon and MTV when you go to Sarah's house," Tami says in a classic jealous-younger-sister tone.

"How do you know that?"

"I heard you talking about it on the phone."

Hands on hips, a replica of her Aunt Jess, Abby warns, "You'd better not tell. Or I'll tell that you were spying on me."

Tami points at me. "She might tell Mom."

"Me?" Hand to heart I promise, "As long as it doesn't involve a crime, my lips are sealed. This is research."

Abby doesn't seem convinced, so I try another tack. "What about your friends? I don't even know them, so I can't tell on them."

"Well, lots of kids don't really watch TV. I mean, they have it on, like in the background. But what's really cool are games like Tetris and Super Mario Brothers."

"Like at an arcade?"

"What's an arcade?" Tami asks.

"Oh, wow. Your mom *is* strict."

"It's a place where old people used to go to play video games," my daughter explains.

Suppressing the eye roll at being called old, I ask, "Where do young people play video games, then?"

"At home on, like, a Nintendo." Abby makes a face. "Of course, we don't have one."

"Or an Atari," Lilah says. "Jennie's brother has one, and she sometimes gets to play. He only lets me watch."

"She's so lucky," Tami says.

"I know."

So, it's not just cable TV shows, it's movies on video cassettes and video games kids can play right in their family rooms. Or bedrooms.

Do kids ever go outside anymore?

"You know who's really lucky, though?" Abby says, answering my unspoken question. "Polly. She got to go to her cousin's farm last weekend and watch kittens get born!"

As she holds forth on the miracle of nature, it becomes clear that changing the pace won't be enough to try to hang on to their attention. Turning the show into a live-action video game could be fun. But if we could also open our audience's eyes to the wonders of the world by taking our cast out where the real drama is happening—in nature—that could be inspirational.

Instead of being limited by the credo "by kids, for kids," we could open up the concept so our cast can model learning by doing. The question is, how?

UNFORTUNATELY, the next day my mom and Lilah wake up with a stomach bug. After getting them both settled in front of the TV with ginger ales, I call the station to let them know that I can't come in.

Thankfully, James tells me not to worry about it. "We do have a small set of letters that I'd like screened by tomorrow. Do you think you could work from home if I can get someone to drop them off?"

I give him the bookstore's address, since I'll be shuttling up and down from our apartment to the shop in case there's a miracle and we actually have customers.

A few hours later, when the bell jingles over the front door, it's not a customer or a delivery, but Henry. Before I can open my mouth to ask what he's doing here, Quinn and Izzy scramble my thoughts and feelings.

You need to tell him right now, Izzy says. *What if Lilah comes downstairs and he sees her? She looks exactly like him!*

How 'bout we skip the confession and shag him on the counter, Quinn counters. *He's a guy. That's all he cares about anyway.*

That's pretty sexist, Izzy snaps.

I'm just telling the truth here, sweetheart. Isn't that what you want?

"Everything okay?" Henry asks, making me realize that I've been listening to the girls yapping on my shoulders rather than him. "You're not getting sick too, are you?"

Wiping a hand across my brow, I send him a shaky smile. "Just didn't get much sleep." I gesture overhead. "We had a rough night."

"You live upstairs?" He knocks on his skull. "Ah, now I get the name of the shop. I thought The First Story referred to the Bible or something."

"Nope. The pun was too much for my parents to resist when they bought the place." I gesture around the shop. "This was my playground growing up. And now I'm back. Pretty lame, huh?"

"Pretty cool, I'd say. Though I was a hyper kid, so I don't know if it would've worked for me. My mom used to make me do laps around the house before I could come inside after school. Then I could sit still for at least twenty minutes." He sets a box of letters on the counter. "That's why I offered to bring these over. Needed to get out of the office."

Before I can thank him, he juts his chin at the inventory list in front of me. "How many jobs do you have, anyway?"

"None of them are full-time." I shrug. "But to answer your question: three. Four if you count being a mom."

"Which you should," he says, leaning against the counter like he's settling in for a chat. "I don't know how you do it."

I hold up my *Comedy of Errors* script, which I've also been studying. "Obviously, I'm used to multitasking, so don't worry. It won't affect my work on the show."

His hands go up in surrender—a gesture he seems to make a lot with me. "I didn't say anything about that. It's just that... I have no patience." Leaning in, he whispers, "I'm terrible with kids."

"Good to know." Hm... how to break the news that he might need to get over this problem he has with kids?

"Girls especially," he adds with a mournful smile.

"Well, since I have a girl..."

"Yeah. Best keep her away from me."

Right there, Quinn crows. *He just gave you permission to not tell him.*

He doesn't know she's his, Izzy argues.

"Unless you want to see her cry," he adds with a sigh. "I'm very good at that."

Oh dear. Maybe you shouldn't tell him about Lilah, Izzy whispers.

I can't believe I agree with you, Quinn says. *I mean, if he doesn't like kids, what's the point?*

He does seem kind of sad that he makes them cry, Izzy protests weakly.

"And yet you've chosen to work with them?" I ask, hoping there's at least a part of him that wants to be around children. "Why?"

"Well, it kind of chose me. Like I said, this was the best job I could get when I decided to leave Raleigh. And I am committed to doing a good job." He straightens. "Which I suppose I should get back to. Can

I do anything before I leave?" Henry asks. "Get you some juice or soda or... crackers?"

See! He can't be all bad, Izzy says triumphantly.

"Oh, that's nice of you to offer, but I think we're good."

Jingling change in his pockets, he scans the interior of the shop instead of moving toward the door. "So, is it always this..."

"Dead?" I finish when he doesn't.

"Yeah. I mean, it's a weekday, but I'd think you'd have *some* traffic."

Straightening the order forms on the counter, I realize that this might be an opening to telling him about Lilah. I hate to be dependent on others, but maybe he'd be willing to pay child support and leave us in peace. "Unfortunately, things have been slow lately, even on the weekends, which is why I took the job at WGBH."

His grin is devilish. "You mean you don't have a burning desire to create a TV show for kids either?"

"Well, now that I'm doing it, I have a burning desire to make it a good one. But more importantly, we need the income. Three people can't live on what this place brings in anymore. I don't even know how long we'll be able to keep it open. My mom has been operating at a loss for some time. Without telling me."

Before I can shift gears to suggesting that he could be a part of the solution, he asks, "But what about your husband?"

"Husband?"

"Doesn't he work?"

"Uh, I don't have a husband."

"Oh. I just assumed."

"Maybe they don't have them down in the South, but there is a thing called a single mom up here," I snap.

Harsh, dude, Quinn says. *No need to bite his head off.*

Hands up again, he takes a step back. "Don't get all Yankee superior on me, now. I think it's a pretty typical assumption."

"I'm sorry." I mirror his gesture. "You're right. Anyway, it's just me and my daughter. And my mom. She gave up a lot for me, so..."

Stop! You can't tell him about being an addict, Izzy warns.

She's right, so I backtrack. "Listen. I don't want to keep you. I'm sure there's plenty to do back at the station. I will go through these and, hopefully, see you tomorrow."

Maybe between now and then you can get your story straight, Quinn huffs.

"Oh, hey, if there are any requests that will get the kids out of the studio, will you let me know?" He grabs a pad of paper and a pen from the counter. "This is my extension. Anything we can possibly shoot outside of the four black walls of that so-called set."

"Will do." Taking the slip of paper from him, I fold it and put it in my pocket. He turns to go and almost trips over Newton, one of the store cats.

"Whoa. There's a cat in here!"

I have to laugh. "There are actually two." I cross from behind the counter to pick up our little silver tabby and give him a kiss on the nose. "This is Newton. He's a terror."

After I set him on the floor, Newton proves me right. With a hop, a skip, and a jump, he claws his way up one of the bookshelf facades that my mom covered in carpeting. Walking Henry toward the door, I point out our long-haired tortoiseshell, arranged artfully in the display window. "That's Desdemona. They're both very popular with customers. She's elegant, and he's a clown."

Henry just nods. "I see."

The cats remind me of Abby's and Tami's excitement yesterday and the idea it inspired.

Tell him, Quinn and Izzy whisper in unison.

I should let him go, but I do as they say. "You know, I did have a little inspiration yesterday, if you have another minute."

He pauses with a hand on the doorknob. "For the show?"

My face heats as Quinn mutters, *Well,* I'm *inspired to—*

"For the show," I say, cutting that thought short. "When I picked the brains of some of Lilah's friends, I realized that we'll be competing with video games too, on top of other television shows, which made me wonder: What if we took a page from gaming and make the show a contest?"

"Like the kids compete with each other?"

"Or they have to meet goals set by some sort of authority figure? Not an adult. That'd never fly with Carol."

"Hm. I like it." The smile that takes over his face reminds me of the first time I saw him.

Kiss him! You know you want to, Quinn sing-songs.

That would be completely inappropriate, Izzy says.

"Anyway, it's just a germ of an idea…" I say.

"I think it's great." Releasing the doorknob, he rocks on his heels like he's picturing possibilities. "Could be just the zip the show needs."

"Also," I continue, energized by his encouragement, "the girls got super excited about a friend who got to watch kittens being born. That tells me that learning about the real world could be a draw."

Still nodding, brow furrowed, he paces the length of the shopfront. The light filtering through the windows highlights the gold in his curls. "How would those two things work together?"

"Well," I say, a nervous laugh coloring the word, "I didn't get any further than that."

Instead of crossing back to the door, he settles in an armchair in the front reading nook and leans forward, elbows on his knees. "Let's figure it out."

"Um, well…" I scoot back to the counter and grab my notebook. Holding it up, I head back to sit in the other chair. "I did make a couple of notes."

"You know," he says, "when James asked me to deliver those letters, he shared that he was worried we didn't have enough viewer suggestions to fill the first season."

"Which might make changes more welcome?"

"Exactly."

At that, we jump right in. Ideas spark back and forth. We finish each other's sentences in an easy rapport combined with a more combustible something that has me rushing to get it all down. He scoots his chair close enough that I can feel the heat of his arm. When I remember to breathe, his familiar scent wafts into my nose, a perfect blend of cedar, sage, and some other thing that reminds me of that night on the balcony.

"Do you want to make the proposal, or should I?" he asks, breaking the spell.

Sitting back in my chair, I stammer, "I—I guess I could bring it up, and you back me up?"

Into a corner, Quinn says with an animal-like groan.

You really have a one-track mind, Izzy says, a hint of amazement in her tone.

"Sounds good." He gets to his feet, obviously much less rattled than I am. When he's halfway to the door and I think I'm safe, he adds, "Oh, I'm finalizing storyboards for the commercial today. If you're in tomorrow, want to take a look?"

You really shouldn't spend any more time alone with him without telling him, Izzy says.

Would you shut up about that? Talk about a one-track mind, Quinn snaps. *Anyway, she has to get her stories straight. As you've so helpfully pointed out, she can't tell him about her time in rehab or her addictions.*

"I'd love to have your input," he adds.

"Um, sure." I give him a stupid little wave. "Hopefully, I will see you tomorrow."

"Call me if you need anything? Seriously, I don't live far from here."

"I think we'll be fine, but thanks, I will," I promise.

I won't, though. No more extracurricular activities with Henry until, as Quinn said, I get my stories straight.

* * *

PASSION HAS ALWAYS BEEN an issue for me. Usually the things I'm passionate about end up getting me in trouble. But this feels different, like producing television might not just be about the paycheck. Maybe it's a way I can do something I'm really into while earning a living wage. Some of my Shakespeare buddies teach; others tend bar or work in restaurants to support their passion for the stage. Others do commercials or other on-camera work. Maybe this could be my thing. In any case, excitement stemming from the possibilities of putting our ideas into action spurs me on for the rest of the afternoon.

By dinnertime, I've done the meager restocking orders for the store and I've sorted the letters into piles: ones I want to work on, ones Henry will want to know about, ones others might be interested in, and—the biggest pile, unfortunately—ideas that are just not doable, like learning to fly an airplane. On second thought, I move that one to Henry's pile. Maybe he could figure that out. By the time I've typed everything up, my mom and Lilah feel well enough that I'm able to get to the evening's rehearsal.

The next morning, both Lilah and my mom seem fully recovered, so I head off to the station running on coffee and hormones.

After checking in with James, I stop by Henry's office. "Here's your list," I say as I hand it over to him.

"Wow, you're organized."

"Told you I could keep up."

"This is great," Henry says. When his eyes meet mine, the thing between us flashes. "Any more thoughts about the competition idea?"

"Not really," I say, backing out of his office. "But I did type up what we talked about."

"You're still up for proposing it, right?"

"Yep." I nod, turning to go.

"Great. You get the ball rolling, and I'll add details as needed."

"Sounds good," I say from the hallway.

"Hey, did you want to see the storyboards for the commercial?" he calls from his office door when I'm halfway to the conference room.

"I should probably go over these with the rest of my team before the planning meeting." Waving the other lists I brought in, I ask, "Raincheck?"

"Sure. See you in a few."

The other APs and I have just enough time to get organized before the meeting. Keeley, Laura, and Tim are all in their early twenties, and they treat me more like a boss—or maybe a mom—than a peer, but I'm not here to make friends. I'm here to make money. And good TV.

Just like at the last meeting, Henry launches right in with suggestions for changes. I always thought that southern people were polite and reserved, but he's like a New York politician with a Carolina accent—or maybe a hound dog. Unapologetically opinionated, a bit of a bully, but with a charming twang. "I'm thinking we'd be more likely to hang on to viewers if there's more of a through line for the show. Something to give each episode a dramatic arc."

When no one else says anything, I jump in. "My research supports this. Any dip in energy can have a kid losing interest and clicking the remote."

"But we don't have commercial breaks like the network shows," James says. "That's when people usually change channels."

"Nickelodeon has ads now too," Tim, the youngest of the APs, notes.

"We do have station IDs and promos, though," Keeley says.

"You think we really have to keep dangling a shiny object to hold a child's attention?" Carol asks, her tone making it clear how she feels. "That just seems counterintuitive to creating a meaningful experience."

"I'm not talking about gimmicks," Henry says with barely concealed impatience. "I'm talking about stakes. Something to get the viewers invested."

"Like a game show or something?" Tim asks, perking up.

"More of a competition," I offer. "Or goals to reach."

"That'd be cool," Keeley says. "Like they could go up against each other to complete challenges, like in a video game."

"And what if they lose? We kick them off the show? I don't like that at all," Carol says.

"The Boomerangs have already been cast," James says. "They've signed on for a show like the original."

"What if they have to work together?" Henry says.

"Like they have to achieve something together," I add, "whether it's taking a physical risk or learning something new."

"And then teaching the others?" Laura asks.

"Yeah, that'd be cool," Tim says.

"We could also use competition to highlight individual strengths," I argue. "It could give them a chance to experience how everyone has something to contribute in a collaboration."

"Oh, oh." Tim raises his hand like Horshack on *Welcome Back, Kotter*. "And they could earn, like, points or something. Or rewards."

"Like in a video game," Keeley points out again.

Carol looks like she's going to explode at the repetition of that particular phrase, so I add, "I bet we can find the positives in the video game format while leaving the negatives behind." Holding up a stack of letters, I play our trump card. "It's clear we don't have enough usable viewer suggestions to fill a season."

Carol raises a brow at James, who nods with a grimace.

"Henry and I came up with a potential new structure for the show." I pass around copies. "The suggestions become goals the kids have to reach before they can move on as a group. Whether that's performing a skit or cooking a recipe, like on the original *Boom*—"

Henry holds up the list I gave him earlier. "Or learning how to use a telescope or training a dog to roll over or running for political office or even flying an airplane."

Before anyone can object to that, I jump in. "Many of these suggestions invite taping outside the studio and involve people in the community. Since Boston is really one big college town, I'm sure we can find willing experts on practically anything.

"Each episode ends with the kids back in the studio, where the points are tallied based on what they learned and achieved. The judge determines whether or not they can move on to the next level." I hold up a hand. "Either way, we see them all again the next week."

"But who is this judge?" James asks. "It can't be an adult."

"What if it was another kind of authority figure, like an animal? Like Mr. Ed?" Henry asks.

Interesting. We have a proposal for this, but maybe he wants to get more buy-in from the others by making them feel a part of the idea generation.

"A horse in the studio?" James scoffs.

"I do know a woman who's an animal trainer," I say, thinking of Lucy Minola. "She did an amazing job with the dog that was in a Shakespeare Boston production last year."

"Who could train an animal to look like it's talking"—James taps his watch—"in a couple weeks?"

"Well, what about a puppet?" Henry asks.

Laura shakes her head. "Too babyish."

"An animated character?" Tim suggests. "That'd be cool."

"Too expensive." James shakes his head. "And it'd take over a year to create."

"A disembodied voice?" Henry asks.

Keeley makes a face. "That's kind of scary."

"A computer?" Laura offers.

"Ha! We could name it Hal," James says with a smirk.

"Why is that funny?" she asks.

"Like the movie? *2001*? Where the computer takes over?" James says.

"Never heard of it," Tim says.

"I'm not sure that's the best idea anyway," Carol says.

"What if it's a female voice instead?" I suggest.

"Less threatening, right? We could set it up so that the computer 'randomly,'" Henry says with air quotes, "chooses from the letters that are sent in."

"The computer could dialogue with the Boomerangs, either using typed text or a human voiceover," I add, which was our idea in the first place.

"I don't know." Carol sits back in her chair and crosses her arms. "Kids deal with so much judgement and competition as it is."

"But if they're working together to complete, like, missions—" Keeley says.

"That gives the audience a way to root for them," Laura finishes, "against the authority figure of the computer."

Henry shoots me a grin, and I know exactly what he's thinking. The younger APs are making our argument for us.

"But what about what the viewers send in?" James asks. "We haven't asked for anything like that."

"First off"—Henry holds up the list I typed for him—"like Bella said, so many of these beg to be shot outside the studio, and most of them have an inherent challenge. We can also change what we're asking for—or add to it," he adds before Carol can object. "We can ask kids something like, 'What do you wonder about? What do you want to know more about?' Or 'What do you want to see the Boomerangs tackle?' We could use the team-building retreat to shoot footage that we cut into a couple of promos that ask those questions."

James shakes his head. "I still don't know if we have time to make these changes."

Henry's practically bouncing in his chair. I can just picture the kid that had to run around the house before his mom let him inside. "I can get this done quickly, cut together a quick commercial that'll give you a taste of what I'm talking about."

"And the new asks from our audience?" Carol cuts in. "We've already sent out thousands of appeals through the schools."

"Like Henry said, we use what we get, we just change how we use them," I say.

"All right," Carol says, rubbing her temple. "You're starting to convince me. I'll see if I can find room in the budget for filming the retreat—"

"I've got prices on equipment rentals right here." Henry sifts through his briefcase. "I can shoot it myself and—"

"No." Carol stops him short, making a stop sign with her hand. "That's where I won't budge. We'll have to bring in someone from the outside. If we're doing team-building, we all have to join in. I want the Boomerangs to feel like we are all working together." She circles the table with her finger. "That includes you, Henry."

Backing off, he nods. "Got it."

Pointing at him and drawing a line to me and the other APs, she continues, "Someone needs to take the lead on the computer. That would require an additional set piece, someone to voice it, and I don't know what else…"

"And I need to have a shot list for the first episode by the end of the week," James adds. "I was hoping to finalize it today, but—"

"No problem," Henry says. "We can do it. Right, guys? No matter how long it takes."

As a working mom, I do have an actual out time, but I sense that we all need to pull together if we're going to make this work, so I nod.

The smile on Henry's face at the outcome of the meeting is way more rewarding than I'd like to admit.

Now that we're going to spend even more time with him, you really need to fess up, Izzy whispers.

So we can get laid, Quinn adds. Because she's Quinn.

Chapter 7

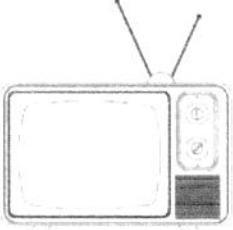

"OFF SCREEN: Dickie Tatum, one of the fine stars on *Private Hospital,* seems to be really making the steady scene with Carla Bayliss from the cast of *Ryan's Wish.* Rumor has it the pair has escaped together for a romantic getaway in the mountains. We also hear that when they can't be together, the phone lines buzz with calls between them." *TV Tattler,* July 1989

HENRY

The days fly by leading up to our group departure for New Hampshire and what Carol delights in calling "Boom Camp." I never went away to any kind of camp—my summers were always full of football practice. New Hampshire in June will be cooler and less humid than North Carolina in August, but that's about the only thing I'm happy about.

It feels like there's a lot riding on this. My bravado and bluster can get me out on a limb sometimes, and that's where I am right now. What if our ideas fall flat? What if I can't create a promo commercial that'll wow both my bosses and audiences enough to launch a successful first season?

What if I'm so distracted by every little thing about Bella York that I can't even concentrate?

If any of these things lead to failure, I'll have flown too close to the sun again, and my melting wings will have me crash-landing back to earth. With nowhere left to start over.

As I drive to the station on the day of our departure, after leaving poor Ribsy at a kennel—another reason I'm not so happy about leaving town—not only am I tense about having to interact with the kids, but I'm nervous about spending so much time in close proximity to Bella. She's been an amazing partner to work with, full of smart ideas and willing to stand up for them. She's also been a useful buffer with the other APs—all so young they feel like kids. In fact, they're as intimidated by me as a bunch of five-year-old girls, so I'm glad Bella has been in all the meetings with them. She's the only one who seems to get that my energy comes from a passion for the work, not anger. Any time I growl with impatience, the other APs flinch.

Bella doesn't flinch, but if I get too close, she scoots away or gets up suddenly or makes an excuse to leave the room. That day I visited her bookstore, we had a moment where I thought a kiss might be possible, but she hasn't let me get that close since. I even changed my aftershave in case that was bothering her. Maybe she's just making it clear that even though she's not married, she's no longer into me.

Which she definitely was the evening we spent together seven years ago. I've tried my best to bury those memories, but her smile, her laugh, her warmth, her gorgeous body—basically everything about her—reminds me of those precious few hours of pure physical passion.

Have I changed that much? I'm not a young buck anymore, that's for sure. I've got a couple wrinkles and my hair might be thinning a tiny bit, but she doesn't seem like she'd be that superficial.

Right now, though, I've got to park those feelings along with my car because I've arrived at the station and the bus awaits. Avoiding the cast members, I chuck my bag in the hold and hustle over to check in with the small crew I've hired to shadow us all week. It's only a camera operator, a sound guy, and a general utility guy, but their equipment fills the back of a Ford Bronco. I make sure they've got directions to the retreat center and a plan to shoot the *Boom* cast and crew's exit from the bus once we arrive, then send them on ahead, wishing I could ride with them instead of taking the bus.

Half an hour later, I'm really wishing I were in the Bronco. Carol must've been a camp counselor in her youth because she's led one inane, repetitive song after another. I know I'm supposed to join in, but since the only seat available was in the very back, I pretend I'm carsick and try to nap.

Next thing I know, I'm blinking awake and the bus is emptying. "Shit," I hiss before muttering a "Sorry" to one of the kids, wide-eyed at my use of the expletive. Jumping to my feet, I press my face to the nearest window. Thankfully, the crew is covering the kids and staff as they climb down the bus stairs and take in the beautiful scenery. The sloping mountains and green trees are a perfect visual contrast to the industrial complex we left behind in Boston.

Blowing out a breath, I grab my briefcase and make my own way down the aisle. Stretching my back before reaching under the bus to get my duffel, I catch sight of a disaster about to happen: a couple of boys are roughhousing right next to the lighting equipment. Not only do I not want to get charged for broken rentals, I doubt we'd be able to find replacements anywhere nearby, so I sprint over to literally pick them up by the backs of their collars.

"What the hell do you think you're doing?" After dropping them to the ground, I point to the light stand they knocked over. "This is expensive stuff. You can't just screw around here, same as when we're onstage. Got it?"

Nodding, both boys back away like I'm the dangerous one.

"Sorry, M-Mr., uh… " the bigger one stutters.

"Henry. You're supposed to call us by our first names," I grumble.

"Oh-k-kay, Mr. Henry."

Before I can snap *Just Henry*, Carol's at my side. "What's going on?"

The smaller boy's chin is trembling, making me feel like an ogre, but I jump in anyway. "They were screwing around and knocked over the equipment. I was just trying to stop them before anything broke."

After she takes in the boys' faces, Carol raises a brow and addresses all three of us. "It is important to show respect for everyone on the team, and that includes any gear that we might be responsible for."

Before I can say, *Exactly*, she continues, "But yelling will not be tolerated. Or physical aggression. From anyone or to anyone. Understood?"

"Yes, ma'am," the boys say.

"Please call me Carol," she says gently.

"Carol," they say with a little bit less enthusiasm.

When all three pairs of eyes track to me, I make myself smile and say, "Yes, ma'am, Carol."

It's gonna be a long week.

BELLA

After we unload the bus—which apparently involved some sort of kerfuffle that I missed because I'd taken two girls as desperate as I was after the long journey to the restroom—we get a tour of the retreat center. I do my best to pay attention, but half my brain is still back in Boston with my baby. This week will be the longest chunk of time I've ever been away from Lilah. I know she'll be fine with my mom, but I feel like I'm missing a vital organ. On top of that, I feel guilty. I'm technically working, but this place looks like heaven and the list of activities promises fun, making it feel like a vacation.

At the end of the tour, we get our cabin assignments. I get one all to myself because Carol's husband will be joining her over the weekend and Laura and Keeley both want to stay with the *Boom* girls.

Tim will do the same with the boys and James and Henry will take the other double cabin, which leaves me with the tiny little cabin closest to the bathrooms. Not wanting to isolate myself completely, I toss my bag on my bed and then join the younger girls to see if they need anything.

What I find in the cabin is the kind of drama we definitely don't want on the show: a roomful of girls in tears.

"Hey, hey," I murmur after closing the door behind me. "What's going on?"

"I'm scared," whimpers the tiniest one. I think her name is Tara.

"Me too," another chimes in.

When I catch Laura's eye, she whispers, "Henry yelled at some boys."

Blowing out a frustrated breath, I dig for patience.

I guess he wasn't kidding when he said he wasn't good with kids, Quinn says. *Good thing you're keeping Lilah away from him.*

That's not the plan, Izzy hisses. *She's just waiting for the right moment.*

Crouching next to Tara, I ask, "Are you upset because the boys got yelled at?"

"Uh-huh," she sniffles.

"Okay. Come on." I park my butt on the floor and wave my hands to get them to join me. "Let's talk it out."

It takes twenty minutes of hearing everyone's version of the story, but we eventually get them calmed down. I'm guessing their feelings are exacerbated by being away from home, by being with strangers, and by the anticipation of having to perform for the camera, but I don't get into all that. "Listen, I've been where you are. Did you know I was on the very first season of *Boom?*"

Jaws drop and emotions shift quickly.

"You were?"

"How long ago was that?"

"Was it fun?"

After fielding all their questions, including how very old I am, I think I've successfully redirected. However, I do want to make one last point before we head out to get to know the rest of the crew and get used to the cameras.

"We're all nervous because we all want the show to be a success—grown-ups and kids. But when it comes down to it, the most important thing is that we work together. Because then whatever we create will be a success. Does that make sense?"

Keeley adds, "Don't be afraid to ask questions or add your own ideas."

Most of the girls look dubious, so I try another tactic. "You know what? Sometimes the best way to get through your own fear is to help someone else get through theirs. Even if that person is physically bigger than you, they might be just as afraid as you—of failing, of looking silly, of getting their feelings hurt. If we keep that in mind, we'll build the best team ever."

Laura jumps up and puts a hand in the center of the circle, chanting, "Boom, boom, boom…"

Seconds later, we're all on our feet shouting, "Boom! Boom! Boom!"

Relieved, I lead a chattering group of girls to the first meeting of the week. But when I catch a glimpse of the cameras setting up, my own belly tightens in panic. My frontal lobe has known for a week that a crew would be filming our every move here, but I guess we forgot to clue in my limbic system. I'm going to need to take my own advice if I'm going to make it through a week of having those lenses aimed my direction.

For better or for worse, the first thing I notice after getting my stomach settled is that Carol and Henry are having a heated discussion. Before I can come up with a distraction so neither the girls nor the cameras will notice, Carol waves me over.

A serene expression on her face, Carol hands me a hat with pieces of paper in it. "The plan is to draw names to create the teams for the obstacle course competition. Henry here"—her smile tightens slightly as she gestures to him, but her voice is calm—"would like to have a hand in choosing who works with whom, but I disagree. Sometimes you have to trust that letting things happen organically will create real events that are more compelling than a manipulation of the truth. I'm willing to sacrifice 'wow' moments in order to get that. In any case, it's time to get this show on the road."

"You're the boss, Carol," Henry says, his tone making it clear that he's not happy about it.

"All right, then. Bella will do the drawings after I introduce your crew. They do understand that they have free rein to film, but no engagement? They're just flies on the wall." She gestures at the campground. "Or in the forest, I should say."

"I could supervise them during the obstacle course, just to get everything off on the right foot," Henry suggests.

Carol shakes her head. "If you're not participating, we won't have even numbers." After patting him on the shoulder, Carol—a hippie at heart—calls for everyone to gather in a circle. "Find a spot where you're standing next to at least one person you don't know," she says. "Or don't know well, at least."

There's some giggling as we jockey for positions. Henry even cracks a smile. Then Carol introduces the camera crew, including one guy who has already climbed a tower on the challenge course to get a bird's-eye view, explaining that we are all to ignore them as much as possible and that part of the purpose of this week will be to get used to having a camera observing us—not to interact with, but to witness whatever's going on. "That way, when we get back to the studio, we'll be comfortable expressing ourselves. Not everything they shoot this week will be used, if any of it," she adds. "If something embarrassing happens, we obviously won't use that. Try to keep your focus on getting to know each other."

"And on having fun!" Keeley shouts.

"Exactly," Carol nods.

We kick things off with a couple of get-to-know-you games that I remember from my time on the show, and then I grab the hat that has all of our names in it: the kids, the producing team, the musical director, the choreographer, the props and costume people—basically anyone and everyone who will interact with the kids on the show. As Carol explains that the hat will divide us into groups of four, the grimace on Henry's face has me stifling a laugh, even as my heart skips in anticipation. I do get why he'd prefer to choose the names, but this process has an excitement of its own. Unlike waiting to be chosen for a team in gym class—a feeling I didn't miss one bit when I left school to go to work—when Fate does the choosing, it feels fairer. And more fun.

When I pull my own name from the hat, I read it aloud and then jog to join a group that already includes Tara and Jared, another cast member. We high-five before I pick the final name to make up our team: Henry.

This should be interesting, Quinn and Izzy chorus.

Refocusing, I finish pulling names. The resulting team makeups may prove Carol right because I don't see a clear winner, though I doubt we four have much of a chance. My only regular exercise is hauling boxes of books in and out of storage, so I certainly won't be scaling walls and diving under nets with ease. I noticed on the bus ride that Jared's a beautiful singer, but I overheard him telling someone that he hates sports. Then there's tiny Tara, still shooting scared eyes at Henry, who is likely our only hope. He's got the makings of a serious athlete: muscular, quick on his feet, and intense.

A memory flashes—Hal sweeping me off my feet and tossing me onto the couch in my old dressing room—and I have to use the hat in my hand as a fan.

When Henry gives me a "You okay?" look, I just nod and smile.

I think we can win! Izzy says, ever the optimist.

I hope we win him, Quinn replies.

HENRY

I can't help it. I'm competitive, always have been. So even though I know my focus should be on the kids—making sure they're warming up to each other and the cameras, making sure moments are captured that I can cut into a fun, fast-paced commercial and opening sequence—all I can think about is winning.

We're so close, I can taste it. I doubt that anyone on my team managed to get a Presidential Medal of Fitness, but what they lack in muscle, they make up for in enthusiasm.

Surprisingly, Bella's the loudest of all, cheering on the rest of us. She was also the one who saved us at the cargo nets. When Jared got stuck, she insisted that I was too heavy to climb back and untangle him, so she did it—quickly enough that we came in second instead of last.

My team is tired, but everyone is. TV people are apparently not big on keeping in shape, and some of them are hampered by clothing not made for running and climbing. James's short-sleeved button-down is soaked in sweat, and the costumer is wearing a dress. We won't be able to use footage of her, of course, but a shot of her teammates' laughter as she gamely struggled to hop through the tires could be gold.

Bella gathers us into a huddle before the whistle blows for the final leg, which every one of us has to complete, to finalize our strategy. Each player's time will count, so if one or two of us can get through fast enough, we could win it, even if the others are back with the rest of the pack.

Tara's small but fast, and I'm big and fast, so Bella suggests that she and Jared try to delay everyone else by getting in the way.

"Pretty sneaky," I say.

"I like it." Tara reaches up to punch me in the arm. "Totally worth the risk."

Earlier, the little girl wouldn't even look me in the eye, so I'm counting that gesture as a win, no matter how we end up doing.

When the whistle blows, we jog over to get into position, chanting "Team Dabba Dabba Doo!" Naturally, Carol made us all come up with goofy team names, but I have to admit it was a good call since that was the first thing that got Jared talking.

Tara and I position ourselves on the outside. Bella shoots me a conspiratorial grin, and I'm hit with a wave of desire. She's muddy, sweaty, and her hair's a mess, but the gleam in her eye is the sexiest thing I've ever seen. The shout of "On your marks!" startles me back to the present, and I pack away the feeling for later.

When I whisper, "Let's do this," to Tara, I'm rewarded with a dazzling smile that I'd love to capture on camera. When the shot goes off, she and I take off like bats out of hell.

Squeals, laughter, and yells of protest echo behind us, but all my focus is on the wall we have to scale. Nobody said we couldn't help each other, so I practically throw Tara over the thing before I haul myself up. Tara's size works for her as we scramble under low-hanging ropes, and then she's ahead of me, nimbly skipping from one rock to another. When I do finally look back, it's clear that our strategy has worked. We're so far ahead of the pack that our scores will give us a good chance of winning this thing.

But just as I'm about to cross the finish line, a cry of pain grabs me by the collar and stops me in my tracks.

Tara, already over it, yells, "Henry, come on!"

Jogging in place, I scan the crowd until I find Bella. She's on the ground, holding on to her ankle. Jared is helping her to her feet, but he won't be able to get her through. Without thinking, I'm off, dodging the other players, until I get back to my teammates. Tagging Jared, I yell, "You go ahead; I've got her."

Nodding, his face serious, he takes off. Without even asking permission, I sweep Bella off her feet and onto my back as I shout, "Hang on!"

BELLA

We don't come anywhere near winning, but we do get everyone cheering and laughing. A heady mix of hormones, the result of being pressed against Henry's strong back, blunts the pain in my ankle at first, but when Henry sets me down and Carol catches my wince, she sends me back to my cabin and orders a couple of kids to fetch a bag of ice.

Twenty minutes later, my ankle is elevated and numbed, but I'm worried. I doubt it's broken, but I need to be at one hundred percent to get through not only the rest of this week, but tech and opening for *Comedy of Errors* next week. I'd thought I was doing the ultimate balancing act when the *Boom* retreat lined up perfectly with my week off from rehearsal, while the rest of the company opens *The Tempest*. But if I've messed up my ankle, my takeaway might have to be "Don't bite off more than you can chew."

Definitely something I need to keep in mind. Not only am I keeping many plates in the air with my tight schedule, but the stress of working with Henry, hanging out with Henry, competing alongside Henry... Every moment I'm with him makes me like him more. Problem is, every moment is also another moment that I'm lying to him.

Only by omission, Quinn scoffs. *He said himself that he doesn't like kids. You're saving him a load of grief.*

We don't know that for sure. Look how great he was with Tara and Jared just now, Izzy points out. *Maybe it's just younger kids.*

The ones about Lilah's age? Quinn asks. *Just because he contributed a few chromosomes to her existence doesn't necessarily make him dad material. If our dad is any example, that is definitely the case.*

Lying is still bad, Izzy sputters. *It really should be his call—*

A knock on the cabin door interrupts the argument between the girls on my shoulders. "Uh, come on in," I call from the bed. "Sorry, I can't get up."

When the door cracks open, I'm temporarily blinded by a ray of the setting sun.

"Hey, you doing okay?"

At the sound of Henry's voice, I sit up and readjust the plastic bag on my ankle, hoping to camouflage a sudden need to squirm. "Yeah. I'm just icing it to make sure."

When he closes the door behind him, the room shrinks exponentially.

"I, uh, brought you a few things." He sets a crutch against the wall. "I could only find one of these, but I figure it's better than nothing. And I brought you some pain relief."

When he pulls Tylenol and Advil from a grocery bag and sets them on the nightstand next to me, his scent wafts under my nose. Clean, crisp, and oh so male.

Searching for a safe place for my eyeballs to land, I attempt to focus on the hands balling up a plastic grocery bag.

Those palms can squeeze me wherever they like, Quinn sighs. *Remember how strong they are?*

Uhhh... is all Izzy can come up with.

He opens a plastic bottle of water and hands it to me. "You might be dehydrated. Come on, drink some of this."

"Thanks." My hand shakes as I take the bottle, spilling water on my lap. Henry grabs a towel from the end of my bed and dabs at my shorts.

When I scoot away from him, he steps back and shoves his hands into his pockets. "Sorry."

I sop up the rest of the water. "It's okay." When I try to reach the end of the bed to hang it up again, he takes it from me. "Thanks."

After what feels like an interminable, awkward pause, I say, "Listen," at the exact same moment that he says, "You know—"

He holds out his hand to me. "You go ahead."

Tell him, Izzy pleads.

But I can't seem to get the words out.

Finally, he lifts a hand between us. "I know what you're going to say."

"You do?"

He nods. "Swooping in and picking you up without asking permission was totally out of bounds."

Since that's not at all what I was going to say, I just shake my head. "It was fine. I'll be fine. It's all... fine."

He laughs. "So, you're... fine."

"Uh. Yeah."

You're just so sex-starved you've lost your native language, Quinn mutters.

Stop talking about sex! Izzy says.

He nods, perusing the cabin. "Layout's same as ours. Except there, James's crap is everywhere."

"Yeah, I, uh… got lucky with a single room."

Which means you could get lucky with him, Quinn sing-songs.

Not without telling him first, Izzy says. *Right?*

Our long-lost libido can be found again, Quinn says.

Not without telling him—

It's only when a cool, dry palm lands on my damp, hot forehead that I realize I've screwed my eyelids shut.

"Bella, are you in pain?"

Yes, Quinn moans. *I'm aching for your touch.*

"No, I'm… just…"

If you're not going to tell him, just ask him to leave, and then we'll all calm down, Izzy says.

I open my mouth to do just that, but what comes out is, "I could use a little distraction. I think there's a deck of cards…" I lean over, open up the drawer of my bedside table, and pull out the deck I noticed when I unpacked.

"Sure." He takes the cards from me.

And then I realize my mistake.

There's no chair in this room! Izzy gasps. *And the other bed is way across the room.*

He can sit on the bed, Quinn says with a smirk.

N-no, he can't—that's too… Izzy stutters.

"I'll just—" Awkwardly scooting sideways, I make room on the bed. "You can… sit."

He doesn't comment on my continued inability to form sentences, just slides the cards out of the worn cardboard box.

I open my mouth, determined to tell him, but when he takes my hand, words fail all of us—Quinn, Izzy, and Bella.

"I just wonder…" He looks away, pressing full lips together for a moment before meeting my gaze again. "Do you ever think about the couple we might've been if I hadn't left that night?"

Not what I was expecting to hear, Quinn says.

Aww, Izzy coos.

He rubs a thumb over my knuckles, silencing them both. "Your life is jammed full of jobs and people, and I don't want to be another problem you have to solve. But... the past few weeks, I can't stop thinking about that night. Every time I'm near you, I... I just want a do-over. Another chance to figure out if we'd be good together."

Who the hell knows what he reads from the expression on my face, but something makes him pull away. "I'm sorry. You're right; I should—"

Stupid me, I grab his hand. "I feel... I have wondered too." I blow out a breath. "But my world is complicated. And so am I. I have a lot of baggage, and I'm not sure you... I mean, it'd be a lot to take on."

One side of his mouth quirks. "As was proven earlier today, I'm capable of hauling around quite a bit of baggage."

I free my hand from his to whap him on the arm. "Are you saying I'm fat?"

"Nah, sweetheart." His sexy-as-all-get-out accent deepening, he captures my other wrist before I can hit him again. "I'm sayin' I'm stronger than I look."

Maybe it's the dare in his eyes, maybe it's pheromones, maybe it's being out in the woods miles from my many responsibilities, but something deep inside me says *Fuck it.* Not Quinn. Some primal part of me wants a do-over too. So I slide my hands to the back of his neck and pull myself up until we're nose to nose, my heart a wild thing in my chest.

HENRY

It's like seven years ago was seven minutes ago when Bella presses her forehead to mine. The desire I've benched since she stepped back into my life three weeks ago takes the invitation and runs with it.

Thankfully, it's quite clear that she's up for carrying the ball. Her lips find mine, urgent and demanding. Worries bubble up briefly: *Am I her boss? What about her kid?* But her breathy moans and impatient groans bat all thought away. When I ask, "Your ankle?" with my last shred of sanity, she just grapples for the bag of ice and chucks it to the floor.

Mumbling "Don't worry about it," she clambers on top of me.

When I pull her Camp Boomerang tee over her head, she breathes, "I'm sweaty."

"Me too."

We're not smooth, we're not polite, we're a scramble of two people who simply need to be skin to skin.

The scent of her is green grass and sunshine, her skin a meadow I want to luxuriate in. My shirt disappears, and her moan has me harder than I've been since… since the last time we did this. Greedy for more, I pull her sports bra over her head. It takes some squirming from her and awkward tugging from me, but finally her breasts are free. A 3D image from my memory—palm-sized boobs with pert pink nipples—is replaced by her new reality. Heavier, fuller globes more than fill my hands. Wider, browner nipples harden between my fingertips. The desperate moan for more and the grind of her pelvis against mine are exactly the same.

"Please, god, tell me you have a condom," she whispers.

"That I do." These days, you have to have a condom. When I lived in New York in the early eighties, women hardly ever asked. One, I always assumed they were on the pill. Two, asking for one implied that the other person might have an STD, so it wasn't polite. But AIDS raised the stakes, so now it's a given.

That's about all the thinking my desire-soaked brain can handle, especially because her hot little hands have found their way to my zipper. "Okay, okay, I got the message."

After rolling her off of me, taking care with her ankle no matter what she says, I free myself from my shorts and boxers, find my wallet, and pull out a condom. Without taking my eyes off her, I lock the door and pull the curtains. Rolling on the condom, I cover her body with mine, and then I'm in heaven.

Warm and slick, she greets me, but too soon, a thrust from me sends her over the edge. The harsh moan of my old nickname in my ear drives me on to the finish. Next thing I know, my forehead's pressed into her breastbone, and we're panting in a pool of sweat.

"Fuck," I breathe.

"Yeah," she answers. "Let's do that again."

Meeting her gaze, I can only agree. "Maybe a wee bit slower this time."

BELLA

When I wake, it's dark out. I'm pressed up against a very warm, very muscular, very male body. I nestle in closer and breathe in his intoxicating scent. Unfortunately, it only takes seconds for all the reasons we shouldn't be in this position—let alone all the other positions we found ourselves in over the past few hours—to slam into my brain.

We work together. We're surrounded by our colleagues, not to mention the preadolescent kids we're responsible for. And then there's the little matter of our daughter.

Our. Daughter.

Shut up, Quinn mutters. *I'm tired.*

I don't know how you're ever going to make this right, Izzy says, suddenly wide awake. *Why did you have sex with him without telling him that he has a daughter? He'll never forgive you.*

Maybe it's just a one-time thing, Quinn says. *But that would suck. That sex was, like... awesome.*

And how do you think you're going to work with him now? Izzy asks.

Same way we did before, Quinn says with a chuckle. *With a side of lust.*

A wave of panic drowns both of them and drives me out of the bed. Wincing at the sharp pain in my ankle, I search the shadows for my clothes. Balancing on my good leg, I get dressed and am about to open the door to escape when I remember that this is my cabin.

Prioritize, Bella, Izzy says. *Slow your breath and your thoughts and solve the problem that's right in front of you.*

Guess somebody was listening in rehab, Quinn snarks.

Tabling worries about what my actions will mean for my future—for Lilah's future—I take the advice and focus on what needs to happen right this moment. Henry needs to wake up, get dressed, and get out of here. We can't have kids witnessing a walk of shame. It's bad enough that James will know he didn't sleep in his bed for... what the hell time is it? When I find my watch, I'm relieved to see that it's only two in the morning.

I'll tell him on his way out the door that this has to be a one-time thing. We scratched the itch, and that's it. We can move on.

My heart rate back to semi-normal, I perch on the edge of the bed and shake Henry's shoulder. "Hey, you need to wake up."

It takes a few good shoves to get his eyes to open, and then he just stares at me. I lean in to whisper, "You have to go," and our foreheads collide. Stifling my own gasp of pain, I cover his mouth.

"Sorry," he whispers. It takes a few beats, but reality finally seems to sink in. "Oops."

Not what a girl wants to hear after a night of sex, Quinn mutters.

Beggars can't be choosers, Izzy says.

Finger in the air, I barrel on. "We don't have time to talk about this. And really, I'm fine. We're cool. This was fun, but... you need to get back to your cabin and figure out a story on your way there."

He opens his mouth, closes it again, shakes his head

There's no time for a protest or an argument. I'm sure once he's fully back to the real world, he'll agree. "How about this?" I suggest. "Just tell James we were brainstorming and you fell asleep on my other bed. Or maybe he won't even be awake, and it'll all be fine."

I don't wait for his response. Instead, I find his clothes. He frowns when I hand them over, but he gets dressed. In fact, he doesn't say anything, just lumbers to the exit. But when I turn the knob to usher him out, he reaches past me to brace a hand against the door, keeping me from opening it. With his other hand, he pulls me in for a long, lingering, hot-as-hell kiss.

When he breaks it, he gives me an equally heated look before slipping out the door.

Wow is all Quinn and Izzy have to say to that.

HENRY

After I stumble back to my room in a sex-soaked haze—where James is snoring away, thankfully, none the wiser that I've been absent—the rest of the week in New Hampshire is so jam-packed that I'm unable to get Bella alone for a few private words, let alone for a repeat. I'd like to convince her that doing over that do-over on a regular basis would be an excellent idea. We're more compatible at the conference table and in bed than anyone I've ever known. So what's the problem?

We work together, yes. But neither of us reports to the other. I'm slightly higher than her in the hierarchy, but her experience with the show and prior relationships give her enough of a power edge that it doesn't feel like that.

There's the kid. I'm sure being a single parent complicates things, especially if the potential new mate is terrible with kids. But it's not that I never want kids or hate them.

There must be other factors that have her keeping me at arm's length. Something to do with her past, maybe. Maybe it's the kid's father? Maybe she had a bad experience with him that has her wary of all men?

The thing I have going for me: I can be patient when I want to. It's just that I rarely want to.

At least the week in the woods is productive. The never-ending list of activities may have me grumpy, but they do provide ample opportunity to capture moments I'm already slotting into storyboards. When we get back to Boston, I'll have to spend more hours than I want to contemplate logging timecodes and labeling takes before tackling the actual edits, but at least we've got plenty of material to choose from, which eases my anxieties about the final product.

When it occurs to me that I could use help with all that and that Bella's perspective would be ideal, my path seems clear. I'll just convince the team—and her—that the elder AP's time is best spent in the editing suite.

At my side.

Chapter 8

"TV'S SEXIEST ACTRESSES TELL WHAT TURNS THEM ON! When we asked Felicity Johnson (Raven on *One Way to Live*) about her ideal man, the daytime actress paused before answering, 'That's hard to say.'" Pressed further, she finally admits with a rueful smile, 'I've done such a rotten job at picking my men. I just wonder if I wasn't looking for all of the wrong qualities.'" *Soap Chat*, July 1989

BELLA

The rest of the bonding week, I manage to avoid being alone with Henry, but both Izzy and Quinn never stop reminding me that there's a lot of unfinished business between us. Unfortunately, when we reconvene back in Boston for a production meeting, James kicks things off by suggesting that I spend my days collaborating with Henry in the editing suite until the opening sequence and commercial are completed.

Despite my efforts to send him bat signals, Henry either misunderstands my widened eyes and shakes of the head or he doesn't agree that us spending hours side by side in a darkened room is a bad idea, because he just smiles and nods.

When I argue that I don't want to leave the other APs hanging, they claim they're on top of the letters and other preproduction duties. When Carol points out that using material from the retreat was my idea, I'm sunk.

I'm going to spend the week either figuring out how to fess up to Henry or avoiding all talk about my daughter, not to mention either giving in to the off-the-charts chemistry between us or fighting it off like a communicable disease.

On top of all that, I've got a show to open, so I'll be skipping out early and driving directly to the outdoor theater for rehearsals every evening. Thankfully, my ankle healed up quickly. That's about the only thing I've got going for me right now.

I feel like I'm totally neglecting my family, but my mom seems relieved to have real income coming in, and Lilah's busy playing with friends she made in kindergarten, whether it's holding court in the bookstore or going to other kids' houses for the day.

After the meeting, when Henry and I settle in next to each other in the editing room, I'm given a reprieve in the form of Sam, the actual editor. Turns out we need someone to operate the equipment. Henry must've spent the entire weekend culling the hours and hours of footage shot up in the mountains because he's got a to-do list a mile long.

"Do you really need me here?" I ask. "You seem totally organized."

"I am," he answers, that too-damn-charming accent lengthening his vowels. "But I've been staring at this stuff for the past forty-eight hours, and I need fresh eyes. Plus, I trust your instincts."

I trust his *instincts,* Quinn says with a grin.

He needs us, Izzy squeals.

"We've got to whittle all this down to a sixty-second spot, a thirty-second spot, and then the opening," he continues.

"Which will also have to include the kids singing and dancing onstage," I say.

"Does it? Does it really?" He sighs.

"What do you mean? Of course it does. They have to sing the *Boom* song."

And then we're off. And dammit, arguing with Henry is as sexy as being naked with Henry. Good thing Sam is here or my hands would be stripping us both down so we could do both at the same time.

HENRY

By day three of working shoulder to shoulder with Bella I feel like my balls are going to explode. I don't know what it is about this woman, but a whiff of the flowery scent of her shampoo has me wanting to bury my nose behind her ear. A whisper of a touch when she reaches across the desk for a pen or to point out a detail on the screen and all I can think about is every soft spot I kissed that night in her cabin. Even the sound of her voice when she returns from a break has my ears pricking up like Ribsy's when he hears another hound baying.

So when Sam takes off for lunch and she spins around to face me, I can't be blamed for what happens next. This woman's a heady cocktail, and I'm drunk on her presence. My hands grab ahold of her rolling chair the minute the door clicks behind Sam's retreating body.

"We have at least twenty minutes," I growl. "I need to kiss you more than I need my next breath."

Before my heart beats twice, her lips crash into mine and her nails scrape the back of my scalp.

I want to inhale her, feel every inch of her, but I take what I can. My hands rove over the swell of her hips and ass, then find their way under her skirt. She's sucking on my lower lip when my thumb sneaks under her soaking wet panties. One quick swipe and she's bucking against me, her chest arching into mine, her teeth biting back a moan so sweet and soft I want to—

The slam of a door freezes us both mid-dry-hump.

"Fuck. What the fucking fuck just happened?" Bella hisses, pushing away from me and pulling her skirt down.

Luckily, the door slam was down the hall, and I have time to whisper an unapologetic "Sorry" before the handle of the editing suite clicks.

"Did I leave my lunch in here?" Sam asks. "Oh, yeah. There it is."

The look Bella shoots me is so angry, so hot—so *aroused*—that I know I have to finish what I started. And my patience is quickly running out.

·

BELLA

In the restroom I press a damp paper towel against my flushed face like a goddamn Blanche Dubois. This man turns me on in a way that I honestly have no idea how to turn off.

I still haven't figured out how to worm out of the edit with Henry when Keeley and Laura burst into the bathroom, giggling.

When they see me, Laura covers her mouth. "Oops, sorry!"

"What's so funny?" I ask, eager for a distraction, but the young women shoot each other a hesitant look. "Listen, I'm not your boss and I'm not your mother. And I may be older than you, but I still have a sense of humor."

"Okay," Keeley says, pausing to scope out the bathroom.

"No one else is in here," I reassure her.

"We were just trying to decide if Henry would be hotter without the beard," Laura says, her pale cheeks pinking up.

My cheeks flame as a slideshow flashes through my mind in Sensurround. The tickle of that beard along my neck, across a naked breast, on the inside of my thigh.

"I like the beard," Keeley says.

"I don't hate it," says Laura. "But I think a Don Johnson five-o'clock shadow would be even better. There could be a dimple under there."

"Either way, I wouldn't kick him out of bed for eating crackers." Keeley sighs.

"Too bad he's off-limits," Laura says.

"What do you mean?" I choke out. "Off-limits?"

Is he married? Izzy yelps.

Who cares? Quinn chimes in. *This debate is fascinating.*

"Well," Laura says, fussing with her hair. "I mean, you can't have a thing with someone at work."

"Totally inappropriate," Keeley agrees.

"Plus, he's old. No offense," Laura adds.

"None taken," I say, probably too brightly.

"I gotta pee," Keeley says, and both girls go into the stalls.

I use the opportunity to exit, but then I remember that I still have to face the man. I'm no longer hungry, but I go to the kitchen anyway and force down my peanut butter sandwich. The clock ticking away on the wall goads me.

You are here to do a job, Izzy reminds me.

But no one said you can't enjoy the view while you do, Quinn adds.

When I return, both men are in the room. Sam's focused on the two video consoles. The units are as big as a washer and dryer, so he has to stay on his feet. Unfortunately, this gives Henry the opportunity to slide a folded piece of paper across the desk to me without being detected. Suddenly, my heart's pounding like the cute boy I've had a crush on all semester has finally noticed me.

Oooh, wonder what that says? Quinn asks.

Slide it back! Izzy yells.

I can't help myself. Stealthily unfolding the piece of paper, I read:

WE NEED TO DO THAT AGAIN.

IN PRIVATE.

My fingers want to find a pink marker and draw hearts and exclamation points all over the damn thing, but my brain hasn't yet given up the ship, so I crumple it up, shove it into the bottom of my purse, and shake my head as I mouth, *We do not.*

He just raises one brow and sends me the sly smile. The you-know-you-want-this-as-much-as-I-do smile.

I mouth, *I do not.*

And kick him under the table for good measure.

He winces, but the smile stays.

Thankfully, Sam asks a question that requires our attention. We spend the next few minutes flipping back and forth between a few cuts, discussing which is more dynamic, and I think maybe I've done it. Shut him down. Shut *us* down.

When it's time for me to leave and pick up Lilah from a friend's house before I head home for a quick meal, Henry stands and walks me to the door.

As he says, "See you tomorrow," he shakes my hand.

Leaving another folded piece of paper in my palm.

I make it all the way to my car before I open it. Along with an address that I happen to know is halfway between the station and the Shakespeare Boston outdoor stage, he's written:

COME OVER ANY EVENING.
I'LL BE WAITING.
HAL

*

FOR THE NEXT TWO DAYS, every single thing about Henry has me wanting to take him up on his offer. The scruff of beard contrasting with full lips as his mouth quirks in a rare smile, the bulge of muscle straining the sleeve of his button-down shirt when he reaches across the desk, even his damn accent taunts me. Spending my workdays in a small room with him? Excruciating.

As my track record clearly shows, I can't handle anything that makes me yearn for more. For me, rehab was mostly about being removed from temptation and then "screwing my courage to the sticking-place" as Lady M would say. Once I got through withdrawal, which was painful, I made a vow to stay away from anything that made me feel too much. Better to be numb than dead.

It worked. At least until Henry showed up.

Today, thankfully, I get an assignment that requires all of my attention and removes me from his presence. We have the go-ahead to add the computer to the show and the kids have finished recording the music for the opening number, so Carol wants me and the other APs to lead the kids in a brainstorming session to name this new character and get their buy-in.

We gather in a conference room. Armed with an oversized pad of paper on an easel and a set of colorful markers, I lay out our assignment.

As soon as they hear the words "computer" and "challenge," they get it.

"Awesome!"

"It's like we'll be in a live video game!"

"Totally cool!"

I explain that we're going to do a "yes session" to help us come up with a name for the computer. "Meaning every idea is a good one. No saying no—to yourself or anyone else. In fact, while I write the idea, everyone's going to yell, 'Yes!'"

This comes from an improv class I took long ago in New York. Before I spent all my time drinking and drugging, I actually took acting classes in the evening.

"Let's throw out words that seem computer-y," Keeley suggests.

When no one says anything, I prompt, "Yes!" and pump a fist in the air. "That idea can help us because a lot of computer names are acronyms. Who knows what that means?"

Tara raises her hand.

"You know what? I say we just yell things out. Hand raising is for school."

Tara grins and yells, "An acronym is a word that is made up of the first letters of other words."

"Yes!" I give another fist pump. "Let's hear some words that sound like computer stuff."

"Computer?" suggests Amy, who has already taken on a leadership role in the group.

Only the other APs and I yell "Yes" at this, but the ball's rolling.

Soon, I can't keep up, so I toss another marker to Laura, who jumps up to join me. When the suggestions start to slow, I say, "Let's add some other words that describe the show and what we're doing. Like 'Boom.'"

Once we've covered the paper, I step back. "Okay, can we spell a name from these words?"

Before long, they've come up with J.A.I.N. (Junior Artificial Intelligence Network), D.I.N.A. (Data Input Network Analysis), C.A.M. (Computer Activated Microphone), E.R.I.C. (Expert Robot Information Calculator) and B.E.T.T.I. (Boom Experimental Technological Thinking Intelligence).

"Should it be a boy name or a girl name?" Mike asks. I've secretly named him Motor Mike in my head because he's always moving.

"Female," a deep voice answers. Henry steps into the room, and all heads turn in his direction. "Carol thought that would be less threatening."

Thankfully, the kids find *him* less threatening after the week at camp, so after I welcome him to the yes session, they ignore him. I'm not quite as successful as they are, but I do manage to wrap things up and facilitate a vote.

After BETTI wins by a landslide, everyone cheers. Then the kids are off to learn choreography. I'm headed to deliver the name to the set designer so it can be added to the plans, but Henry stops me on the way out. "You're really great with them. I bet you're an amazing mom, too."

Man, Quinn shudders. *How does he make even a lame compliment like that sexy?*

Lame? Izzy protests. *That's the best thing he could say.*

Me? I just smile like an idiot, nod, and run away.

Chapter 9

"Last week on *The Daring & the Divine*: Cathy tries to make some headway (or should it be *bed*way?) with Tim. Being the liberated woman that she is, she openly suggests to Tim that she'd like to sleep with him. Later, Tim makes a mistake." *Soap Opera Land*, July 1989

BELLA

Getting through the days leading up to and including opening night of *Comedy of Errors* has been almost as hard as getting through Lilah's colicky first couple of months on this earth. Awesome moments and truly awful moments, with the whole thing leaving me completely wrung out.

Two things keep me going. One, I sleep like the dead whenever I get a chance. Two, I truly love everything I'm doing. Playing Adriana is a blast, especially since the director encouraged me to let her ride an emotional roller coaster. Ripping into her sister and servants one moment, drooling over the man she thinks is her husband the next, she's a great emotional outlet for everything I'm feeling in real life. And at the station, my creative juices are flowing. I'm excited about the editing we've done, and I can't wait to shoot my segments.

Last, but not least, Lilah's handling all the changes like a trouper.

Except for the one she doesn't know about, of course.

Every morning I wake to the same conversation in my head:

Izzy demands that I tell him. *Today.*

Quinn counters with a reason why I shouldn't, which I use to justify putting off the discussion.

Just one more day.

On top of all this? Even though I'm running on empty, even though my brain and heart and imagination are fully engaged, Henry's goddamned address is burning a fucking hole in the zippered pocket of my purse.

So, the Friday night of our second weekend, when a downpour has us canceling a show, I decline the invitation for an impromptu game night with the cast and crew. Agreeing with Izzy that I need to go home and go to bed, I nevertheless let Quinn take the wheel. She turns left instead of right when I exit the parking lot, having already memorized the address, having already located it on the map of Boston in my glove compartment.

Before I know it, I've parked on the street, taken a set of porch steps two at a time, and knocked softly on the door. With Izzy hissing that I should leave and Quinn howling with need, I'm frozen halfway between dread and desire.

When the door opens, I push my way inside. "Just. One. More. Time."

•

HENRY

Angrier than a wet cat, she drops her bag and kicks off her shoes. Before I can offer her anything—a drink, a snack, a towel—she finds the bedroom. By the time I cross the threshold, she's stripped out of the thin tee and cotton skirt that I couldn't help but notice clinging to her curves like I've fantasized my hands doing every moment of every day since the last time I was allowed to.

If I'm going to be let in once more, I want to slow down and savor this. In case it never happens again. But she has a different idea.

Pointing a finger up and down my body, she orders, "You too. Take it all off."

What can I say? I obey.

Once I do, she pushes me onto the bed, drops to her knees, and proceeds to play me like a fucking saxophone, her mouth and fingers working up and down my pipe in perfect harmony. Hanging onto the bedspread for dear life, I manage to stop her before the horn blows. Her mouth is awfully talented, but if I'm to have a ghost of a chance of changing her mind about that "just one more time" pronouncement, I need to make her come before I do.

Grinding out a "Hang on there, missy," I pick her up and chuck her onto the bed before spreading her knees, planning to bring her to the edge I'm teetering on. But my fingertips have barely grazed her inner thigh when she growls, "Inside. Now, Hal."

"Your wish is my command."

Rolling on a condom in record time, sliding my torso up hers—both of us already slick with sweat—I'm inside before she can say another word. When I tweak her nipples, her nails scratch my ass. When my mouth finds her neck, she orders me to bite.

She wants it a little rough? I'm happy to comply. One hand traps her wrists, the other pushes her knee practically to her armpit. Circling my hips, I rock into her. She arches to meet my thrusts, inner walls tightening, heel driving into my butt cheek, driving me to the edge of pleasure, of control, maybe even the edge of my sanity.

BELLA

When I open my eyes to the darkness of a strange room, a heavy male arm draped over me, I'm thrown back to the worst of my junkie days: when I was out of control and a danger to myself and everyone around me.

Even when my brain stutters awake and clocks that I'm neither high nor hungover and that the body is Henry's, it doesn't change the threat level. I obviously can't control my urges with this man. I don't have time for sex addict rehab—if such a thing exists—so I'm just going to have to go cold turkey. Somehow.

Right now, though, I have to get home.

As quickly and quietly as possible, I pull on still-damp clothes, write him a quick note, and make the short drive home.

Sneaking into the house the way I used to sneak into the apartment I shared with my dad after partying late as a teen—at least until I figured out that my dad usually stayed out carousing later than I did—I think I've gotten away with living on the edge. Again. But when I reach my hand into the den to turn off the light, I find my mom on the sofa. Awake. And angry.

"Isabelle."

So much subtext in just three little syllables.

"Mom." Before she can launch in, I raise my hand. "I'm fine. Everything's okay. I'm really sorry if I worried you. We had a rainout and..."

Izzy urges me to tell her the truth, but with Quinn telling me it's not really her business and, besides, *Are you really going to tell her you just had head-banging sex with the father of your child?* even Izzy concedes, *Good point.* So I lie like the addict that I have to admit—even if only to my two inner selves—I still am. "There was a game night at Deb and Pam's, and I fell asleep on the couch. Burning the candle at both ends these days, you know."

My yawn is real, and fortunately—or unfortunately?—my mom buys the story.

Hand to her heart, she shakes her head. "I'm sorry I doubted you. I was just so worried, and I didn't even know who to call."

Reaching out a hand to help her up, I say. "You have every right to worry, Mom. I put you through a lot. But I'm okay."

As I pat her on the back and trail her down the hall, I really hope that I'm right.

HENRY

I haven't seen or heard from Bella since she showed up at my apartment all hot and bothered Friday. Did I dream her late-night visit? Since I can't find her phone number, I go by the bookstore Saturday, but she's not there, just an older woman who has to be her mother, the resemblance is so strong. When I tell her I'm a colleague from WGBH, I learn that her name is Doris and that Bella has shows all weekend. She gives me a brochure for the theater, so Sunday afternoon, instead of taking my dog for a hike outside the city somewhere or finding a pickup basketball game or going to James's house for a barbecue—in my defense, the thought of eating any kind of barbecue cooked up by a Yankee holds no appeal—or doing *anything* that might lead to meeting new people here in Boston, I go to a play.

It's just down the street from me. I can ride my bike there. It's convenient.

I'm not exactly a cultured person. Raleigh supposedly has a decent theater scene, but I wouldn't know. The two years I lived in New York, I only went to the theater when my mom visited.

But I go to this one. I'm that desperate to see her again.

After locking up my bike and buying a ticket, I find a spot in the temporary bleachers. Others spread blankets and set out picnics on the grass. I enjoy the people-watching until a man sits next to me—a little too close for comfort—and starts talking in what sounds like another language. Edging away, I'm looking for another seat when someone nearby laughs at a guy speaking a similar language.

Scanning the crowd, I notice brightly dressed people pushing their way down the aisles, even stealing food. All of them are speaking what seems to be a made-up language, like Ooobee-Doobee, the *Boom* language, but even less comprehensible. I've never heard of a play where the actors show up in the audience, but like I said, I'm not an expert.

Then I see Bella, and everyone and everything fades into the background. She's arguing with a shorter, curvier woman. When the other woman cries, Bella stomps away to pick a fight with someone else. Soon all the actor-people are arguing, and things get louder and more frantic until a blast of trumpets sounds. Everyone—on and off-stage—is silenced.

An elegantly dressed woman steps to the center of the stage and seems to point right at me, but it's the guy next to me who stands and responds. At her prompting, he tells what is clearly a tale of woe. It's Shakespearean English now—still Greek to me—but I get the basics. He's been in a shipwreck and lost his family. This doesn't seem to please the woman onstage, because a guard comes and takes him away.

After that, most of the action continues onstage. The slapstick humor is entertaining, but I'm not fully engaged until Bella returns. When she throws herself on the floor in a tantrum, I see more of the snarling cat from my bed the other night than the got-her-shit-together woman I've worked beside for the past month. The passion that she's brought to this role rarely flares at the studio, and when it does, it's about ideas, focused on the work at hand.

Here she splashes each and every raw emotion all over the stage. The rest of the audience loves the goofy servant pranking his master, but I only have eyes for her. I'm as confused by the plot as the char-acters seem to be, but I don't care. When it's all over, I clap along with everyone else, even as all I can think about is kissing her. Making love to her. Convincing her that we're perfect for each other.

First, I have to find her.

As the rest of the audience gathers up their things while chatting about the show, I keep an eagle eye on the stage. When a sweaty man with makeup only half removed emerges from behind a screened-off area, I conclude that it must be the equivalent of a stage door.

By the time I step off the bleachers, I've got some arguments lined up. I just need to persuade her to take a chance—to believe that I can be a support in her life, rather than yet another demand on her time and energy.

Distracted, I almost trip over a little girl who pushes past me. An older woman calls, "Lilah, watch out!" from behind me.

"Sorry," she says. "She's a handful."

"It's fine, I say." Recognizing her from the bookstore, I wave. "Doris, good to see you again."

"Oh, it's you," she says.

"Yeah, Henry. From WGBH." She just nods, so I babble on. "I'm glad you gave me the brochure. I live nearby and it's a beautiful day, so I thought I'd check out the show."

"And did you enjoy it?"

We chat for a moment about the play, but she keeps looking over my shoulder. When I follow her gaze, she says, "Sorry, just keeping an eye on my granddaughter."

Nodding politely, I move out of the way and let her precede me toward the stage, but when we get close enough to see the girl clearly, I stop in my tracks. Daylight is fading, but she may as well be in a spotlight.

Because she's the spitting image of my twin sister the summer after kindergarten.

Chapter 10

"All the Daytime News: If you've been keeping up with *All His Children* of late, you'll believe that viewers are shocked and electrified by the latest plot twists. We're getting letters by the hundreds wondering what those writers will be up to next!"
TV Tattler, July 1989

BELLA

When I finally get out of costume for the final show of the weekend, I feel like I could sleep for a week. I can't do that, but I can go home and enjoy a quiet evening with my family before going to bed early. Lilah's voice echoing off the scenery prods me to pack up my things faster. *Comedy of Errors* may be Shakespeare's shortest play but sitting still for two-plus hours is a big ask for a not quite six-year-old.

Propelled by the idea of cuddling with my kid and letting her read me to sleep tonight, I take the corner of the outdoor stage with a smile on my face. My life may be exhausting at the moment, but I'm lucky. I've got an amazing little girl, a mom who supports me in so many ways, and now I'm able to literally support her.

But what I see on the other side of the scenery has me frozen in place. Eyes flicking from my mom's confused expression to Henry's furious one, I watch in horror as the drama of my real life unfolds right before my very eyes.

Lilah jumping up and down in front of me yelling "Mommy" brings me crashing back to reality. To the web of lies I've spun that only I can untangle.

HENRY

As clearly as when she was onstage, the emotions that cross Bella's face when she rounds the corner tell an unmistakable story.

Shock at seeing me here. Panic until she locates her daughter. A brief sliver of hope that I won't notice the family resemblance between Lilah and myself. Resignation when she sees the anger I'm not even trying to hide. Then a grim determination as she approaches us, her arm hugging her daughter close like I'm going to grab her and run.

"Bella is this man—" Doris begins.

With a warning glance, Bella interrupts her. "Mom, I really need to talk to Henry right now." Squatting, she takes Lilah by the shoulders. "Lilah, I so want to hear what you thought about the show, but I just need to talk to your—um, I mean—my work friend Henry about some important, uh, work stuff. I promise I will be home for dinner and then we can hang out. Okay?"

"Can we have Chinese takeout still?" the little girl asks.

Bella nods. "Of course. Just like I promised."

"Okay."

Grabbing her grandmother's hand, Lilah drags her toward the parking lot. Doris gives Bella a clear you-and-I-need-to-talk brow raise before giving in.

When I turn back to Bella, the tears in her eyes disarm my anger momentarily, but then I remember that she's been lying to me. For weeks.

Years.

"Either we do this here or at my place, but I am not leaving your side until you explain to me why you thought it was okay to not tell me I had a daughter," I grind out.

Panic crosses her face as she checks the surrounding area. "Can we go to my car? I just"—a hand flaps in the air—"don't want this aired in public."

Throat clogged with questions, I throw up my hands. "Fine."

The parking lot is nearly empty at this point. Her steps slow as she approaches an older Corolla, and she takes a ridiculously long time to unlock the trunk and stow her bag inside.

"Bella," I warn.

"I'm sorry," she says quickly, her voice shaking. She unlocks the passenger side and then walks around to the driver's side like she's walking to her execution. Steeling my heart against pity—the woman lied to me, for god's sake—I climb in. And wait.

Hands trembling, she grabs the steering wheel. "You don't even like kids."

"That's your excuse?"

"It's not an excuse, it's—"

"You didn't know that years ago," I cut in, "when you found out you were pregnant." Then something else occurs to me, and jealousy jumps to the head of the line of uncomfortable emotions battling for control of my mouth. "Did you not know she was mine?"

She hesitates, but then answers, "No. I knew she was yours. I mean, I wasn't a virgin or anything—"

"Obviously," I growl.

"But I hadn't been with anyone since I got out—I mean, since I decided to leave the show."

"So, you just chose to keep the news to yourself."

"No, Henry." Shifting in the seat, she points a finger at me. "You left, remember? How was I supposed to get this news to you? I didn't know anything about you. Where you worked, where you lived, not even your fucking last name."

"Smith," I mutter.

"Right, which wouldn't have helped me find you."

"I'm… I'm sorry I left. And I'm sorry, I…" Picturing her reading a pregnancy test and not knowing how to contact me has my heart squeezing with empathy, but indignation slams that out of the way. "What about the past few weeks? It didn't occur to you that it would be a good idea to tell me I had a kid? Before we slept together again?"

Fingers claw through her hair, a sweaty mess from the exertion of the play. "I did—I mean, I tried, but"—her hands flap in the small space, her head shakes—"it was… I didn't know how. It's all so fucking complicated and an unbelievable mess, and I love how things are with just the two of us—Lilah and me, I mean. I didn't know how to deal with this"—her hands draw lines between us—"and I couldn't figure out how or what to tell you."

She bangs the back of her head against her seat. "I am sorry." Facing me, tears run down her face and I have to steel myself against the feelings the sight stirs. "I know I fucked this up, but I was afraid."

"Of me?"

Her hands circle in the air. "Not of you, like, personally but of… I guess of the unknowns. Mostly, I guess I was afraid of losing her."

"You think I'd try to take her away from you? What kind of asshole do you think I am?"

"I don't know what kind of asshole you are," she snaps. "I hardly know you at all, Henry."

"Well, I may be the kind of asshole that kids don't like, but I'm not the kind of asshole that sues a perfectly good mom for custody. Okay?"

After an excruciatingly long silence, she meets my gaze. "Okay."

⬚▪

BELLA

A perfectly good mom is what he called me. But am I?

The weight of one lie has lifted, even as the other hangs over my head like an anvil. And not like in *Looney Tunes*, where the character gets squashed only to shake it off moments later. If Henry knew I was—*am*—an addict, would he still think I was such a good mom?

You've done it now. You may as well tell him everything, Quinn says.

But what if—what if he thinks she's unfit as a mother? Izzy asks. That she's a danger to Lilah? He could go to court and try and take her away. That could scar Lilah forever.

If my conscience can't even figure out what's right, then there's no need to do all the confessing right now. It doesn't really have anything to do with Henry or with Lilah's paternity, anyway. Not really.

So… one problem at a time, right?

I suppose, Izzy sighs.

Works for me, Quinn agrees. *But what about sex with Henry? Is that back on the table?*

Hanging onto the one-problem-at-a-time mantra, I force words to leave my mouth. "Okay. Um. So, what do you want? How… I mean, in what way do you want to be Lilah's parent? You shouldn't feel pressured to do anything. We are fine as we are. She's fine. She has my mom and me."

"You want me to back off?" he asks, like he's telling me to back off.

He's sexy when he's mad, Quinn whispers.

"No, I'm not saying that." What I'm doing is trying to keep my voice calm, like a good mother would. "I'm asking what you want. From everything I know about child psychology, it seems important that we be clear before we rock Lilah's world with this information. It's not fair to her if you just, like, pop in with 'Oh, hey, I'm your dad now' and then 'Whoops, I'm not really interested,' or 'Sorry, I'm moving back to Raleigh, and I'm not going to be around anymore.' You know?"

He opens his mouth like he's ready to continue arguing, but after a quick headshake, he closes it. Opens it. Closes it. Finally, he says, "You're right."

Before I can plow on, he holds up a hand. "You weren't right to lie to me. You're not off the hook for that. But this is all… big news. For me, for the rest of my family."

"As it will be for Lilah, who is about to turn six," I remind him.

"It's not like I want to punish her because you screwed up," he says, testy again.

"Excuse me. Did you wear a condom when we had sex in New York?"

He drags a hand over his mouth before answering. "No. I didn't. I assumed you had it covered."

"Just because I thought I did doesn't mean—"

Hand up again he interrupts me, "You're right. Okay? Can I finish?"

When I nod, he says. "I'm angry because you've been lying to me since we met again. We've had sex twice, and you still didn't tell me. I think I have a right to be pissed." He takes the grab bar and hangs on like it's the only thing that'll keep him sitting still. "But I agree. We should think this through before we tell Lilah. And figure out what to tell her."

When he meets my gaze, I pour everything I've got into making myself clear. "Which means you should think about what you really want. That's what I'm trying to say. Please don't take her on out of obligation or anything. She'll be fine with the status quo."

He nods and his eyes soften slightly. "She seems like a great kid."

Tears threaten, but I swallow them back. "She is. She really is. And you're right too. She shouldn't have to pay just because I screwed up."

HENRY and I don't really resolve anything. He promises to think through what being a father would look like to him, and I promise to meet him after work tomorrow, where we will ostensibly decide on next steps.

A bitter laugh coughs out of me as I watch him swing his leg over his bike and ride away. I thought I was tired before, but after that encounter, I'm not sure I can make the drive home or haul my body up the stairs to our apartment above the shop, where I have more emotional heavy lifting to do. Hang out with Lilah for the evening while pretending that everything's normal. Then once she's in bed, facing my mom.

For the first time in years, I want a drink. I want the oblivion of a high. I want escape, however I can get it.

One little drink wouldn't hurt, Quinn says.

It's never just one, Izzy says.

A couple of drinks, Quinn shrugs.

And then what? Izzy demands. *Then she really could lose Lilah. That man doesn't know about our past. If he did—*

How is he going to find out? Who will know? Quinn scoffs.

Anybody could take a picture, sell it to a paper, Izzy says.

Nobody cares about us anymore, Quinn snipes.

Squeezing my temples between my palms, I drown their voices with my own. "One step at a time. One thing, one moment, one second at a time. That's all I can do."

"Are you talking to yourself?"

Hand over my exploding heart, I roll down the car window. "Jesus, Jess! You scared the shit out of me!"

"Sorry!" She leans closer. "Whoa, you look like you saw a ghost."

"Worse." I don't know how long I've been sitting here, but I remember Jess saying she was meeting Cal for dinner. "Wait, didn't you leave?"

"I left my makeup bag." She scans the empty parking lot. "But everything's locked up. Damn." Eyes back on me, her brow furrows. "So, what's going on? Are you okay?"

"Honestly?" I'm not a big sharer, but Jess is the closest friend I've got. Maybe it'd help to get her perspective. "I don't know."

"Do you want to come to my place and hang out?"

"I thought you were having dinner with Cal."

She waves that down. "I was, but I can let him know you need me. He'll understand."

"He's a good guy, isn't he?"

"The best. Plus, we'll be spending a lot more time together very soon."

"Are you moving in with him?"

"Yep."

"Wow. That was quick."

"Do you think? My sister's worried about that."

"What do I know?" I shake my head. "I am definitely no relationship expert."

"Well, let's take advantage of the privacy while I have it. You can follow me. It's not far."

"I would love to, but I haven't seen Lilah much lately and my mom is expecting me home."

"Okay. Then let's talk here." She jogs around to the passenger side and hops in the front seat. She waves around the interior of the car. "Nothing you tell me leaves this vehicle, but take it from me, keeping everything inside is no way to move forward."

Dragging a palm over my face I groan, "I don't know what to do. I have to figure out how to unravel all the lies I've been telling."

"About?"

The kindness in Jess's eyes tips me over the edge, and I take in a huge breath to just spill it out. "I've been working with the father Lilah doesn't know she has for the past month. He didn't know either until he saw her after the show."

"Oh. Wow." There's no judgement in her tone, thankfully. "He works on *Boom?*"

I nod. "Yeah. I've lied to him, to my mom, to everyone at work, and to my daughter. I'm such a fuckup." The clog of emotions in my throat has my nose filling, so I grab my purse and dig through till I find a tissue.

"Bella, you've just done the best you could." Jess's hand on my shoulder is as kind as her eyes and voice, but it somehow makes me feel even shittier.

"It doesn't feel like it." After I blow my nose, I add, "I was just trying to protect her."

"Which is a good instinct."

"Or was I really trying to protect myself?"

She tips her head to the side. "From what?"

"From… embarrassment? Shame? Having my mistakes plastered across the pages of gossip rags."

"It's understandable that you'd want to avoid that."

"But in the process, I've dug myself into a hole."

"Where you don't trust anybody?"

I make myself meet her gaze. The warmth and acceptance I see there gives me the courage to keep going. "Not even my own mom."

She nods slowly. "You're trusting me now. Why?"

Good question. "Well, because…"

"Because I've made mistakes and you know all about them?"

Is it because I know things about her? That kind of transaction doesn't feel right. "I hope not. I mean, that's kind of icky." I meet her gaze again. "I think it's more that you set an example. You overcame your fears, so maybe I can too."

"Okay." She smiles, her eyes shiny. "What are you afraid of?"

"It just felt—feels—like the stakes are so high with Lilah. I didn't want to ruin her life. But I did anyway."

"Her life looks pretty good to me. She's a smart, happy kid."

Despite my worries, I have to smile as I picture Lilah's face. "I hope so."

"Whatever happens, she'll be okay. Do you believe that?"

"I want to."

"What else do you want?"

I roll my heavy skull against the head rest. "What I really want is to go to sleep and have this all disappear."

"Okay, fwoop." She waves a hand in the air. "All gone."

"Thanks. I appreciate that." I cough out a laugh and then press my palms over my eye sockets. "Ugh. What *do* I want?"

"Seriously, if everything were to fall into place…"

"Well, I do want her to have a dad. But I want her to have a dad that stays. That she can trust."

"I guess you can't guarantee that, but you could make it clear to… What's his name? The dad?"

"Hal. Henry, I mean. We both went by different nicknames when we met."

"Which was obviously some time ago?"

"I hadn't seen him since Lilah was… you know. Conceived."

"And what about the two of you? Do you want to have a relationship with him?"

"I don't know. He's… he makes me feel things I haven't for a long time." Just the thought of our last encounter has me jonesing to do it again. Which is a problem.

"Nothing wrong with that. You are both adults."

I shake my head. "The way I feel with him is out of control in a way I feel like I can't afford."

"Okay." Her hands sweep invisible items off the dashboard. "Maybe put those feelings on the back burner for now."

"I wish I could. My body just gets kind of crazy around him. Plus, I've got to tell my mom. Not to mention Lilah. And the people at work."

"Is it really their business?" Jess asks, interrupting my panic spiral.

"I guess not. But Carol's a mentor. A friend, too."

"Let's break it down so you don't get totally overwhelmed. The most important person—Lilah." She draws a circle in the air between us. "Then gradually open that up. Lilah and you." She continues to expand the circle as she adds people. "Lilah and you and your mom. Lilah, you, your mom, and Henry. Figure out what those relationships are before you share this with anyone else."

"That's a good idea." I nod, picturing us nestled like Russian dolls. It does feel a tiny bit more manageable. "I don't know why it feels like an all-or-nothing thing. Lying, that is."

She places a hand on my knee and squeezes it lightly. "Keeping parts of your life private isn't lying."

As she opens the car door, I give her wrist an impulsive squeeze. "Love you."

Telling someone I love them isn't habitual for me. My parents, while caring, weren't lovey-dovey types, with each other or with me. Jess is the only girlfriend I've felt close enough to that the words feel true.

Jess doesn't skip a beat, though. She just squeezes me back. "Love you too."

I think I might actually believe her.

Chapter 11

"Last week on *Private Hospital*: Bill threatens to tell Laura the whole story because of his anger at Shelley from telling everyone his business. Identical twins Judy and Jane continue to argue bitterly, but neither Rod nor Callie can find out what's going on between them, nor can their mother, Louanne." *Soap Opera Land*, July 1989

HENRY

After I walk away from Bella—mind blown—all I can figure out to do is bike back to my apartment, which is not what anyone would call a home, I have to acknowledge when I walk in the front door. Bare walls and minimal furnishing do not scream "Welcome." What would a little girl think if I brought her over here? The only sign that someone actually lives here is my dog.

What if she's afraid of dogs?

Since I haven't made it beyond the doorway, Ribsy takes matters into his own paws—or jaws, rather—by pulling his leash off the hook. Whining, he circles me until I grab it. After a brief tug of war, I clip it onto his collar, and we head out to the park. As I watch him sniff for doggie news, my heart rate slows and my thoughts unwind.

When Ribsy came to live with me, he was a whole different animal than the puppies my family had adopted. Big eyes and bigger needs made bonding easy with them. Even though Ribsy was fully grown, I doubt he'd ever seen the inside of a house before he found me. It took a lot of patience to train him to stop treating my apartment like a kennel. He'd jump onto the bed, the couch, even the kitchen counter. He marked his territory in the corner of my office. I'll admit there were a few times when I rued the day I let him hop into my truck. But now, I wouldn't trade him for the cutest puppy.

Seeing Lilah was… like Ribsy running at my truck. A deep-seated feeling barreled into my heart the moment I laid eyes on her. I've watched my cousins and siblings go all goo-goo eyed over their babies in a way I can't picture myself ever doing. And it's not like my heart is magically bursting out of its frame like the Grinch's when he learns the true meaning of Christmas.

It's more like a drive. To protect her.

Even if it's from myself.

It's pretty clear that I can't just barge in and demand that she love me—or even trust me. Like Ribsy, she's no big-eyed baby. She's a kid. She's spent years on this earth without me. If I'm going to have a relationship with her, I have to be patient and let it evolve. And I guess if she decides she'd rather not have a dad in her life, I'll be her father in name only: mail a check every month and a card on her birthday.

Still, as Ribsy and I pass the playground where dads are pushing kids on swings and teaching them how to ride without training wheels and picking them up and kissing boo-boos, I'm insanely—if irrationally—jealous of what they have. Of what they've had the opportunity to build from day zero with their kids.

The chance I didn't have.

But as my jaw tightens with anger, I have to ask: *Whose fault is that? Really?*

The night Bella and I met and had sex like I'd never experienced before, I could've found my way back to that dressing room after I got the message about my dad. I could've given her my phone number. Hell, she could've been a support while I stumbled through the grief of losing him.

I just assumed that she wouldn't be interested.

She seems to have done fine parenting without me thus far. I guess I owe it to her not to mess things up.

"Thanks for the walk, Ribsy. I just wish you could talk too," I say as we climb the stairs to our place. He barks in response, but that's probably because it's dinnertime.

After I hang up his leash and feed him, I survey the contents of my fridge. It's as empty as the living room walls. Sifting through takeout menus—the one thing I've managed to accumulate since I moved to Boston—I wonder how I think I'm in any way prepared to be any sort of a positive influence on Lilah. When I pick up the phone to call the Chinese place—hey, at least I know my daughter likes that—I'm tempted to call my mom to get her advice.

In that moment, I kind of get why Bella didn't tell me right away. I mean, what do I say? *Hey, Mama, guess what? I had sex with a girl the night Dad died, haven't seen her since. But I happen to be working with her now, and apparently, I fathered her kid. Small world, huh?*

The way that my little girl got to this earth is a mess. If nothing else, I need to avoid adding to it.

I just wish there was somebody who could tell me how to do that.

BELLA

It takes every ounce of acting talent I have to pretend that everything's fine and dandy as I go through the motions of parenting my child for the rest of the evening. I almost fall asleep as my baby reads to me from *The Boxcar Children*—okay, I do fall asleep—but Lilah wakes me to say goodnight.

"Sorry, baby," I yawn. "Mommy's a little tired."

She nods as if she understands all. "You ran around a lot on the stage."

"I did," I say, wishing that were the only thing wearying me.

"And it's bedtime now," she says, pointing to the clock. "The big hand is on the twelve and the little hand is on the eight."

Squeezing her tight, I bury my nose into her neck and kiss her cheek with a loud smack. "Love you, girly girl."

"Love you too, mommly mommy."

I have to make myself roll out of her bed. After I blow her a kiss from the doorway, I trudge to the den to face my mom.

Before she can say a word, I raise my hand. "I know I screwed up." After giving my mom the bare bones version of how Henry and I found, lost, and found each other again, I sink into the couch and throw my arms over my face. "Now I have no idea what to do."

When my mom shifts closer to me on the couch and puts her arm around me, I let her, even as part of me resists. After all, my own parents gave me a pretty sketchy template to work with. A question surfaces from that resentment and worms its way out of my mouth on a whisper. "Why did you let me go?"

The arm draped across my shoulder tenses. "Go where?"

"To New York." I shift away so I can see her face. "You must've thought it was a terrible idea."

She presses her lips together and closes her eyes. When she opens them again, she looks ten years older. "You were determined. So was your father. With your agent, it was three against one, and you all wore me down. You gave yourself a year, and honestly, I thought that'd be it, that you'd be back."

Old grudges resurface so fast my head spins. "I was right. You didn't believe in me."

"That's not it, sweetheart." She takes my hand, and her expression softens. "If anyone could do it, you could. The odds were so slim." Her shoulders twitch, as if she's shrugging off a scratchy sweater. "But you beat them."

"And you trusted Dad to take care of me? I mean, George." I haven't called that man my father for years. He abdicated that title.

She nods slowly. "I did."

"But he didn't," I press.

Her sigh is heavy as she says, "No, he didn't. He had his own—"

"Parties to attend?" I ask bitterly.

"His own demons to deal with." She takes my hand again. "Listen, sweetheart. I'll always regret that I didn't know what was happening sooner, that I let my own insecurities keep me from checking in more. I'm just grateful that I got there in time." She tugs on my hand until I meet her gaze. "I didn't protect you enough, but sometimes I worry that you're protecting Lilah too much."

"Protecting her from her father like I should've been protected from mine?"

"That's not exactly what I meant. Your father wasn't a danger to you, he just—"

I swipe that thought away before she can finish it. "I don't want to talk about him. Henry seems like a decent guy. I should've told him about Lilah the minute I saw him again. I was just scared."

She shifts to face me on the couch. "Scared of what?"

I drop my gaze to my lap. "That he'd find out the truth about me and try to take her away."

She squeezes my knee. "Being addicted is a disease, not a failing, Bella."

"That's not how most people see it."

She shrugs. "That's their problem."

Even if she's right, the stakes still feel way too high because I *am* going to lose Lilah. Maybe not in court, but we're likely to lose what she and I have. Despite all that, I have to laugh. It's that or cry. "I'm just a selfish bitch. I don't want to share her."

"Every mother feels that way." She tips her head to the side. "Except during the terrible twos."

"Lilah never went through that."

"She is kind of perfect. Which has a lot to do with you being such a good mom."

"Nature or nurture. Who knows?" Worry and guilt haven't completely left me, but I feel less overwhelmed than I did when I walked in. Then something occurs to me. "Why did you never ask about Lilah's dad when I found out I was pregnant in the first place?"

She considers for a beat before answering. "It wasn't my business."

"Are you sure it wasn't that I was too fragile? That if you pushed, I might start using again?"

She shook her head. "No. I could tell you were determined from day one to put Lilah first." She takes in a deep breath and lets it out again. "It was something else. You were… I guess I recognized the expression on your face."

"From something you'd seen in George?"

"Maybe."

When she doesn't go on, I probe, "What did you see?"

"That you had secrets that you couldn't even face."

"I get that honestly, anyway," I say, my voice laced with so much sarcasm it's veered into Quinn territory.

"Some secrets are necessary," she says, without a trace of accusation or even indignation. "The problem, I think, is when you keep them from yourself."

I'm not sure who she's talking about now—me, my dad, or herself—but I'm suddenly exhausted. I lean over and give her a hug. "Thanks for listening and understanding. I think I need to go to bed now."

Unfortunately, when I do, I drift in and out of sleep laced with nightmares featuring that haunted expression on a face that morphs from my dad's to my own to Henry's.

The bigger the secret, the harder it is to hide.

HENRY

I can't sit still. I need to talk about this with someone. Not my mom. It's too late, and besides, she'd freak out and hop on the next flight, ready to smother me and her new grandchild with love. Not a bad impulse, but before that happens, I have to figure out what I want and give Lilah a chance to do the same.

Not Ralph. He's the last person I'd ask about any kind of long-term relationship.

My brothers are a no-go. One, they can't be trusted not to tell my mom because they work side by side with her. She'd sense something was up and get it out of them. Two, they're as useless as Ralph.

My twin sister has better mom-defenses. In some ways she's the obvious choice because she knows me better than anyone. I'm just afraid of what she'll say because she won't hesitate to tell me the truth: that I'm a terrible candidate for instant fatherhood for a whole host of reasons. One, I have a quick temper. Two, I lose patience too easily. Three, I'm a workaholic and Lilah would be better off without me if I'm just going to follow the next job out of town.

I guess if that's all true, it'd be better to face it before I meet her so we can be clear about what I have to offer. Which isn't much.

Pacing to the kitchen, I check the clock on the oven. It's after ten. It's a little late for her to be up, but—

My thoughts are interrupted by the phone ringing. As I sprint to answer, my heart rate soars. A call this late can only be bad news. "Hello?"

"What's up, Jack?"

Another of Jill's bazillion nicknames for me, this one because of the nursery rhyme. She doesn't sound upset, but I need to make sure. "What's wrong?"

"Nothing," she says. "What's wrong with you?"

"Is that why you're calling?"

"Yeah. I felt weird and I haven't talked to you since you moved—you jerk—so I figured you needed to talk to me." Before I can answer, she continues. "Spit it out. Long distance may be cheaper after ten, but it ain't free."

There's no way to ease into this, so I do as she says. "I just found out I have a daughter." When she doesn't say anything, I ask, "You still there?"

"I'm sorry. I thought I heard you say that you have a daughter."

"That's what I said."

"Here in Raleigh? Did you cheat on Christine? Oh man, that's going to be a problem. I can't lie—"

"I didn't cheat on Christine," I cut in. "The mom's here. We had a fling right before I left New York, but she lives in Boston. She works on *Boom*."

"I don't even know where to start. Did you tell Mom yet?"

"No. And you can't tell her—or anybody—until I figure out what I'm going to do."

"What do you mean what you're going to do? You're a dad. You have to take care of her."

"Well, obviously, I'll take care of her financially. But she's almost six years old already. What if she doesn't like me?"

"Isn't that, like, a kid's job at least half the time? But—hang on. Rewind. Who is the mom? Do you like the mom? Like, *like* her like her? Is this why you dumped Christine?"

"I didn't—we're not having that conversation again. But maybe."

"To what part?"

"To all of it? I don't know. We have a pretty strong… connection."

"You've slept with her."

"Obviously. Did you miss that week of health class or something?"

"No. You've slept with her *recently*."

"Sometimes I hate that you can read my mind."

"What's the problem, then? Other than the fact that I've been waiting to get pregnant for you to be married. Now you've totally lapped me, and I'll never catch up."

"Well, I'm pretty pissed off that she didn't tell me about the kid. We've been working together for weeks now. And yeah, we had sex again. And she still didn't tell me."

"Maybe she had a good reason. You are pretty grouchy. Did you scare some kids?"

When I don't answer immediately, she does it for me. "You did. So maybe she was worried you'd be a mean dad. Who could blame her?"

"Thanks for the support. Always good to have you on my side, J."

"I *am* on your side. I'm on the side of you getting back to the fun-loving brother I used to have."

Not able to deal with this at the moment, I remind myself that I did call her for advice, so I may as well let her give it. When she doesn't launch into that, I get worried. "Do you think I'll be a bad dad? A mean one?"

"No, but…"

"But what?"

"Maybe you need to think of her as a dog, not a kid."

"Treat my daughter like a dog?"

"No, *think* of her as a dog. You're great with Ribsy. I think you're just prejudiced against kids. You did have to deal with a lot of little assholes on the cowboy show."

"And the clown show before that."

"Right. So, to avoid your ogreish tendencies, just pretend she's an abandoned dog."

"Full of fleas and buckshot?"

"Exactly. Except hopefully less smelly."

"Huh."

"I know, I'm brilliant. You have five days before I tell Mom."

"Why do I only get five days?"

"Because we have a staff meeting Friday. I can't promise anything if I see her in person. You know how she is."

"Okay, I get it. Hopefully, I can figure out how this is going to go by then."

"No matter what, this little girl's family just got a whole lot bigger. And that's a good thing."

"Yeah. That is a good thing."

"Oh, hey. Can you take a photo? Or get one and send it?"

This has me smiling. "You don't need it."

"What do you mean?"

"Just find one of yourself from first grade. She looks exactly like you."

"Aww. Now I definitely need to meet her. When are you going to see her again?"

"I don't know. The mom and I are going to try to come up with a plan after work tomorrow."

"You'll be fine, Henry."

"I want to be better than fine."

"That's why I love you and why you'll be a good dad. Call me tomorrow."

"Love you too."

After I hang up, I'm not exactly confident, but I have more hope. Whether or not I'm able to change my personality, Lilah will be welcomed into the loving—if pushy—arms of my extended family. Maybe I'll even feel more like I belong.

BELLA

Henry said he'd meet me outside the station at the end of the workday, but I've been sitting in my car for ten minutes and he hasn't shown.

See, he doesn't really care about Lilah, Quinn says.

Maybe something important held him up, Izzy counters.

I'm just about to go back in to ask if he forgot when he pushes out of the front doors. When he scans the parking lot, I wave until he sees me. "Sorry," he pants after sprinting to my car. "I was in a meeting with some Boston Brahmin types that just wouldn't stop talking."

"Foundation people?"

"Yeah. I hope I convinced them to meet our larger budget asks."

"That'd be good." I nod.

He sighs and drops his head, hands on his hips. "Do you, uh, want to go somewhere and talk?" He meets my gaze, his expression unreadable. "I don't suppose my place is a good idea.'

"Yeah. No. Not a good idea right now." I drag my hands off the steering wheel. "One thing at a time."

He nods. "Right. So…"

"How about we go over to the park that runs along the Charles? We can walk and talk there."

"Sounds good. I'll follow you?"

"Sure." I peek at the entrance to the studio to make sure no one is watching us leave together. Another thing we have to figure out: what and when to tell our coworkers.

Izzy and Quinn are strangely silent during the short drive to the River Basin parking lot. Then Henry and I are awkwardly silent as we get out of our cars and find our way to the path along the river. I'm not sure what's going on in Henry's head, but I'm still paralyzed by the contradicting thoughts and feelings bouncing around in my own after that conversation with my mom last night.

"I'm still angry," Henry finally says. "But after talking to my sister last night—"

This has me stopping in my tracks. "You told your sister? I thought we were keeping it between us until we—"

"You talked to your mom, right?" He shoves his hands in his pockets, his expression unyielding.

I nod, begrudgingly.

His hands fly out again. "Well, I'm sorry, but talking to my dog wasn't enough. Jill is my twin. She knows me better than anybody."

"Okay." A hand up between us, I make myself meet his gaze and mean it when I say, "I'm sorry. But I—"

Fingers swiping his hair out of his face, he interrupts me. "Just listen. Please?"

After I mime zipping my lips, he drops his hands to his sides and continues walking. "She convinced me that you probably had good reasons for not telling me. So, whatever they might be, I want to let you know that I'm willing to trust you and your judgement, despite the fact that you didn't trust me." He blows out a breath suddenly. "Sorry. I do have a bit of a quick temper."

"Which is worrisome to me," I say, a little out of breath from trying to keep up with his long strides. "Kids push your buttons like you wouldn't believe."

"Oh, I believe it." He shakes his head. "You can't imagine the shit kids tried to pull on set down in Raleigh."

"Lilah's a good kid. But she's a kid. Your expectations will have to adjust. Patience is something you'll have to work on."

He nods vigorously. "I know, I know."

I stop walking and take his elbow to stop him. "Be honest with me. Have you ever even pictured yourself having kids?"

Hazel eyes tinged with sadness meet mine. "Not really. I mean, I had a longtime girlfriend in Raleigh. My twin sister's best friend. The two of them have had us married since elementary school, our lives all ticky-tacky and sewn up." He blows out a breath. "And I couldn't do it."

"Is that why you left Raleigh?"

"Nah, that was about work." He winces as he stares off over the water. "But maybe it was part of it. My parents had such a perfect relationship that maybe I expected too much, but I just... it wasn't right. Any of it." He shoves his hands in his pockets and heads up the path, mumbling something.

Again, I have to jog to catch up with him. "Sorry, I didn't hear you."

He walks backward. "I said, What if she doesn't like me?"

"So what? She hates me at least twice a week. It's part of being a parent."

"It's not fair. You've had years to figure this shit out." He winces. "Shit, I guess I have to work on the cussing."

"If you don't want to lose your entire salary to the swear jar."

He laughs. "Swear jar?"

I shrug. "Part of being a parent."

"Me, a parent." He shakes his head. "I'm still not quite used to the idea."

I stop him again with a brief touch. I don't trust myself to do more. "Like I said, you have to be all the way used to it before you meet her. So, if you need time—"

"I don't. I want to be a part of her life, if she'll have me. I felt robbed when I saw her." He flings a hand in the air. "Like, how is it possible there's been a piece of me out there for almost six years and I didn't even know? Family is important to me."

His tone is full of passion, not anger. Passion that I can't be the focus of. This time, I lead the way up the walk. "It's important to me too."

He catches up quickly and takes my elbow. "What have you told her? About her dad?"

I have to slip out of his grasp to think straight. "That she doesn't have one. So far, she's been okay with that."

"What do we tell her now?"

"I think the most important thing is to be honest."

"Honest? As in tell her *everything*?"

Hands in the air, I backtrack. "Everything in a way that she can understand. I read this article about talking to kids about sex—"

"We have to have the sex talk?"

His voice has climbed to the top of his register, and I have to stifle a laugh. "No, but I think the approach should be similar. This article suggested that you don't sit your kid down and have this big sex talk. You just answer their questions openly and honestly when they come up."

The panic on his face is priceless. "*Have* those questions come up?

I just nod, enjoying torturing him more than I should. "Some. Like, 'Where do babies come from?' But the trick is to only answer the exact question the kid asks. Don't launch into an extended explanation. They'll only ask what they're ready to hear about."

"So, we sit her down and tell her that I'm her dad. Then what?"

I shrug. "And that's it, unless she asks for more."

"But what if she asks, like, how we know?"

"Well"—I run a hand up and down his face and body—"she looks like you."

His expression shifts from alarm to wonder. "She looks just like my sister at that age."

"Exactly. Tell her that."

"And if she asks more? What words do I use?"

Slowing my steps, I take my time grappling with his question, too. "Well, what is the truth?"

He gestures between us. Just like that night on the balcony. "We met…"

"And we…" I add.

"Had a really strong…" he continues.

"Connection?"

"We connected, all right."

I can tell from his devilish tone that I shouldn't meet his gaze, so I keep moving. "But then you had an emergency and had to go to Raleigh, and I didn't know how to get in touch with you. And then we saw each other and we weren't sure, but then we…"

"Had that connection again."

His grin is merciless. Remorseless.

Hands on hips, I say, "This is not useful."

He just keeps grinning. "Sorry. I'm nervous."

"And you make jokes about sex when you're nervous?"

"Only with you."

"Great." I shake my head. "Let's just… uh, have you decided what you want? What your parameters are?"

He nods sharply. "I want what she wants."

"What if that's not possible?"

"I guess there are reasonable boundaries. I mean, I can't give her a pony, right?"

"Right. No ponies." We've come to a turnaround on the path, so I face him again. "But what if she wants the mom and dad and two-point-four kids? And a dog and a picket fence?"

"Well, I've got a dog. You guys have a picket fence. We could try to make the rest happen."

I can't tell if he's pulling my chain or if he's serious. Either way, it's too much. "Let's take it one step at a time. The relationship between you and Lilah has to be our primary focus. In the meantime, I think we need to keep whatever's going on between us simple."

"Seems simple to me." He shrugs. "But you're welcome to come to my place soaking wet again anytime."

My smile in response is tight. "Thanks, but I'm going to try and avoid that."

Chapter 12

"Daytime Close-up: Melanie Benson (Jeanie on *Ryan's Wish*) makes a very welcome return after taking time off to spend time with her brand-new baby. She says she'll miss snuggles with the little one, but she's glad to be back on the set." *Soap Chat*, July 1989

HENRY

Last night, after a discussion that was testier than I'd hoped but more positive than I expected, we decided that the bookstore was the safest place to meet Lilah, so I'm supposed to meet them there this evening, which can't get here fast enough. I've been useless at work all day. For one, my relationship with my own dad keeps haunting me—the good and the bad, the ideal and the not-so-ideal. I've put him and my mom on a pedestal, but there must be a reason why I don't feel like I belong in my family. My dad did have a kind of a "my way or the highway" attitude, and he had a temper, too. At least with us boys. Jill had him wrapped around her little finger.

Not only has my brain been mired in memories, I've found myself staring at the Boomerang kids, wondering about their relationships with their fathers. Wondering if I'll measure up. At least Lilah's not a baby that I'd probably drop or hold wrong or make cry. Or a toddler that I'd lose patience with. Or a preschooler because, as experience has shown, we do not get along.

At least I'm no longer terrifying to Tara, because when she caught me staring, she came right up to me and said, "Stop being creepy, old man!" When I didn't respond, still lost in thought, she punched me so hard in the bicep it made me yelp.

That got me laughing. And, oddly, made me feel better. And got me focused enough that I was able to get through the day's shot list without any more gawking.

Now though, I'm literally shaking in my boots as I join Bella and Lilah in a little nook at the back of the quiet bookstore. As I sit like a prisoner waiting for a jury's verdict, heart pounding heavily in my chest, Bella tells Lilah that my name is Henry, that we work together, but that we also knew each other from New York.

"You remember I told you that I lived in New York before you were born?"

Lilah nods, her expression more serious than any I've seen cross my twin's face. "On 96th Street and Riverside."

"Right," Bella says, wiping her hands on the sides of her shorts. It makes me feel better to know that she's nervous too. "So, I met Henry there. We only knew each other for a short time, but when a baby really wants to be born, that's all you need."

When we talked about what to say, I suggested we add, "If you're not careful," because I certainly don't want my daughter knocked up by some teenage horndog. But Bella insisted that Lilah shouldn't feel like an accident.

Right now, I don't think it's clear to Lilah that we are talking about her.

"But then I had an emergency in my family, and I had to move away from New York," I explain. "Your mom and I didn't get a chance to talk before I left."

"Which meant I didn't have a way to contact Henry when I found out that I was going to have a baby," Bella adds.

"But the other night, when I saw you at the theater, you reminded me of my sister, so I asked if maybe you were my daughter."

"And I said that I believe he is," Bella says.

Lilah's eyes have been pinging back and forth between us, but when it's clear that we're finished, her penetrating gaze lands on me and I have to work hard not to squirm under her scrutiny.

Then she frowns and turns to Bella. "But you said I didn't have a father."

Bella opens her mouth and takes in a breath but doesn't speak. I can't help here, so I just keep quiet. Finally, she says. "I did say that. But I was mistaken."

I'm not sure whether or not to be impressed at Bella's admission. Is it a good idea to have your kid believe you make mistakes? Just when I'm thinking I might've won this round, the little girl shifts her focus back to me. She tips her head to the side to study me again. "Did you miss me?"

Not what I was expecting. Nothing about the birds and the bees, which is what I was dreading. At least I dodged that one. "Um, well, I didn't know that you were, uh, here, but you know what? I did miss you. I missed out on your first five years, and I'm sorry for that."

"Six and a half, if you count the time I was in Mommy's uterus."

Good at math and apparently the talk has already happened. At least that part of it. "You make a good point, there. When is your birthday, by the way?"

"August fifteenth. I'm going to have a party. Do you want to come?"

"Yes, I'd love to."

"Do you want to read a book?"

"Uh, sure."

She hops up to get one, presumably. We are surrounded by them. "So, that was it?" I whisper to Bella.

"I doubt it, but"—she shakes her head—"I've never done this before."

I'm sweating like I just ran five laps around the football field. "Yeah, well, me neither."

"Do you want me to stay?" she asks. "Or do you want time alone?"

"I don't know. Uh, I guess we ask her?"

When Lilah returns with a stack of books, Bella asks, "Do you want me to hang out with you guys, or do you want to read just the two of you?"

Lilah trains her assessing gaze on me again for a moment before answering. "You don't have to stay."

It's hard to tell what Bella thinks of this verdict. "Okay. I've got some paperwork to do, so I'll just be up front." Looking like she's prepared to be disappointed, she leaves us be.

Lilah sets the books on the coffee table in front of us. The cat, the little gray one, jumps up on the table, and she strokes his back as she speaks. "These are advance reader copies. It's my job to read the ones for kids so I can make recommendations." Pointing at the stack, she says, "You can choose."

The first one that catches my eye is a brightly colored picture book called *Chicka Chicka Boom Boom*, but when I pick it up, she says, "That's for little kids. We can read it if you want." Her tone makes it very clear that it's *not* what she wants.

"Maybe I'll read that later to myself."

She shrugs, but I feel like I passed the first test.

I flip through a couple of thicker books that must be for kids in junior high at least: *The Winter Room* and *Number the Stars*. "I'm sure these are more your speed, but I'd hate to get into them and not get to finish."

Her brows go up.

"Today."

She waits.

"Before dinner."

She narrows her eyes at me and then holds up a book that I'd've thought was closer to her reading capabilities, *Wayside School is Falling Down*. "I guess we could read this one. I haven't decided exactly what to say about it."

"Have you read all of these books already?"

"Once. I read them twice before I write my review."

"Can you show me your reviews?"

"After we read. Scooch over."

She sits down next to me and opens the book. "I read fast, so you can turn the page when you're ready."

"Okay." At first it feels odd to sit next to this child—my child—and just read silently to myself. But it's pretty clear that this is the best way in. It's not having a catch, but it's not pretending to drink tea with dolls and stuffed animals either.

The book is a collection of short stories, so we take a break to discuss them after each one. I've never been in a book club, but I'm guessing this is what it's like. It's the strangest sensation to simply talk about literature with this tiny person who happens to be made of a chunk of my DNA, but when Bella says it's time for Lilah's dinner, I'm not ready for it to end.

Lilah asks, "Would you like to come back tomorrow to finish it?"

Without hesitation I answer, "I'd love to" and am rewarded with two of the most beautiful smiles I've ever seen. At least until Bella schools her expression to neutral.

*

I GO BACK to the bookstore the next day, and the next, to read with Lilah. I'm afraid that she'll get bored with this, but when I make suggestions for outings like playing mini golf or going to the movies, she politely declines.

After I say goodnight for the third time—an awkward wave because she doesn't seem ready for a hug—I decide it's time to check in with Bella.

"So, is Lilah really shy?" I ask.

Her head ticks back and forth slowly. "Not at all. But she hasn't had a lot of men in her life."

Now I'm wondering if that means that Bella doesn't date, which make me inordinately happy. Even though she's keeping me at arm's length at the moment, it makes me feel like there could still be a chance for the two of us.

"Do you think she's afraid of me?"

"You are a bit… intimidating."

I can't help but sigh. "I don't know how to be any other way, I guess."

"Give her time. This is her safe place. It just may take a while for her to trust you."

"Yeah, okay. That makes sense."

When I get back to my apartment, Ribsy greets me enthusiastically. Going to the bookstore after work instead of coming straight home means that he's alone for even longer. "Sorry, buddy. Let's go for a walk, huh?"

He's grabbed his leash even before I get the "w" word out. I guess we both need the time outside because by the time we get back, I've not only sorted out a few niggling issues with my shooting plan for the next day, I've calmed down about Lilah.

It makes sense that she needs time to get used to the idea of having a father, and to get used to me specifically. I just don't want her to get bored. Plus, sitting still for an hour every day after so much time at my desk has me itching to move.

When we step into the kitchen, the red button's blinking on the answering machine. After I dump kibble into Ribsy's bowl, I play the message.

BEEP. Dude, it's been three days. What the heck? What's happening? I'm seeing Mom tomorrow at work. Have you told her? Call me.

Ribsy whines at the sound of Jill's voice, but I'm not sure whether he agrees with her or just misses her.

"She's right," I say to Ribsy. "I just haven't known what to say."

I dial her number anyway, and she answers with, "I have been waiting patiently since Sunday, you asshole. What is going on?"

"Sorry," I say. "It's just been crazy at work—"

"I don't care about work! Did you meet her? What's her name, anyway? Do you like her? Can I tell Mom?"

"Jesus, Jill. Give me a sec."

"She's been driving me insane here, Henry." My brother-in-law must've wrenched the phone away from my sister. "If you don't fill her in, she's going to fly up there this weekend."

"What he said," Jill's voice comes back on the line.

"Okay, okay. The family owns a bookstore, so I've been going there after work every day and we read together."

"That's it?"

"Pretty much. She's a brainiac, this kid."

"I guess the mom must be smart."

"Seriously. Didn't get it from me. She just finished kindergarten, but she reads books for junior high kids. And writes reviews for the store. She even leads a story time on Saturdays."

"Oh, Henry." My sister's voice sounds uncharacteristically sentimental. Maybe even teary.

"What's wrong?"

"I've just never heard you talk about anything this way before."

"Well, she's a pretty special kid. But I feel like I don't know what I'm doing, and really, it's not fair. Bella's had years to figure her out while I'm jumping on a moving train."

"I think it's time to call Mom. She'll have some good ideas."

"You're probably right, but—"

"Besides, I'm seeing her tomorrow, so I can't guarantee—"

"Yeah, yeah." I check the clock. Already eight. I haven't had dinner yet, but my mom's generation believes it's rude to call after nine o'clock unless there's an emergency. "I'll do it now."

"Love you, ya lug."

"Love you too, stinky."

Three laps around the couch, and I've worked up the courage to call my mom.

She answers on the first ring. "Henry. What's the matter?"

"Uh, nothing. Well, I do have some news."

"Something to warrant a weeknight call? Must be big news."

"It is." Now that I've got her on the phone, I realize I should've written out what to say. "Pretty big news."

"Well, what is it? Long distance is expensive, and it's almost bedtime."

"So, well…" Yep, definitely should've written something down.

"You're not sick, are you?"

"No, no. Nothing like that. It's just a big surprise. Well, it was to me, and it probably will be to you too."

"Good lord, Henry. Spit it out."

Here goes. "I found out that I have a daughter."

Silence on the other end of the line, so I continue. "Up here. In Boston."

"How in the world did that happen? You've never been to Boston."

"The mother is someone I knew in New York. Right before I came home." Swerving past the details to avoid talking about sex or my dad's death, I plow ahead. "When she found out she was pregnant, she didn't have any way to get in touch with me because I'd moved." I quickly explain that Bella moved back here and how we ended up working together. I skip the part where Bella didn't tell me at first, because I don't want my mom to think poorly of her. "I just met her for the first time Tuesday. My little girl, I mean."

I hear a sniffle on the other end of the line. "What's her name?"

"Delilah. But they call her Lilah."

"Lilah. That's beautiful." A swell of emotion rides her voice, so I just let her absorb the news for a moment.

"She's Jill at age five or six—looks-wise anyway. She's one of a kind, personality-wise."

My mom clears her throat. "I'm coming up there. I need to meet her."

"I want you to, Mom, but I think we have to take it slowly. It seems like she's a bit… wary of me."

"I hope you're not being too gruff with her."

"I'm doing my best," I grumble.

"Hmm," is all she says.

"I could use some advice, though."

"Of course." As I expected, her tone brightens.

"She's a big reader, and that's what we've been doing together so far. I've asked if she wants me to take her to do fun things, like roller skating or bowling, but she doesn't seem interested."

"Children don't always need to be entertained, you know. Walk the dog, take her to the grocery store. Things like that."

"That won't be too boring?"

"Just listen to her and include her in your life. Trust me, that's what she needs. Especially right now. Baby steps."

"Yeah. I missed that stage."

BELLA

When I was in rehab, the therapist said that my ability to focus was not only my secret weapon, it was the thing that saved my career. My ability to be in the present allowed me to work no matter what nonsense was going on around me, no matter what poison was coursing through my veins.

That ability is the only thing keeping me going right now.

When Lilah hangs out with Henry, I have to tear myself away from them. Even then, my heart remains right there between them while I rearrange books to spread out the dwindling stock, since my mom's current survival tactic is to cut down on supply. It would make sense in any other business, but when a customer does come, then asks for a book that's out of stock, they don't want to wait a week to get it. They give me a pained smile and walk out the door. I'm sure their next stop will be the bookstore at the mall. Next time, they'll skip coming here altogether.

Being busy from dawn to dusk helps, too. We've begun shooting the location segments and steering the kids through them takes every skill I've got in my toolbox. On top of that, I'm performing three nights a week in a comedy that moves at lightning speed and has me pulling out all the emotional stops. I can't spare a thought for Lilah until we take the last bow. But then I can't wait to get home, even though she'll be asleep. I need to see her sweet face, know that despite the fact that she's spending every evening with her father, she still needs me.

That's where my mind is as I peel off my sweaty costume, just as Jess leans in close to ask, "How's everything going at home?"

We share the dressing tent with the other actresses in the show, so I send her a subtle shake of the head before answering. "Good. When's the big move?"

Thankfully, that successfully redirects the others' attention. They jump in with questions about Jess moving in with Cal. Everyone's happy for her, and the advice is mostly good, as far as I know. It's not something I've ever done with a guy, so I have nothing to offer.

I didn't even know that you could get free boxes from the package store since I've never purchased alcohol in Boston.

Fifteen minutes later, I've almost made it to my car when Jess calls out, "Bella, hang on."

I send an apologetic wince her way. "I didn't mean to give you the brush-off back there, I just need to—"

She holds up a hand. "No need to explain. You must be juggling a lot right now." After sprinting to catch up to me, she gives me a hug.

"Oh," is all I can say. "Thanks."

Squeezing me tight, she whispers, "I just want you to know that I love you and I believe in you. Whatever you're struggling with, you can do it. And if you need me, call me. Anytime." Stepping back, she says. "I mean it."

I'm still getting used to having a friend I can trust who doesn't seem to want something from me. Her offer means more to me than I can explain, so I just nod and whisper, "Thanks."

When I finally do get in my car, I'm also grateful that the drive home is short, because Quinn and Izzy have opinions about all the secrets I'm still keeping and lies I'm still telling—misleading my colleagues at WGBH, keeping my addictions from Henry, and even lying to myself about how I feel about him.

Was he just kidding about the picket fence? Would he marry me just to make Lilah happy? Even if he did really care about me, what would that mean? I've never been in a real relationship with a guy. I've had flings, and I've had fake boyfriends that the PR people set up to bolster ratings. Half the time those men weren't even into women. I didn't give a shit as long as they kept me happy in other ways.

I'm still mulling over these questions the next morning when Lilah bounces into my bedroom. "Mommy! Guess what? Henry has a dog, and guess what his name is?"

Giving my girl the most genuine smile I can, despite the fact that the day has only begun and I'm already exhausted, I answer, "Um, I don't know. Spot? Rover?"

"No, silly. His dog is named Ribsy!"

"Henry and Ribsy." I nod. "That's pretty good."

"He really is a book person," she says, her face so full of awe and joy and love that it makes my heart break a little.

HENRY

It's the big night. I'm actually taking Lilah away from the bookstore and the supervision of Bella or Doris. Per my mom's advice, I'm keeping it simple. We're going to walk the dog, then go to the grocery store, cook dinner, and eat it. I'm a bit nervous to spend this much time with Lilah on my own, but hopefully Ribsy will be a good distraction. She seemed excited to meet him, anyway.

I'm really glad my daughter's not just a cat person.

My daughter. I just can't seem to get used to it. It isn't something I ever factored into my plans and I really don't know what I'm doing, but I look forward to spending time with this kid more than I have any woman I've dated. It's just so mind-blowing that I helped make her, and I feel the weight of responsibility for her now. Not like it's a burden. Like I want to be a part of teaching her about life.

It doesn't hurt that she's the coolest kid ever. She doesn't whine, she's curious about everything, and she's smart as hell. If every kid was like her, I'd love them all.

When I pull up in front of the bookstore and see her face in the window, it makes me ridiculously happy. But when she and Bella approach my truck, the frown on Bella's face puts me on the defensive. Like it always does.

"Don't worry. We're not doing anything dangerous, and I won't keep her up too late," I say as I round the front of the car. After I open the passenger side door, I gesture inside. "She's a bit of an antique, but there are seatbelts and everything."

Bella pastes on a smile, probably for Lilah's sake. "Do you have everything you need, sweetie?"

"Yep."

As she climbs up into the truck, Bella asks, "So what are you guys going to do?"

"Just take my dog for a walk, then make dinner. Chinese food."

"My favorite!" Lilah says.

"I heard."

"That a thing down in North Carolina?" Bella asks.

I laugh. "Nah, I learned from one of my roommates in New Jersey."

"Was he Chinese?" Lilah asks.

"No, he was Jewish. He just loved Chinese food. All Asian food. Thai, Japanese, Vietnamese. All I really do is stir fry. Not fancy. Not too spicy," I add for Bella's sake.

"I like spicy," Lilah says.

When Bella frowns again, I say, "Well, that's the good thing about making it yourself. You can try it and add more spicy stuff if you want." Before closing the door, I ask, "You all set?"

After pointing to the seat belt she fastened on her own, Lilah blows a kiss to Bella. "Bye, Mommy."

Bella shoves her hands in her pockets like she really wants to grab Lilah out of my car and drag her back into the store, but she smiles and says, "Have a good time, sweetie. Be good."

Before I get in myself, I give Bella's shoulder a squeeze. "I promise that I'll take care of her."

Lips pressed together, she nods. "See you later, then."

Before I can say anything else, she disappears inside.

·

EVERYTHING GOES to plan until it doesn't.

Ribsy politely gives Lilah his paw to shake when they meet, charming her instantly. Then we go to the dog park. Lilah wants to know the names of all the dogs and we meet a few people in the process—all female people. Weirdly, a little girl is even more of a chick magnet than a dog. More than one woman practically has hearts floating out of her eyes when we introduce ourselves. One even asks if I'm a widower. My relationship, or lack thereof, with Bella is way too complicated to explain to a stranger, so I just shake my head and announce that we have to get to the grocery store.

There, Lilah doesn't pester me for junk food, not even in the checkout line where the candy begs to be tossed onto the conveyor belt.

It's when we get back to my kitchen that things fall apart.

I just didn't think about how unsafe cooking could be until I put Lilah on a stool next to me at the counter and notice how small her hands are. How vulnerable her skin seems.

"My mom lets me use the big knife," Lilah asserts when I say that I'll be doing the chopping.

"I can stir," she complains when I insist on doing the actual stir frying, worried that she'd get burned by popping oil.

I try to distract her by getting her to set the table and even feed Ribsy, but by the time we sit down to eat, patience has run out for both of us.

When she grabs the hottest of the hot sauces from the counter and I suggest that she might want to try a different one, her brows come together and she says, "I told you I like it spicy," before dumping half the bottle on her dinner.

When I tell her that it's way too much, she shoves a forkful into her mouth. She chews once before spitting the food back onto her plate.

Unfortunately, I explode with, "Dammit, Lilah, I told you not to use that sauce! Now you've wasted it."

She tries to prove me wrong by stuffing more food in her mouth, to the point that she starts choking. Panicking, I pour her a glass of milk, but before I can give it to her, she runs to the bathroom and throws up on the floor. And then bursts into tears.

I try to clean up her and the floor while she sobs that she wants to go home. By the time I get her settled, the food is cold and we've both lost our appetite. Feeling like a complete failure, I bundle her back into the truck and drive back to Bella's. By the time we get there, Lilah has fallen asleep. I manage to get her out of her seat and up the back stairs to the apartment without waking her, so when Bella answers the door, I whisper, "Can you show me her room?"

She nods, and I follow her up another set of stairs. Bella opens the door to a little room tucked under the eaves of the big old house, then hustles to move stuffed animals and turn down the covers on the twin bed.

"Did she brush her teeth?" she whispers.

I wince and shake my head.

Bella frowns. "Just sit her down. I'll get her in her jammies and take her to the bathroom."

When I whisper an apology, she hesitates but then says, "Don't worry. We've done this before."

BELLA

I just spent the night with nothing to do for the first time in six years. Mom was out with friends, I didn't have a show, and Henry took Lilah to his place. So I cleaned the kitchen. Took everything out of every cabinet, scrubbed the interiors, threw away expired cans of pumpkin puree and chickpeas, as well as plastic containers missing lids, and then put everything away again.

But I can't do that every time he takes her.

When they show up at the back door, Lilah's asleep in his arms, and I'm suddenly so angry I can't meet his gaze. Angry that he's taken my job from me. Angry that he hasn't been here for her whole life. Angry that he is here now.

As I get Lilah ready for bed, she sleepily whines about dinner being too spicy and something else about Ribsy. After I've tucked her in, reassured that she still needs me, I make myself face him. Before I can apologize for snapping at him—it's not his fault that I'm not able to deal with sharing my daughter—he says the worst thing possible.

"I don't know if I can do this."

My apology goes out the window. "What do you mean? You can't quit on her now. It'll break her heart."

He rubs a hand over a face that's aged ten years in one night. "I fucked up."

"What happened?"

He launches into a story that involves a temper tantrum, a bottle of hot sauce, vomit, and tears. I can't help but laugh. "Welcome to being a parent, dude." I point upstairs. "She survived. You'll survive. You do your best and move on."

When he meets my gaze, his expression is dialed to dumbfounded. "You're not mad at me?"

"Well, I was mad at you."

"Because...?"

Be honest, Izzy urges.

About everything? Quinn asks.

About Lilah, Izzy clarifies.

Forcing my lips to separate from each other, I spill out the only confession that I tell myself really matters. "I will be extremely angry with you if you give up on her after one bump in the road. I was mad at you earlier for no good reason. I was really jealous, I guess"—gesturing at the kitchen—"so discombobulated by being on my own that I reorganized all the cabinets."

He laughs. "That's desperation."

"Tell me about it."

He shoves his hands in his pockets and looks everywhere but at me. "I wish there were a manual."

It takes me a minute to figure out what he means. When I do, I have to laugh. "For Lilah?"

"Yeah." He shrugs. "I don't want to screw her up any more than I already have just by not being there."

My hand lands on his muscular forearm and squeezes, but when our eyes meet, I jerk my hand away. "Sorry, I, uh…"

He grins. "Apology not accepted. You can touch me anytime you want."

I squeeze my eyes shut. "I'm trying to keep things simple here. You want to do what's best for Lilah, right?"

"Having a sexually satisfied mom isn't good for Lilah?"

I knew I liked this man, Quinn sighs.

Ticking a finger in the air between us, I aim a glare at him. "It's not that simple, and you know it. Anyway, don't distract me. In fact, follow me."

Grabbing the keys from the hook, I lead the way downstairs. After unlocking the door that connects our apartment with the shop, I turn on a few lights and head for the Parenting section. There, I gesture like Vanna White. "Voila: manuals."

Henry steps up to a shelf and runs a finger over the spines, reading the titles out loud. "*Raising Positive Kids in a Negative World.* Not sure about that. *Making Children Mind Without Losing Yours.* That sounds like what I need." He gapes at me. "Have you read all of these?"

I don't get it, but this is turning me on for some reason, Quinn whispers.

I get it, Izzy says breathily. *A man who wants to be a good father? That is so... beautiful.*

Hot as fuck, you mean, Quinn snickers.

Kiss him, they say in unison.

And I do want to. But… it's too much. Too complicated. Using the parenting skills I did acquire by reading, I school my thoughts to the topic at hand. "Some, but not all."

Unfortunately, my arm brushes his as I reach for a book, and my body's reaction is as heady as if I'd copped a feel of his butt.

I guess we get what we get and we don't get upset, Quinn mutters.

"I've heard good things about this," I say, handing him *Your Child's Growing Mind.*

"What about this one?" He holds up *The Secret of Happy Children.* "Too good to be true?"

"With a title like that? Probably. But I haven't read it. Um…" I scan the shelf. "I feel like we got one recently that had really good reviews. I hope I didn't send it back already."

"Because a customer returned it?"

"No, bookstores have this business model where we can return stock if it doesn't sell. It's the only way we have room to keep adding new books. But now we're returning books because— Oh, there it is. Someone put it on the wrong shelf." I hand him the book.

"*Raising Self-Reliant Children,*" he reads. "Sounds like a good premise."

As he flips through the book, that flop of curls falls across his brow, begging me to brush it out of his eyes. Full lips framed by a trim beard the exact same color as his caramel irises remind me of the night in the cabin when their contrasting textures woke up nerve endings I'd forgotten existed. Every bit of me yearns to revel in those feelings again, and when he looks up from the book, I'm tempted to indulge.

Thankfully, all the reasons why I shouldn't have me taking a big step back.

In response, both his eyes and the book's pages snap closed, and he makes a beeline for the door. "I'll take it. See you at work."

Chapter 13

"Last week on *One Way to Live*: Ronin interrupts his conversation with Norah by calling Brandy to break a date. Seems he's promised to take little Tommy to the country. Brandy misunderstands Ronin's call and rushes off in tears. Laney has a premonition that something tragic will happen." *Soap Opera Land*, July 1989

HENRY

The entire drive home, I take my frustration out on my poor truck, slamming on the brakes and taking corners entirely too fast. Christine used to use sex to manipulate me—seducing me when she wanted me to agree to go away for the weekend, withholding sex once we got there because I said something wrong at dinner. I didn't like it then, and I don't like it now.

Once I step inside my apartment, Ribsy whines and noses his leash. I hook it onto his collar. Going over the events of the evening as we go for a final walk of the day, I find calm. Perhaps Bella wasn't being manipulative. Like me, she could be struggling to do what's best.

I mean, what were we going to do? Have sex up against a bookshelf or the checkout counter?

The look in her eye before I closed the parenting book and stepped away wasn't about getting something she wanted. She was fighting to control her own desire. Because she is a good mom, and her kid—our kid—was asleep alone upstairs.

We can't screw around and then break up. We have to be in it to win it. Maybe I have to prove to her that I'm as concerned about Lilah as she is before she can trust me. Not just as a co-parent, but as a potential partner.

When Ribsy and I return, he steps on The First Story bookstore bag that I dropped by the front door. After I rescue it from his scrabbling paws and pull out the book inside, it's clear what I need to do: study this parenting book and every other one I can find and prove that I can be the perfect dad.

That's got to be the way to win any single mom's heart.

■

THINGS BETWEEN BELLA and me personally may be up in the air, but at work we are a team that can do no wrong. Today is the day everyone meets the computer—which has turned out even better than I could have imagined due to an inspired crew—and I'm going to pull out the stops to convince Bella that she needs to be the voice of BETTI.

It seems obvious to me. She's the actress on the team. She knows the kids. But for some reason, she's against it.

When I ask if she'll join me on stage to see the setup, she argues, "I really think we should hire a voice-over person to do this. My friend Jess would be great."

"*You'd* be great. And you're right here. Already on salary. As a producer, you can do it without us having to pay someone else. I even checked with the union."

Crossing her arms over her chest, she frowns. "I think it'll be confusing for the kids."

"They won't see you, and besides, we have it set up so you'll sound like a computer."

When her hands go to her hips and her head drops, I wonder if there's more behind her resistance than what meets the eye. I don't want to be a jerk; she's simply the best person for the job. "How about this? We just try it out. We need to work out the kinks anyway, make sure all the moving parts work like they're supposed to. We'll record it, and if you watch it and really hate it, we'll hire someone else."

She gives me an assessing look, like she doesn't really believe me. I raise my right hand in the air and place it over my heart. "I promise. We won't use what you do unless you completely agree."

Eyes holding mine for one final beat, she finally throws up her hands in surrender. "All right. I'll be the rehearsal computer." Her focus on the set, she asks, "Do I stand behind it, or what?"

"You'll be in a booth with a monitor, a mic, and headphones. The mic gets run through a synthesizer called a vocoder. What the kids—and everyone else—will hear is a robot-like voice. Here, I'll show you." Taking her by the elbow—a seemingly innocuous spot, but any touch gets me going with this woman—I lead her to the large set piece that is our computer, BETTI. "Wait here."

I jog to the booth nearby, close myself inside, and put on the headphones. When I say, "Hello, Bella," she whirls around to face the camera and speaker I've set up behind BETTI, her hand covering her mouth in surprise.

As I speak, hopefully, lights are going off on BETTI. That's what's supposed to happen.

"This is BETTI's brother, Hal. You wouldn't want me to scare the kids, would you?"

She scans the set to see if anyone else is around and then gives me the finger. "Bella!" I say, keeping my voice modulated to get the best robotic effect. "How terribly rude of you."

Hands on hips, she finally cracks a smile. "All right, all right. You've convinced me."

"Then join me here at the mic so Hal can hand the reins over to BETTI."

Moments later, the soundproof booth door cracks open and Bella steps inside. It takes every bit of self-control I've got to yield the space to her. What I want to do is turn the mic off and press every inch of me up against every inch of her. But I need to be patient. And the show needs her.

"Why can't Laura or Keeley do this?" she asks as she takes the headphones from me.

"One, their voices are pitched too high for the synthesizer to create the best effect. Two, they're not actresses. We don't have a script, remember? You're going to have to make this up on the fly."

I risk a touch to her forearm when I make my final appeal. "You're the only one I trust to get it right on every take."

"No pressure, then."

A brief squeeze from my overheated palm has her meeting my gaze. "You'll be great. I believe in you."

And then I get out of there before I do anything stupid.

·

BELLA

I'll never admit to Henry how much fun I had playing BETTI during today's shoot. From the improvisation it required to the kids' faces when we finally revealed it was me to the feeling of accomplishment —Henry and I pushed for this change, and it actually seems to work —I had a blast at work today.

The kind of fun that gives you energy instead of drains it. I'm still raring to go when my friend Ben pulls up to give me a ride to the theater so we can both see *The Tempest* for the first time. We worked together at Shakespeare Boston last fall, but since then he's been working out of town. I've been juggling way too many things to get to it yet, so when he called this afternoon and asked if I'd be his date, I readily agreed.

Timing is everything, as they say, so of course Henry pulls up and parks right behind Ben. The glare that he levels at the internationally famous model appears to be fueled one hundred percent by jealousy.

Oh, he still likes you, Izzy sighs.

Likes you? Quinn sniffs. *He's ready to kill for you.*

Calm down, ladies. This is an easily cleared up misunderstanding.

Before I can intervene, however, Lilah grabs Ben's hand and drags him down the walk to Henry. "Daddy, guess what?"

Ben's head practically spins on its axis, and his eyeballs bug out like a cartoon's. The man really is a clown inside that gorgeous exterior. After I mouth "I'll explain," he refocuses on Lilah and Henry.

"Ben had a dog called Puck that was in a play with him and Mommy," she explains breathlessly. "Ben's friend Lucy taught Puck tricks for the play, and she's super good. I bet she could help us teach Ribsy to do high fives and play dead and everything! Can we get Lucy to train Ribsy? Please?"

I have to bite my lip to keep from laughing at the procession of expressions that cross Henry's face. To his credit, he finally shakes Ben's hand. "Henry Smith. I am Lilah's biological father."

Since we seem to have neglected to discuss what to do when Lilah outs us, I'm impressed with his quick thinking. Luckily, I trust Ben more than most people, so he's a good out-of-town tryout. I step in to add my bit. "Henry and I lost touch, but we're now working together on *Boom*, so..." That's when words fail me. I end up just gesturing back and forth between Henry and Lilah.

"I'm spending time getting to know my daughter. Good thing," Henry finally jumps in, his tone icy. "It seems like her mom has a date."

Ben seems oblivious to Henry's obvious jealousy. Maybe because he's in a committed relationship and assumes that everyone knows it since it's actually been announced in *People* magazine. He just slings an arm around my shoulder. "She sure does. Got to have my favorite scene partner by my side when we go to see the play they didn't put us in."

I roll my eyes and bump hips with him. "First of all, Ben didn't even audition for this season because he's been too busy acting on Broadway and in a television show. And I told them I only wanted to be in one play." I check my watch. "But we do need to get going. Can't be late, or we'll get a thrashing from the house manager."

Squatting, I give Lilah a kiss. "Be good, honey."

"You too, Mommy."

"I will."

Why didn't you explain that you're not really going on a date with Ben? Izzy asks, affronted.

Because it's important to keep a man on his toes, Quinn advises.

And me? I haven't a clue. About any of this.

THE MOMENT we get in the car, Ben asks, "What the heck was that all about?"

I just point at the steering wheel. "Drive. I'll tell you on the way, but I seriously don't want to be late."

He narrows his eyes at me. "Okay, okay, but I want to know all."

Because, like Jess, Ben has shared secrets with me, I owe it to him to give it to him straight. Everything that I can talk about anyway. So, after making it clear that it's something I haven't yet talked about publicly, I give him the quick and dirty version of the story. Well, not too dirty.

He just shakes his head when I'm finished. "You know, it's weird. I wondered about Lilah's father when I first met her, but then you two were such a perfect duo that it was like a father was extraneous."

"Like she just popped out of my armpit fully formed?"

"Maybe not exactly like that."

"Yeah, well, he was kind of extraneous. Until he wasn't. Isn't," I correct. "She's getting pretty attached pretty fast."

He shoots me a sly look. "And what about you?"

"What do you mean?"

My attempt at an innocent tone clearly falls flat. "You may be a good actress, but you're a terrible liar. And that guy. I've never felt laser rays of jealousy shoot at me like that before."

"Well, you didn't help."

"Really? I thought I was playing gay best friend for you."

A snort of laughter escapes out my nose. "You're not that good of an actor. Speaking of which, how is the love of your life? How are you two doing with the long-distance thing? Are you going back to North Carolina?"

"Not unless there are reshoots. The film's wrapped."

"And you and Lucy…?"

"Things are great." His smile is so wide as he goes on to talk about her and their busy lives and how they're making it all work, I'm the one with a jealous heart—not of him and Lucy, but of what they have. The kind of relationship I wrote off years ago but has been dangling in front of my nose as a possibility of late.

"And how about you? What's this I hear about you working on the other side of the camera?"

"It's true. An opportunity came up, and I couldn't say no."

"Because it's something you've wanted to do? Like from when you were working on the soap?"

"No. Not at all. Frankly, it was because we needed the money."

He nods as he steers the car into the park that serves as the company's summer home. "I get it. Shakespeare Boston doesn't exactly pay the bills. It's basically gas and beer money. I'd hate for you to give up acting, though. You're so talented."

"I appreciate that, but… I'm not sure it can be a career for me. When I was a full-time actress, I wasn't healthy. Doing it for the love of it is one thing, but having to show up nine to five—"

"You mean five to ten?"

"Right. AM to PM. You know what I'm talking about. How do you deal with the stress? Having to create on demand? Putting your whole self on the line like that?"

After parking, he asks, "Was that hard for you?"

Legally, I can't share the details of my addiction and stint in rehab with anyone, but that doesn't mean I can't share with a close friend how it all made me feel. "It was. When I got pregnant, it was way too easy of a choice to give it all up. It was actually a relief." We have a few more minutes before curtain, so I ask, "How did you deal with it? How do you now? Having your life out there for everyone to see?"

"Well…" He looks out over the trees that frame the lot. "When I was modeling, I didn't really care about any of it, so I always kept a little part of myself back."

"But you can't do that as an actor. At least I can't."

"Yes and no. I mean, the part of me that loves Lucy, that belongs to her, that's always tucked away. I think our relationship keeps me grounded too. So I don't start thinking that what I'm doing is really important."

"You don't think it's important? Making people feel things?"

"*That's* important. But the chasing after work, the schmoozing? That isn't. When I'm actually acting, then I put my whole self on the line. But the rest of it—that's when I'm pretending."

What he's saying makes sense intellectually, but… "I'm not sure I know how to do that. Maybe it's because I missed adolescence."

"Lucky you. How'd you manage that?"

"I didn't go to high school or college. I didn't have that time to figure out all this stuff you're talking about. All my screwups were potentially in the public eye, so I had to hide them. And since nobody was making sure I came home by a curfew or passed classes, I had plenty of opportunities to screw up."

He nods. "I knew people at school who messed up so badly they got kicked out."

"Exactly. But nobody was kicking me out of anything. There were absolutely no boundaries. I acted like an adult, so everyone treated me like one. As long as I maintained a thin veneer of professionalism, there were no consequences for anything I did. When I went out partying, that just created great PR ops."

When you showed up for work high, no one even noticed, Izzy says, her voice even sadder than usual.

Or they gave you another drug to counteract whatever thing you were on, Quinn adds, her tone somber as well.

"Anyway, I know we won't be able to hide this story for long, but while we're still figuring it out, I'd appreciate your discretion."

"Of course." Hand over his heart, he says, "Your secret's safe with me."

"Thank you. And thanks for listening." I point to the clock on his dashboard. "We should head in."

As we walk toward the theater, I bump shoulders with him. "I'm happy for you and I'm envious that you've figured it out, but it's just not for me. Acting is something I do for fun once or twice a year."

He grins. "And you'll spend the rest of the year working as a big-time producer, telling other people what to do?"

"Well, I am pretty darn good at that."

"I've noticed," he says, and then squeals like Lilah as I chase him all the way to the ticket booth.

Chapter 14

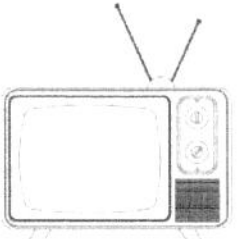

"MORE CHANGES? *ALL HIS CHILDREN* SHEDS FELICIA AND CHARLES! This pair's exit means that the love triangle including Delia, played by Sharon Roundtree, falls apart. Who will Delia set her sights on next?!" *Soap Chat*, July 1989

BELLA

The following week, on a night that Henry has Lilah and I don't have a show, my mother corners me in the kitchen. "Sweetheart, I'm sorry things are so complicated all of a sudden. I wish..." She trails off, eyes tracking to the windows above the sink. "This probably isn't the best time to tell you, but I'm running out of time."

My butt hits the nearest chair. "Now what?"

"I'm selling the shop."

"What? To whom?"

"A woman who asked about buying it almost a year ago. She's got money, has always wanted to open a yarn shop and loves the location. I called her Friday, she called me back this morning and we're going to talk to a lawyer tomorrow."

"But... where will we live?"

"We'll have to figure that out. And I know this will be a big change for Lilah. But she's willing to pay enough that I'll be able to pay back the mortgage and walk away with a decent sum. I figured we could rent a place while we figure out what's next."

Resting my cheek on my hand, I let my gaze rove over our tiny kitchen. The wallpaper's fading, the linoleum is peeling in the corners, but it's the only one Lilah's ever known. In this room, she took her first bites of baby food and dumped bowls of mashed peas on the floor. Her artwork covers the surface of our ancient fridge, so you can barely see that the color's a no-longer-fashionable avocado.

"I'm sorry if this adds to your problems, but I didn't want to keep it from you either."

My focus snaps from memories to the present. "Like I did, you mean?"

"Well, yes." She sits with a groan. "I guess we both have a lot to learn about sharing burdens before we dig ourselves into trouble." Reaching across the table, she takes my hand. "Again, I'm sorry. I just don't know a better way forward. The shop is not going to magically save itself."

Nodding, staring at our hands, I mutter, "Yeah. Okay. I'm sure you're right."

HENRY

I seem to have worn my daughter out again. To me, it's a good thing that she biked so hard while Ribsy and I jogged that she falls asleep on the way home, but from the look on Bella's face when I carry her upstairs, I've screwed up somehow.

She may be giving me the cold shoulder, but she gets Lilah changed into pajamas and tucked into bed with more patience than I can imagine mustering. When she closes the bedroom door, I follow her into the kitchen.

"I'm sorry if it's a problem that I'm wearing her out. She seems to love acting as my so-called trainer, and she had Ribsy and me running for a half hour while she—"

Bella holds up a hand and interrupts me. "It's fine, Henry."

"Then what's wrong?"

She shakes her head. "It's nothing."

"Bella, come on. I can tell something's up."

She shakes her head. "I can't. I'll cry."

"Can I just give you a hug?"

She frowns, which at least brings us back to normal. "I thought we weren't doing that."

I hold up a hand. "You said you wanted to keep things simple."

"Which nothing ever is," she says on a sigh so deep it breaks my heart.

"Bella, I—"

"You know what? Maybe you should just take Lilah and move her in with your perfect family down in North Carolina." She flaps a hand out to the side. "She won't have her childhood home for much longer and neither will I, so—"

"Whoa, whoa, what is going on? Is Doris kicking you out?"

Pacing the length of the small kitchen, hands in fists, she spits out, "She's sold the shop and the building. We can't live here anymore."

I can tell she's trying to hang onto anger. I do it myself when I'm trying not to cry. I'm not sure which feeling is worse, but I want her to be comfortable sharing both with me, so I just hold my breath.

Spinning to face me, her expression anguished, she says, "Lilah's favorite thing in the world is the Saturday story time. It's the place she shines. If she doesn't have that—" She breaks off, lips clamped together, and shakes her head.

"Can I please give you a hug? I know it won't solve the problem, but..."

After a long, stubborn pause, she shrugs. Taking that as permission, I wrap her in my arms. Her shoulders heave, and she finally lets go. I do my best to just hold on and let her cry, but it literally hurts my heart for her to be in pain.

I have no idea what to do with the feeling.

Eventually, she lets out a long, shuddery breath. When she steps out of my embrace, I let her go. The emptiness I'm left with? Even worse than feeling her grief.

"Ugh." Pointing to my shirt, she grabs a box of tissues from the counter, takes one, and gives me the rest. While she blows her nose, I dab at the mess she left behind on my shirt.

Grimacing at the wet spot, she says, "I'm so sorry."

The tissues don't do much to dry my shirt, and I have to laugh. "You've been storing those up for some time."

"I guess I have." She blows out a breath and scans the kitchen like she wants to do dishes or sweep the floor or something. "I… I don't know what to say."

"You don't have to say anything. You don't have to be Supermom. Let me help."

She coughs out a half-laugh. "I'm hardly a supermom. I'm just hanging on by a thread."

"Is it financial? I'm happy to help if you need money to get resettled."

She leans on the counter. "That's part of it. But—" She blows out a breath. "Oh boy."

Obviously overwhelmed with emotion again, she slaps her cheeks with both hands. I grab them to stop her, but she resists, so I let loose with, "You know my family isn't perfect, right? I mean, my parents' relationship was pretty awesome, but I had nothing to do with that. I'm the black sheep. The only one who doesn't work in the family business, the only one who left."

"Hal. Henry, I mean—"

"It's okay." I squeeze her hands, which she's relaxed enough to let me hang onto. "I like it when you call me Hal."

That has her tugging away. "Sorry, I can't focus when you…"

"Touch you?"

An impressive grimace taking over her beautiful face, she grits out a "Yes."

I do my best to squelch a smile. "I'll try not to take advantage of that."

"I'm trying to be serious here, Henry."

"I'm serious. Serious as a heart attack."

She rolls her eyes, and I take the tiny win. I'll take any emotion other than deep sorrow.

Facing the counter, she braces her arms and drops her head. "There's a lot you don't know still. Things I need to tell you."

"About Lilah?"

"About me and my past."

Her tone is so full of self-disgust and self-loathing I can't stand it. I have to hug her again. This time, I don't ask. I just wrap her in my arms as gently as I can. It only takes a moment before her stiff posture relents and she melts into my chest.

"One thing at a time, remember?" I whisper. "We've all made mistakes. Whatever yours are, you've done a great job with Lilah. And we'll get through the bookstore closing. Together. You can lean on me whenever, however you need to."

She doesn't say anything for a long time, but when she finally whispers a wet "Okay" into my shirt, the word touches my heart in a place so deep I didn't know it existed.

Two people depend on me now. My priorities are clear. I'll do whatever it takes to make things right for them.

THE NEXT DAY IS SATURDAY. I have pre-edits to do—combing through the footage of the previous days' shoots to prep for our editing time Monday—but I have an idea for an adventure that I think will kill a few birds with one stone. No pun intended, but I think a very special tour with a very famous family of ducks might help prove to both Bella and Lilah that I'm a good dad and give both of my girls something to smile about. Luckily, it's the younger one that answers the phone.

"York residence, Lilah speaking."

I decide to play along when I respond. "Yes, Miss York, this is Mr. Smith. Is your mother on the premises?"

"She's sleeping."

"Excellent. I need an accomplice, and I think you just might fit the bill."

"For what? Is it a super-secret crime?"

She sounds a little too eager, so I dial it back a bit. "No, no, it's not illegal, but I think it should be secret. A surprise for your mother." I doubt that Lilah knows about the bookstore closing, so I don't want to say that Bella needs cheering up. "I think she deserves a fun day, don't you?"

"What is the surprise?" she asks.

When I tell her the basic idea, she gasps. "I've always wanted to do that!"

"The question is, how do we get your mom to go along?"

"I could tell her that I want to take pictures as a project for story time."

Even though this might make Bella upset, it does seem like the best plan. "How about I pick you up after lunch? Can you keep your mom home until then?"

"Okay. She doesn't have to do the play today."

"Great. I'll see you later."

"Okay. Bye, Daddy."

She hangs up, but the dial tone buzzing in my ears barely registers because all I can hear is the echo of my little girl's voice in my mind. When Lilah called me "Daddy" in front of that guy Ben the other night, I was so jealous of him that it didn't really land. Not to mention the fact that we were scrambling to explain ourselves.

But now, all I want is to hear her say it again and again. And to be worthy of the title.

BELLA

Lilah has been acting strangely all morning. I'm worried that she's somehow picked up on the fact that we're having problems with the store because after story time she insists that we need to take pictures for a project for next week's presentation. I'm not ready to tell her that I don't even know if there'll be a story time next week, so I agree to let her use the camera. Thing is, she won't tell me the project or where she needs to go. All she'll say is that we have to eat lunch.

My mom waves us off with a sad shake of her head when I ask if she needs any help in the store, so Lilah and I go upstairs and make macaroni and cheese. She doesn't say anything more about the project, so I figure maybe it was just a passing whim of an idea. After I finish up the dishes and get a load of laundry in, I go looking for her to see if she wants to invite a friend over. I find her back in the bookstore, Henry at her side.

"Um, hi." There's a gleam in his eye that has me worried. "Did we—are you taking Lilah somewhere?"

"I'd like to," he answers with an all-too-innocent grin. "But only if you'll join us."

"Please, Mommy! We have a really good surprise!"

So, this is what was going on. The two of them have cooked up something. I gesture overhead. "I just put a load of laundry in, so I think—"

My mom cuts me off. "I can put it in the dryer. You should go."

I give them all a glare. "Are you guys ganging up on me?"

Henry wince-smiles. "A little bit? But in a good way. I promise."

I hang on to my irritation for a moment, but then decide, what the heck, spend the afternoon making my girl happy. With her father. How bad can it be?

Quinn and Izzy are uncharacteristically silent.

I have to admit, it's a relief.

FIFTEEN MINUTES LATER, we're stuffed into the cab of Henry's truck with Ribsy at our feet. He rests his chin on my knee, and I stroke his soft ears. I've always been more of a cat person but working with a dog in *Two Gentlemen of Verona* with Ben last year, I got close to a dog for the first time. Puck is one of a kind, but with his big brown eyes, I could see how Ribsy could worm his way into anyone's heart.

Like dog, like owner.

The smile on Henry's face as he heads down Storrow Drive toward downtown is the exact same expression he had on his face the night we met. Pure joy. He ruffles Lilah's hair as they chat, and she snuggles into his side unselfconsciously. How did this closeness develop in just a few short weeks? Is it genetic? Some sort of animal instinct?

Or is it that he's been putting in real effort to win her over?

He's definitely done some parenting homework. Just getting into the car, he set clear expectations and reminded her that it's not safe for her to push all the buttons or try to help him steer. When she kicked the dashboard, obviously full of nervous energy about whatever this surprise is, he just set a hand on her knee and squeezed it once, settling her without losing his temper.

I'm wishing he'd squeeze my knee or ruffle my hair by the time we've parked in the lot beneath the Public Garden, but as we emerge into the warm sunshine, I simply enjoy the view. Flowers sway near graceful arches of wrought iron, and sunlight sparkles on the surface of the pond. "Wow. I haven't been here in a long time."

"I've never been here," Lilah exclaims.

"You have," I tell her. "But I guess you were too young to remember. So, is this the big surprise?"

"Almost." Lilah grabs my hand. Instead of pulling me into the park, she leans toward Henry and whispers, "Um, I don't know where to go now."

He takes her other hand. "That's okay; I do."

HENRY

I may not have Robert McCloskey's *Make Way for Ducklings* memorized like Lilah does, but I have a map and I've prepared by marking not only the bronze statues of the mother duck and her eight ducklings, but just about every location depicted in the book. If I could fly a helicopter, we could take in the aerial views, but I'm happy as can be to stroll through the streets of Boston with my two girls.

When we find the statues, Lilah poses for a photo astride Mrs. Mallard. Then she calls out the name of each of the ducklings: "Jack, Kack, Lack, Mack, Nack, Ouack, Pack, and Quack!" After that, she wants to operate the camera, and I'm all for it. For one thing, my little girl seems to have the instincts of a documentarian because she's taking the time to frame shots like a pro. For another, it gives me a chance to walk with her mom.

As Lilah crouches pondside to photograph Duck Island, she yells, "This is where Mr. and Mrs. Mallard spent the night!"

"But they didn't find much to eat," Bella recites.

I point to a kid on a bike. "And then Mr. Mallard almost got run over."

"That was after they saw the swan boat, Daddy," Lilah says.

Seems I've earned the title Daddy in Lilah's mind, but I still have to convince Bella that I'm worthy of it because I'm convinced that it's the only way into her heart. I have a feeling she'd let me into her bed if I really tried, but that's no longer enough. I'm greedy, and I want it all.

"Right," I say. "Let's go check that out."

We can't ride the swan boat with Ribsy, but we do buy some peanuts and feed them to some real-life ducks. After that, we hike to check out Beacon Hill, the State House, and Louisburg Square. Lilah photographs each spot, and we all agree that there's no water in any of these locations, as the ducks in the book discovered. Next, we troop over to the Charles River and find the little island where Mr. and Mrs. Mallard eventually settled.

"I wish we could go over there," Lilah says, a whine creeping into her tone.

I want my kid to be happy, so my first instinct is to give her what she wants. There are boats to be rented, after all. But I remember reading that it's important to set boundaries for kids and I want Bella to see that I'm not just trying to buy Lilah's love, so I squat down and point at the island. "Well, first of all, we can't fly."

Lilah sticks her lower lip out in a pout. Cute, but could lead to a tantrum if I don't do this right. "Second, we didn't bring our swim trunks."

She opens her mouth, but before she can suggest that we try wading across in our clothes, an even better argument comes to me. "And third, we don't want to disturb any wildlife over there." I point to the Esplanade where families have spread out picnics and folks are running and biking. "See, that's a park for people. We should leave the smaller islands to the wild animals."

"Okay." Lilah sighs. "Can we go see if there's a policeman named Michael?"

We don't find a policeman, but we do find an ice cream truck and enjoy our cones while Lilah recites the part of the book where Mrs. Mallard teaches the babies how to behave like good little ducklings. After that, we walk back to the park, taking the route the ducks followed. By the time we make it back to the pond, Lilah's getting droopy, so Bella takes Ribsy's leash and I give Lilah a piggyback ride to the car.

Once we're in the car, Lilah snuggles in next to me and whispers, "I'm glad we found you again, just like Mrs. Mallard and the ducklings found Mr. Mallard."

"I am too, Lilah," I say. I meet Bella's gaze over her head, blinking back a sudden rush of emotion. "I am too."

ON THE WAY BACK, Lilah falls asleep with her head on my shoulder and Ribsy falls asleep curled up on Bella's feet, but the moment I park in front of the shop, child and dog perk right back up, scrambling out of the car to chase each other around the front yard.

I'm trying to figure out how to invite myself to stay, when a man exits the front door of the shop followed by two dark-haired girls. Lilah squeals and runs over to hug them before introducing them to Ribsy. By the time I've caught up with Bella, she's hugging the guy. I have to suppress a growl. This woman has too many good-looking guys in her life.

It's only when he extends his hand in greeting that I notice the scars covering the left side of his face. "You must be Henry. I'm Cal, Jess's boyfriend."

Relieved that he's taken, curious about his scars, but most of all intrigued by the fact that he knows who I am, I shake his hand. "Good to meet you."

He turns to Bella. "We're here to see if we can kidnap Lilah. We're watching the girls this weekend. Jess has the show, but they really want your daughter to join us for a movie night."

"Oh, Mommy, please, can I?" Lilah presses her little hands together in front of her heart. I'm glad I'm not the one in the line of fire. I can't imagine saying no to that face.

Bella just crosses her arms over her chest. "Lilah, you know that tone doesn't work on me. In fact, it makes me think you might be overtired already."

"I'm not tired at all," Lilah promises, whine erased from her voice. "I just had a nap in the car."

"Please, Miss Bella," the older of the two girls chimes in. "We won't stay up too late."

Bella considers for a moment—or at least pretends to, it's hard to tell—before giving in. "All right. Run upstairs and pack a bag for the night."

I put Ribsy on his leash so he won't be tempted to follow the girls inside and chase the cats, and then let him do his business on a light pole or two while Cal and Bella work out details. By the time I've put Ribsy back in my truck, the three girls are getting settled in Cal's car. I blow a kiss to Lilah as they drive away.

Left alone with Bella, I feel as awkward as I did back in junior high when I was a pimply-faced, skinny kid. On the one hand, everything seems so perfect. We get along great, we have a great kid, and we've had some great sex. I'm trying to convince her that I'm fully on board with being Lilah's dad. Today was idyllic. I could sign up for more.

But she seems determined to be self-sufficient, and it's not like I have a great track record myself. I'm not even sure if I've ever been in love. The way my mom and dad used to look at each other… I've never felt close to a woman like that. I've had glimpses of it with Bella. Not just in bed, though sex with her is definitely more mind-blowing than it's ever been with anybody else. It's the little moments. When I catch her private smile and she lets me in for a moment. When I make her laugh. When I surprise her with a cup of coffee at work, just the way she likes it. The fact that each of these little connections just makes me want more.

Maybe that's love?

"Henry?"

"Uh, yeah?" She's staring at me, and Ribsy is pawing at the car window. Shaking my head, I say, "Sorry, lost in thought."

"Oh. Well, if you've got too much going on, then—"

"Wait. What did you say? Did you ask me something?"

"I just wondered if you wanted to get dinner." She shrugs, and her cheeks flush. "After what happened with Ben the other night and seeing Cal just now… I feel like we need to get our story ready for prime time, as it were. We might have to tell people at work soon about you and Lilah." She pauses to search my face. "But we can talk on the phone or whatever later if that's better."

She turns abruptly and walks toward the house leaving me at a crossroads of indecision, confusion, lust, and longing. How is this woman's mind still so hidden from me? Does she really not feel any of the things I'm feeling? Or is it that she's afraid of something? I don't want to lose her by pushing, but if I don't catch her now, it'll feel like I've given up.

"Bella!" I shout just as she opens the front door. "Yes." When she turns, there's a hairline crack in that facade of hers. "Yes. Let's have dinner."

Chapter 15

"Last week on *Private Hospital*: Things have come to a head for Matt. The realization that he's Tricia's father has stirred his memory. Jim urges Mandy to marry him, but she says she's made too many mistakes in the past. Meanwhile, Betty gets a difficult diagnosis." *Soap Opera Land*, August 1989

BELLA

This may not be the right time, but even though I gave Henry an out, he insists on doing dinner. I don't want to talk in public, for obvious reasons, and my mom is having some friends over, so Henry's apartment is the only option.

And the riskiest, Izzy says.

In all the good ways, Quinn counters. *Can we please sleep with him just one more time?*

You sound like Lilah, Izzy grumbles. *You should know by now that whining doesn't work with her.*

Whatever, Quinn says. *I just don't see why you're so against this man.*

I hate to admit it, but I kind of agree, Izzy says. *He's being so good with Lilah. Maybe you should give him a chance.*

He's saying something about needing to feed Ribsy anyway as he turns onto Storrow Drive. "Did you feel like anything in particular?"

Oh, just your hands everywhere, Quinn says sweetly.

It takes me a moment to realize he must be talking about food. "Oh, no. Whatever you want is fine."

"Well, if you don't mind leftovers, I've got some tuna casserole."

This makes me laugh. "Seriously? Did your mom mail it to you or something?"

A hand to his chest, he moans. "You wound me! You don't think a grown man can mix up frozen peas with mushroom soup and a can of tuna?"

"All I care is, does it have potato chips on top?"

"It wouldn't be tuna casserole if it didn't," he says with the smile that gets me every time.

The smile that's just for you, Izzy coos.

Ugh, you people. Quinn shudders. *Gross.*

After he unlocks the door and ushers me and Ribsy inside, Izzy thoughtfully reminds me that we do have some important things to discuss before we get too cozy, even as every sight, smell, and sound of this apartment reminds me of the last time I was here.

Work out the kinks between you, and then we can enjoy some kink, Quinn offers. *What's the big deal, anyway?*

Because you work with him? Izzy reminds me. *Because what happens if you have a fight and break up? Because you haven't yet told him all of your truth?*

Dude, Quinn cuts in. *Makeup sex is the best sex.*

I groan, and Henry shoots me a look. "Everything okay?"

"Yeah. Just... hungry all of a sudden."

That's one word for it, Quinn says.

"Just got to feed the dog, and then we can heat up dinner.'

I offer to help but regret it immediately. Henry's kitchen is way too small for two people to work in it without running into each other. By the time we sit down at his tiny dining table, I'm so wound up I've lost my appetite.

Henry frowns after taking a bite. "Sorry, I guess the potato chips got kind of soggy."

"It's fine. It's good," I say, shoving a forkful into my mouth. "We do need to talk, though. It's not fair to Lilah for you two to have to worry about running into people we know, like what happened this week, whether it's my friends—"

"Or people from work."

"Right."

He takes my hand suddenly. When I flinch, he winces as if in pain.

Covering my face with my hands, I can't help but groan.

"Really? Really, Bella? Can you honestly tell me you're not feeling any of the things I'm feeling?"

Don't lie to him, Izzy warns.

I kind of have to agree, Quinn says. *Just tell him, for god's sake. If he judges you, then fuck him.*

Not how I would put it, but... yeah, Izzy says.

I'm too rattled to do this sitting down, but they're right. I need to do it. "It's not that, Henry. It's... there are other things about me—about my past—that I still haven't told you."

HENRY

There's pain in her eyes, and I hate it. I want to fix it. When she lurches away into the living room, I trail her like Ribsy on the hunt. Then something awful occurs to me, and I reach for her, needing to be in contact. "Are you... are you wanting to hurt yourself?"

"Not the way you're thinking." Twisting out of my grip, she puts a few steps between us before whirling to face me. "I'm an addict, Henry. I got hooked on pills and alcohol when I was a teenager working on the soap. I wasn't self-medicating because of some trauma or anything—it was just a bad habit that got out of control." She points at me, stabbing a finger in the air. "I went to rehab, got my shit together, and I've had it under control until you showed up."

I take a step back and bump into the coffee table. "Are you saying that you're doing drugs again?"

"No!" Her expression is as fierce as any mother bear's. "I would never endanger Lilah like that." Squeezing her eyes shut, she grits out, "But I want to. For the first time in over seven years, I want to."

"And you blame me for this?"

"No. Yes. It's everything. I thought I was fixed." The laugh that explodes past her lips is caustic. "But I guess I was just fooling myself. Or it's been in there, dormant, just waiting for me to let down my guard."

Like a caged animal, she paces in front of the living room windows. "All I know is each change has made it harder to resist the temptation. The job at GBH, you coming into our lives, and now the store…" Seeming to run out of energy, she melts to the floor. "It's just one thing too many."

Every part of me wants to wrap her in my arms, but I don't want to shut her down. "How did it happen in the first place?"

"After my year on *Boom*, I was hooked," she grumbles into her hands, shocking me.

"You were doing drugs *then*?" I ask, dropping to a squat next to her.

"No. Sorry." After rubbing her eyes with her palms, she shakes out her hands. I shift to my butt and get as close to her as I dare.

She doesn't look at me as she continues, but she doesn't flinch away either. "I was hooked on performing. I wanted to spend my whole life in front of the camera. When an agent approached my parents, I begged them to let me sign with her. My dad was teaching high school drama at the time and was totally on board, but we had to talk my mom into it. Somehow, we—my dad, my agent, and I—convinced her to let me give it a try. I know now that I was incredibly lucky. Right off the bat, I got an *After School Special*, a bunch of day player jobs, and then the soap."

"Did your parents move too?"

She shakes her head. "My mom felt that she had to stay with the store. I thought that she didn't believe in me and she was just waiting for me to fail and come home." She raises a finger in the air. "That was problem number one. Number two: My selfishness broke up my parents' marriage."

Before I can process that, she plunges on. "But at first, it was all great. Conveniently, my dad got hired as the on-set teacher. I was the only child actor regular, so it did make sense. And I was like everybody's little sister. When I wasn't needed on stage, I was bugging people about their jobs. I barely got through the high school curriculum, but I got a PhD in making TV. Plus, I took acting classes at night. I loved everything about it.

"But then, when I turned sixteen, I didn't need supervision anymore. Legally, anyway. There weren't any other minors on the show at the time, so my dad took a teaching job elsewhere." Her gaze shifts, and it's like she's watching a movie of her past. "Without him around, people treated me differently. Suddenly there were all these invitations, and I said yes to them all. Parties, clubs, openings, fashion shows—"

"You were only sixteen?"

"No one gave a fuck." She waves her hand in the air. "Typical stupid story: Before I knew it, I was caught in a vicious cycle. I'd party all night, then I'd need something to get me through the day. Somebody always had something—"

"Somebody? Like people who worked on the show?"

"Yep. From the script supervisor to the prop guy, somebody always had a pill for this or that. I didn't know what they were half the time." She chokes out a bitter laugh. "I was so proud that I never did coke. When I was working," she clarifies.

I can't muster words but the shock must be plain on my face.

"Lots of people did. Sometimes I'd have to take a Valium to calm down because I took too many uppers." She shakes her head and gazes back out the window. "My poor body."

I want to say, *That poor girl.* I want to strangle each and every asshole who helped get her hooked, but I don't want to interrupt.

"Anyway," she continues on a sigh, "no one said anything at the time, but a lot of money was spent to keep photos of drunk teen me out of the papers." She makes air quotes. "'To protect their invest-ment.' What they didn't do was actually protect *me*. After a couple years of partying, I looked so awful that the show gave my character cancer. Unfortunately, that made things worse. Not only was I stuck in a hospital bed, Quinn couldn't be a villain anymore because people couldn't hate her if she was dying. I was bored to tears, so I started drinking at work."

"Where was your dad during all this?"

"He was doing his own partying thing. I didn't care." She shrugs, but there's something sharp beneath the feigned indifference. "We were like roommates who barely knew each other."

"How long did you keep this… lifestyle going?"

"A few years." I must look horrified because she adds, "It wasn't like I was alone. It seemed like everyone took something or other to get through the day. That's what people did in New York in televi-sion. Back then, at least."

She leans back against the wall so abruptly she almost slams her head into it. "But then my mom came to visit, and it was like she was the only adult in the room. By then, my parents had divorced. I assumed she didn't give a shit about either of us at that point, but she took one look at me and took over. Before I knew it, I was in rehab." She continues with a hollow laugh. "And I was pissed."

"I thought I was fine. I thought it was normal to lose track of big chunks of time. And I hated it there at first, all the admitting that I was powerless and the education sessions. I thought it was dumb. And I was in a lot of pain, like the worst flu you've ever had."

A sigh so deep it must come from the floor beneath her judders through her body. "But I eventually gave in. My mom had done her research. It was not only a really good place, but it was totally locked down. No one knew I was there. My agent floated this story that I had cancer, just like my character on the soap. 'So tragic, so horribly ironic, blah, blah, blah.' They kept me hidden away for a bit after I finished rehab, then executed this whole re-emergence where they leaked photos of me looking sick and then gradually getting better.

By the time I went back to work, everybody believed I'd kicked cancer. Jeez, I almost believed it."

She takes in a deep breath and lets it out like she's run out of steam. It's a terrible story, but then it occurs to me it might not just be pain or shame that has kept her from telling me.

"Did you not tell me because you thought I'd take Lilah from you?" Her face is an open book, so it's clear that's what she was thinking. "You really think I'd do that?"

"I would if I were you." Her laugh isn't bitter, it's sad. It breaks my heart.

"Bella, I would never do anything to get between you and Lilah. She needs you."

"But what if I'm a danger to her?"

The pain in her voice, in her expression—in her entire posture—takes my broken heart and rips it in two. As much as it hurts to feel her pain, I'd rather have it than nothing, so I scoot as close as I can, pressing my thigh against hers. "I don't know much about addiction, but I'll help any way I can. I'll watch her if you need to go to a meeting or… whatever you need."

"That's the thing." After a few beats, eyes on the floor, she says, "There is another reason why I didn't tell you. I don't go to AA meetings or anything like that because I'm not allowed to. It's always been a carefully kept secret. The circle of people that know about this is very small. The network paid for all my rehab, but I had to sign away so many things." Her lips flatten into a hard line. "They didn't want to be blamed for the fact that I was underage and using while working on a set, and my parents and agent just wanted to get me clean. They also felt like keeping it secret would protect my reputation, so we agreed to never talk about it. Any of it."

She sits up abruptly. "I mean, I don't want it to get out either. I don't want Lilah to get dragged into whatever circus it might create. Plus, how do you think Carol would feel if she learned there's a drug addict working with the impressionable preteens on *Boom*?"

"You're hardly a crack mom, Bella."

"That's because I'm lucky! Because I got cleaned up before that was an option. Because I'm terrified of needles. Because I was a rich white girl. If any of those things were different, I'd be dead."

Clearly, she's not exaggerating and I fear that she's right. After holding my breath for a few beats, to make sure she's finished, I just hold out my hand, palm up.

She just stares at it. "What's that mean?"

"It means I want to be your partner in this. I'm here for Lilah, but I'm here for you too, Bella. I'm here to give you a hug, a shoulder to cry on, or whatever you need."

BELLA

This man has me so discombobulated my conscience has given up. I've got no fight left, so I let him take a bit of my load. Literally. I just lean in his direction, and he catches me. His arm drapes over my shoulder, and—*dammit*—it's just right. Not heavy, not tentative. It just pulls me into his side where I fit perfectly. Our breathing slows, and the familiar scent of his aftershave calms my wildly beating heart. I'm not sure how long we sit there on the floor of his apartment. I feel safe tucked under his chin, but my butt is not happy on the hardwood floor. When I wiggle in an attempt to find a more comfortable position, he grunts, "C'mere."

Just like he did at camp, just like he did the day we met, he scoops me into his arms and carries me to his bedroom. Setting me carefully on my feet next to the bed, he pulls down the covers and points at the phone. "Call and leave your mom a message. I'll sleep on the couch if you want me to, but you're staying here tonight."

I open my mouth in an attempt to argue, but when nothing comes out, he wraps his palm around the back of my neck and pulls me in for a hug. After he whispers, "You don't have to do it all alone," he releases me. "I'm just going to take Ribsy out. I'll be right back."

It terrifies me to even consider letting go of control, but I don't have the energy to push back anymore, so I do as he says. My mom doesn't answer the phone, meaning she's probably still entertaining. I leave a message, not caring what she thinks. I go to his bathroom and borrow his toothbrush and then strip down to a tank and underwear and crawl under the covers. I'm suddenly so very tired, but when he gets back, I can't help speaking a string of words more truthful than any I've uttered in recent memory. "I want you to sleep here."

The moment his arm pulls me in to nestle against his chest, the only thought I have left is that I could sleep here forever.

Chapter 16

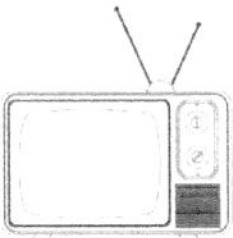

"TALENT TODAY WITH… Belinda Goodwin. After our waitress stops by to offer more coffee, the beautiful leading lady from *Weeks of Our Lives* (she plays Carol) emphasized that physical beauty was not the only consideration for her when looking for a partner, though she does admire a man who has a fit physique. 'Truly, a beautiful mind is far more important than surface appeal,' she claims. (Though readers who pay attention know that her most recent beau was the ruggedly handsome Trevor Wright from *One Way to Live!*)" *TV Tattler*, August 1989

HENRY

In my dream, Bella rolls on top of me and drops kisses up my neck until she gets to my earlobe, which she takes between her teeth. The sensual nip has my hands gripping her ass, pulling her into my rock-hard erection. Her moan matches mine before she drags her teeth away from my ear to bring her lips to mine. I'm just thinking that this is the best dream ever when she gasps and breaks the kiss.

"Shit," she whispers. "What the fuck?"

My eyes flutter open to discover that the dream seems to have slid into the home base of reality.

"I am so sorry, Hal," she says, starting to pull away.

"Hey," I whisper. Gripping a perfectly round butt cheek with one hand, I cup her flushed jaw in the other until her eyes meet mine. "Maybe we should listen to our bodies. They seem to know we've got a good thing here."

She drops her forehead to my chest with a frustrated groan, but she doesn't move away. "I want to, Hal—Henry, I mean. I want to so much. But I'm afraid."

Stroking her soft hair, I ask, "Tell me. Get it out of your head. What's the worst that could happen?"

"I become more addicted to you than I already am, and then we can't make it work."

My ego needs to hear more, so I convince myself that it's in the service of Bella to ask, "You're addicted to me?"

"Look at me. I can't be near you without wanting to get naked with you. You're like diet pills."

"Because sex with me helps you lose weight?"

She shakes her head and rolls off of me but doesn't move away from my side. "Diet pills are a baby junkie's high. Problem is, they just scratch the itch in a way that makes it burn. Touching you is the same."

Facing her, I trail a finger across her clenched jaw. "But there's a difference, right? Or there could be?"

She glances in my direction briefly before training her gaze on the ceiling again. "I don't know. That's the thing. I've never..."

When she doesn't fill in the blank, I say, "Never had sex like we do before?"

Crossing her arms over her face, she grumbles, "Yes. And that's the problem."

"Why is it a problem?"

"Because I'm afraid that's all there is."

"You think I'm that shallow?"

Her arms flop back down again, revealing a face full of pain. "No,

I'm that shallow. I've never been in a real relationship before. I don't know how to do it, what to do. And the stakes are too high. If I fuck this up, then Lilah has to deal with parents who hate each other."

And it suddenly makes sense. "Like your parents do?"

Lips pressed together, tears leaking from her eyes, she just nods.

Her distress is a vise squeezing my heart to the breaking point. How do I convince this woman to take a chance on us? I've tried to prove that I can be a good dad. Maybe it's time to let her in on my own fears. When I slide an arm behind her back, she tenses momentarily, but then her body seems to instinctively relax, giving me the courage to go on. "You know," I say softly, "I'm kind of the same. I work long hours and I'm grumpy, so women give up on me. And it's always been easy to just let them go because I didn't really care."

My heart is beating fast, telling me that I'm stepping into dangerous territory. What if I tell her that I'm already in love with her and Lilah, and then she says she can't handle it? What if she's right and we can't make it work? But what would be worse? To try and fail, or to never try at all? I've taken chances in my career. The cost of failing is much, much higher here because a little girl's well-being is at stake, but the potential reward is more than I ever dreamed possible. So I leap.

"Bella, with you, I've cared since the moment we danced on that rooftop. Every day, every moment I've spent with you makes me care more. I care about Lilah more than I've cared about anything in my life. I can't give up on this. Not this time. If you can look me in the eye and tell me that there's no possibility for us, I'll do my best to accept it. But if there's a chance, I'm ready to do anything and everything to figure out how to be..." Taking her hand, I press it to my chest so she can feel my heart. "Our bodies know. I think our brains just need to catch up."

She doesn't move for what feels like forever. Doesn't breathe. But she doesn't remove her hand from my chest either.

Finally, she nods and whispers, "Okay."

It takes a moment for me to get what she's said. And I need more. "Okay? Okay to..."

She pulls our joined hands to her own chest. "Okay to... listen to our bodies, and we do our damnedest to make this work."

I can't help but grin. "So, maybe we let them give us a lesson right now?"

She shakes her head, but she's smiling too. "I guess we could use a little reminder. Of what we're good at already."

"Oh, I can always use that reminder," I say, rolling on top of her. "And the practice, of course." Nuzzling into her hairline, I brush kisses across her soft skin from cheekbone to jawline. "I figure the more we do this... and this," I say, dragging my lips down her neck and then to her breast, taking a pert nipple between my teeth through the thin fabric of her tank top and rolling it with my tongue until she groans, "the more our bodies know, the less our minds have to get involved."

Sitting up, I meet her heated gaze. What I see gives me an idea. "What about this? When we're together, just the two of us in this safe space, you call me Hal. I mean, it's good that I left his tunnel vision and arrogance behind, but he was also..."

"Not jaded?" she asks when I don't go on.

"Hopeful," I clarify. "Optimistic."

She nods, and then shakes her head. "You can't call me Izzy, though. She's too..."

"Vulnerable?"

She nods. "Yeah."

"How about Bel?"

She laughs. "Your southern belle?"

"Nah, you ain't no southern belle, honey. But you ring my bell," I growl as I crawl over her luscious body. "You're the siren that tempts me to toss myself on her shores."

"I think I can play that role." Nodding, she slides one finger under my T-shirt and the other under the waistband of my boxers. "Time to get naked," she whispers.

BELLA

Henry's right about our bodies knowing what to do. The moment we shed the scraps of clothing separating us, instinct kicks in. Can you get a high from sex? Would it be so awful to be addicted to whatever hormones are released when this man's lips touch my skin?

Pleasure doesn't have to be bad murmurs in my head—in what I'm pretty sure is my own damn voice—before I relinquish control. Worries fade into the background, and all I do is feel.

The brush of his beard and chest hair over my breast and belly wake up every nerve ending. The calluses on his fingertips part the curls above my sex and set me on fire from the inside out. My nails scrape across his ass and my teeth sink into his trapezius as he brings me right to the verge of pain and pleasure before tipping me over the edge. He produces a condom from somewhere, and next thing I know he's pounding into me, roaring his own release until we're little more than a puddle of sweat and heaving breath.

Sex with him forces me to be in the present. Unfortunately, the moment it's over, apprehension kicks back in. Throwing an arm over my face, I groan, "Everything was less complicated before you showed up."

He peeks under my arm. "But a little boring?"

"Boring is safe," I say, gently elbowing him away.

He just rolls me on top of him. "What if you had a safety net?"

When he stretches his arms overhead and folds his hands behind his head, all I can see is the flex of his perfect biceps.

Fingertip on my chin, he redirects my focus. "I could be your safety net."

Folding my elbows over the shelf of his pecs, I rest my chin on my hands. I've never understood pillow talk, but it's surprisingly easy to have a discussion with Henry like this, like we're equally vulnerable and safe. Still, I'm not letting him off the hook. "What do you get out of this deal? Besides more sex with me."

"Family."

"But you have a family. That you love."

"Not my own family."

"You didn't want that with what's-her-name in Raleigh."

"I didn't want that with *her*. I wasn't sure if I'd ever want it, to be honest." He drags my finger over his mouth, and a sound like a purr rumbles from his chest beneath me. When his eyes pop open again, I'm completely caught by their unusual copper-brown. "But with us, I can have mind-blowing sex and a partner I love working with and the smartest, cutest little girl in the world. It all feels like the perfect package. And it feels like..."

He pauses, seeming almost afraid to continue. I hold my breath to give him space, trying to ignore the flutter in my chest at the word he just used. He loves working with me, but does he love me? Can we just will that into existence?

"Home."

Caught in my own mental loop, it takes me a moment to hear what he's said. Not love, but home. Which might be even better. Just as I'm about to agree, though, Ribsy jumps on the bed and sniffs my butt, which has me shrieking in surprise and then laughter.

"Way to ruin the mood, Ribsy," Henry says. But there's a smile in his voice like this is all a part of that home he was talking about.

"What about him?" I ask.

"Ribsy? What about him?" He pulls me into one side as Ribsy settles down on the other.

"My cats don't like dogs."

Scratching behind Ribsy's ear, he says, "Ahh. My dog is like me. He can convince anybody to love him."

Again with that word. Scary, but maybe in a good way. "Pretty cocky, mister."

"But true?"

"We'll see," is the best I can answer.

There's still a lot to figure out. But maybe it is better to risk taking it on with a partner, rather than on my own.

Making a home might be safer than falling in love.

HENRY

After I take Ribsy out, I use the early morning light to get to know every nook and cranny of Bella's body while wringing another couple of orgasms out of her. As we both drift off to sleep again, I'm feeling pretty darn good about life—great job, amazing kid, and a chance at a promising relationship with an equally amazing woman.

Then the phone rings, and she's instantly on alert.

Heading her worries off at the pass, I announce, "I'm not answering. It's Sunday. I don't need to talk to anybody."

We lay there until the answering machine picks up in the kitchen. My recorded voice message is muffled, but after the beep, the words echoing through the apartment are all too clear.

"Henry? Henry Cornelius Smith?"

Bella giggles. "Cornelius?"

I groan the way I do every time someone learns my middle name.

"I need to hear the story of that." Bella pokes me in the side, which has me tensing even more than my mother's voice.

"If you're there, you need to pick up," my mother drawls. Somehow, she manages to sweetly chide and urgently demand at the same time.

Even though she can't hear me, I cover my face with a pillow and groan even louder.

"All right, then," she says. "I suppose I'll just have to book this ticket and fly on up there so I can make sure you haven't lost my grandchild again."

"Goddammit," I grumble, throwing on my boxers—because you can't talk to your mother naked—and sprinting for the phone. She's going on about her friend Francine who's a travel agent and how she's got the flight all lined up but wanted to check with me when I interrupt her monologue. "I'm here, Mama. Sorry, I was—"

"Spare me the details," she says, cutting me off with a sniff. "What I do want is the four-one-one on this grandbaby of mine. We are all dying of curiosity down here."

"I know, I should've called. My days at work are nonstop, and then I've been spending almost every evening with Lilah."

"Well, that's all well and good, but what I want to know is when do I get to meet her? Can y'all fly down here? This is our busy season, you know, so I can only come for a few days if I have to go there."

"I can't get away. The summer is when we shoot the show, when the kids are out of school."

"And Lilah's out of school too? What is she doing all day?"

"She's with her grandmother—her other grandmother."

"Oh." So many emotions fill that one little word. "Well, I'll just have to come up, then. It'll have to be during the week, so I'll come tomorrow night."

"Tomorrow?"

"Francine did some magic and got me a good deal. I'll stay till Saturday. What's the weather like up there? I imagine it's a bit cooler than here. The humidity has been ridiculous this summer. Good for growin' things, but—"

"Mom," I interrupt. "You're coming *tomorrow*?"

"Yes. You have a two-bedroom apartment, right? I'll stay with you and I'll spend time with Lilah during the day and I'll cook y'all dinner. I'll get to meet her mama. It'll be fun."

"But—"

"Oh, shoot, I've got to go. I'm opening the Fuqua Varina store today. All right, then. I'll call you this evening with the flight numbers and all. Can't wait to see y'all! Bye now!"

All I'm left with is the dial tone in my ear and a knot in my stomach. Dropping the phone back on the charger, I plod back to my bedroom.

"Everything okay?"

I flop onto the bed face down and groan.

"Henry? Henry Cornelius?" Bella asks, in a horribly accurate imitation of my mom's Carolina accent. "Do they call you Corny?"

I swat in her direction, but she grabs my hand and then pokes me in that ticklish spot again. "Stop it!"

She just pokes me again.

"Hey! Stop tickling me."

"Then tell me what's going on," she says, grinning wickedly.

"I'll tell you what's going on." Grabbing her hands and pinning them both to the bed, I straddle her and grind my pelvis into her. "We're going to have as much sex as humanly possible today."

She grins and then frowns. "But I have a show at two. So—"

"So, we'll have some sex now and some after your show."

"What's the big hurry?"

"The big hurry is that I'm going to have a houseguest the rest of the week." I pause to make the drama of the situation clear. "My mother."

"Oh." She blinks. "I guess we need to…"

"Have sex?"

She coughs out a laugh. "I mean, yeah, but also we should figure out what we're telling people about—"

Stopping her mouth with a kiss, I do everything possible to derail her thought process. "Figuring out later. Sex now."

And then I do my best to make that happen. Which she enjoys immensely, if I do say so myself.

Chapter 17

"BACKSTAGE WITH… Pearl Raynor. Asked if there was anyone in her life right now, Pearl admitted, 'People have me dating so many different people… it's all just a lot of rumors.' She also confides that while she can 'sparkle' when she needs to, she's essentially a solitary person and loves nothing more than curling up with a good book!" *Soap Chat,* August 1989

BELLA

When I get home from the Sunday matinee, my mom catches me at the front door. "I think we have to tell Lilah tonight. The new owner wants to come in to take measurements."

"So soon?"

"She can close at the end of the month. The sooner we do it, the sooner the debt is over and done with."

"Which means we need to find somewhere to live."

Something crosses her face that makes my stomach drop. "Mom. Do you have plans you haven't told me about?"

She winces. "Nothing definite. But you remember my friend Joanie who lost her husband a couple of years ago? She doesn't want to move but also hates being alone in that big house. She invited me to move in and stay as long as I need to."

"Is that what you're going to do?"

"I hate to leave you and Lilah on your own, but it would help me to save some money. And with Henry here—"

"Mom," I hiss. "I slept over at his house *one* night. I'm not ready to play house with him yet."

She raises a hand. "I'm not suggesting that. But if he's paying child support—which he should be doing—then you can afford a little place for you and Lilah. There are those cute townhouses near the school, for instance."

Taking a deep breath, I do my best to let go of frustration. My mom's just doing the best she can with the situation my dad left us in. "Okay. Let me call Henry—he wants to be here when we tell Lilah —and wash my face and grab something to eat."

"Joanie sent me home with some of her tomatoes. I'll slice those and some cucumbers. And I've got some cold cuts if you want a sandwich."

Twenty minutes later, the doorbell rings. I send Lilah to let Henry in while I finish setting the table for supper. It's a little surreal to have him sitting down with us, but maybe it's good practice. I'm definitely happy to have him here as a distraction.

Once everyone's seated and has filled their plate, I dive in. "Lilah, honey, we have some news."

Without missing a beat, mouth full of ham sandwich, she asks, "Am I getting more family?"

Henry mouths *Should I?* and I shrug. Maybe it's better to share good news first. "Well, as a matter of fact, you are. Your other grandma is coming to visit this week."

"She is?" my mom asks.

"Is that okay with you, Grandma?" Lilah asks.

"Of course," Mom says. "I know I'll always be your first and best. But don't tell her."

"Okay," Lilah agrees. Before I can try and segue to talking about the store, she asks, "But what about more moms and dads and grandads? Some of my friends have two moms and dads and even four grandpas."

"Uh, no," I say. We've kind of skirted around the existence of my father, and that's not something I'm ready to talk about now. "No extra moms and dads."

"But you'll get some aunts and uncles and cousins," Henry says. "Maybe we'll go visit them at the end of the summer."

"Where are they?" Lilah asks.

"They're all in North Carolina, where I'm from."

Lilah picks up a slice of cucumber but pauses before dipping it in a glob of thousand island dressing on her plate. "What's my other grandmother's name?"

"Linda," Henry says.

"What will I call her?"

Henry scratches the beard on his chin. "Well, her other grandchildren—your cousins—call her Gammy Lulu."

"That's babyish." Lilah's nose wrinkles in obvious disgust. "How old are they?"

"They're around your age, but one of them called her that when he was a baby and I guess it just stuck."

"Oh," is all she says.

"I bet you could come up with something better."

She takes that in for a moment and then asks, "When is she coming?"

"Tomorrow," Henry says. "I'm going to pick her up at the airport after work."

"Tomorrow?" my mom asks.

"Yeah, sorry." Henry says to her. "This was a last-minute thing."

We need to get down to business before they plan out the week, so I switch tacks. "But Lilah, honey, that wasn't what we meant to tell you. That is some good news, but we have some bad news."

A tiny wrinkle appears between her eyebrows.

My mom takes Lilah's hand. "Sweetheart, Grandma is selling the bookstore."

The furrow on her forehead deepens. "Why?"

"Well, it's time for me to retire."

Lilah slides her hand out from under my mom's. "But Mommy and me can run it."

"I know you could, but the bookstore isn't turning a profit anymore, so we can't afford to keep it going."

"But that's not fair," Lilah says, sounding younger than she usually does.

"I know, honey," my mom answers, sounding much older than she usually does. "It's not fair at all. I hate it."

Lilah blinks like she's struggling to compute all of this information. "What will happen to it?"

"Well, a lady is going to buy it. She's going to sell yarn, things for knitting and crocheting."

"But it's a bookstore."

"It is now, but those are the things she likes and wants to sell."

"But it's ours." With this protest, her voice wobbles, and I can't take it anymore. My mom's doing her best to explain, so I just scoot my chair closer to Lilah's and scoop her onto my lap, hugging her from behind.

"I know, sweetheart," my mom continues. "But sometimes you have to make a change, and this is what Grandma has to do right now."

Lilah takes in a shaky breath. "But what about the books?"

"They're going back to the publishers."

"Even the children's books?"

"Yes, honey." Now my mom's getting teary.

"But can I keep my favorites?"

"Well, sure. We can go through them, and you can pick some to keep."

Lilah's head drops, and I hug her tight. She's being so good about this. Then she whispers, "May I be excused?"

"Of course, sweetheart."

She slips off my lap and walks out of the room without another word. I lean back in my chair so I can watch until she disappears into her room.

Henry leans forward to whisper, "That could've gone worse."

I shake my head. "I don't think this is over."

"Bella, we can't afford to not return most of the books," my mom says softly.

I nod. "It's okay, Mom. We'll figure it out."

She gets up and grabs a tissue from the box on the counter. "I'm so sorry."

"I know you did your best."

"So, what happens next?" Henry asks.

"We wait for it to really hit," I say. "Could be five minutes, five hours, or five days."

FIVE MINUTES IS ALL it takes. When I go to check on Lilah, she won't speak to me. Instead, she slams her bedroom door in my face.

When Henry whispers, "Should I do something?" I stop myself from saying, *It's okay; you can go.* He needs to be here for the ugly stuff, too. He needs to see that it's not all blissful trips to the Public Garden. I crook a finger, and he follows me back to the kitchen.

"Let's give her a little space before we say goodnight," I suggest before offering to make tea. After the kettle has boiled and I've poured three cups of peppermint tea, Henry offers to check on Lilah.

Moments later, he's back. "She's not in her room. Or the bathroom."

Our apartment is small, so it doesn't take long to determine that she's not in it.

"Has she ever run away before?" Henry asks.

"No." After a quick scan of Lilah's room, I say, "But I bet that's what she did. Her backpack isn't here, nor is her favorite pillow or her teddy bear."

One look at my face, and Henry has me in his arms. "It'll be okay, Bel. She can't have gone far."

Letting him give me one more squeeze, I nod and step out of his embrace. "Thanks. We should, um, split up and, I guess, search the neighborhood."

Gripping my upper arms, he dips his head to make eye contact. "Do you want to call the police?"

"My gut says she's not far. Let's just— Oh, wait. We haven't checked the shop."

"But the door was locked."

"She knows where we keep the key." Seconds later, the empty hook tells me that my instinct was right. "She ran away to the book-store. Poor thing."

"Maybe she's trying to protect it from us."

"Or spend as much time as possible there. Whatever it is, we need to make sure." Running back up the stairs, I call out to my mom.

After we find her and fill her in, she grabs the spare key. "Should we go to the front door?"

"I don't want to scare her, but I also don't want her to get out and really run away."

"How about we all go in through the back stairs, then fan out to cover the doors?" Henry suggests. "I'll take the front."

"I'll take the back," my mom says.

"And I'll take the middle, I guess."

Moving quietly so as not to scare her, we creep down the stairs, unlock the door, and enter the shop. A soft glow—probably from a flashlight—tells me someone's here. Henry's palm rests on my shoulder briefly before he moves quietly toward the front door. After I nod at my mom, I walk softly toward the sitting area, where I'm both relieved and heartbroken to find a little tent set up between two chairs, both stripped of their cushions. Easing onto the floor nearby, I whisper, "Knock, knock."

A gasp of breath and some furtive rustling have me thinking that she really didn't expect to be discovered.

"Lilah, honey."

"Go away!"

"Sweetie, I get that you're upset."

"I hate you! And I'm not leaving. I'm going to stay here forever."

My mom emerges from the shadows. "I'm so sorry, Lilah. This is all my fault. Grandma made mistakes. I'm sad too, and I don't want to sell the store. I hate that it makes you so sad. But sometimes life just takes a turn that you don't expect."

I let this sit for a few moments and then chance a peek under the blanket. When Lilah's hand swats at me, I let it drop.

"You can't make me leave!"

Soft footsteps sound behind me, and then Henry settles onto the floor next to me. With a sigh, I lean against him for a moment and absorb the quiet strength of him, appreciating that there's someone else to share this with, even if neither of us really knows what to do.

Sensing that this'll take some time, I whisper to my mom, "You can go to bed. I've got this."

"*We've* got this," Henry's voice rumbles beside me.

THE NEXT MORNING when I wake up in Lilah's bed curled around her, it takes me a moment to remember what happened the night before. Lifting my head to peek over her, I find confirmation.

Asleep, fully clothed, and on top of the covers, Henry's body is barely contained by the other twin bed in Lilah's room. Easing up to a sitting position, I take in Lilah's little tear-stained face. After we waited her out last night, her demands that we leave finally faded away, and she fell asleep curled up on the chair cushions. Henry scooped her up and carried her to bed, with me locking up behind us. Exhausted but unwilling to let her out of my sight, I only vaguely remember lying down beside her. I don't remember what happened next, but it makes my heart stupidly happy that Henry stayed with us.

It's like we all survived a wintry nor'easter together. A storm that brought us all a little bit closer together. I do hope the worst of the storm has passed. There will likely be more tantrums along the way as we pack up books and then pack up the apartment. Moving can be an adventure, too, though, and I'll do my best to foment that feeling. In the midst of working several jobs.

Henry snores softly, reminding me that I now have a partner to help me. It's something I never really missed, but now that he's here, I don't want to let him go. When a voice in my head whispers, *Maybe you don't have to*, it's not Quinn or Izzy—neither of whom has chimed in for days, it seems—it's just me. My own voice.

Bella making choices for herself.

Chapter 18

"Last week on *All His Children*: Rochelle promises to give Kayla all the help she can, even offering hand-me-down clothes from her own child. Nevertheless, she agrees that Kayla should tell Dave. Meanwhile, Irene proposes to Rob, pushing for an elopement. He agrees if they can have an 'open marriage.' Apparently, this pair doesn't need the same thing from marriage that others do." *Soap Opera Land*, August 1989

HENRY

Standing in the gate area waiting for my mom to deplane, I catalog all the ways this visit could go wrong. My mom takes up a lot of space in a room, and I fear that it'll make both Lilah and Doris shrink away. Not just from her, but from me. On the other hand, she's a charmer, and her bustling, bossy energy may be just what we all need right now.

My mom never met a stranger, so I'm not surprised to see her deep in conversation with a younger woman as she steps out of the jetway. After I manage to get her attention, she gives her new best friend a big hug and, probably, a few final words of advice.

Just a warm-up for what she's going to dish out for me, I'm sure.

"Hey, Mama," I say, stepping into a hug of my own. After breathing in her familiar floral scent, I take her carry-on bag. "Did you check a bag, too?"

"I did," she says, hooking an elbow in mine and letting me steer her toward the baggage claim. "I just didn't know what kind of weather to expect. Plus, I had to bring some presents." She looks around pointedly. "Delilah didn't come with you?"

"No, it's almost bedtime for her."

"I just can't wait to meet her."

As we navigate the various tunnels and bridges and highways to get from Logan Airport to my place, I fill her in on the bookstore closing and how Lilah is upset by it.

"Oh my word, that is sad. Well, I'll just have to buy up those books so she can have them close by. I've got plenty of savings, and this is just the thing I want to spend it on. Plus, you owe them child support, Henry." Digging through her enormous handbag, she says, "I wrote down how much."

"How do you know how much I owe?"

"Oh, you know my friend Luanne's husband is a lawyer, so I asked him about it."

"How many people know our business now, Mama?"

"Just a few close friends."

"Mom, Bella is very private. She was a celebrity—"

"I know; it's very exciting. I have friends who are huge fans. Do you think you could get her to sign a few photos?"

"This is what I'm talking about, Mama. We haven't told many people that I'm Lilah's father yet—"

"Well, why not? Are you ashamed of her?"

"Of Bella?"

"Of Lilah."

"No."

"Well, then. No need to hide."

"Mama, you know Bella and I are not married. We never were."

"Oh, Henry. It's not the dark ages. What's important is making that little girl happy. Which is why I am buying out the entire children's section."

"What if their new place can't fit all those books?"

"Are you going to deprive your daughter of books, Henry?"

"No, ma'am."

By the time we pull up to my apartment, it's after nine o'clock. My mother never even calls anyone after nine, so I know she won't want to intrude on the Yorks.

After I haul her very heavy suitcase up the stairs and let her into my place, she accepts an enthusiastic greeting from Ribsy and then makes a few tutting noises about the state of my bachelor apartment. I dutifully offer her tea or coffee, but she declines, saying that she wants to get settled and go to bed.

"I want to see them first thing tomorrow. You can drop me at the bookstore on your way to work, and I'll help out with whatever they need."

THE NEXT FEW days are a blur of work and doing my best to head my mom off at the pass whenever she gets a new idea, but thankfully she and Doris are getting along and Lilah is slowly warming up to her.

I do admit that I've enjoyed my mom's cooking. The five of us even had a remarkably relaxed family dinner last night. After my mom complained to Doris that my kitchen was appallingly ill-equipped, Doris offered up her own kitchen, and my mom put together an excellent supper of pork chops, waldorf salad, greens, and her skillet cornbread.

Thursday night, Bella has a performance, so I go straight to the store after work and find the grandmas packing up books. My mom's impulse to buy the entire section was sweet, but Bella put her foot down—luckily before anyone floated the idea to Lilah directly. Now, Lilah's in the midst of deciding which books to keep and which to let go.

She's not happy about it.

I half-crouch on a kid-sized chair next to her. "How's it going, buddy?"

She slumps even further down in her chair. "Not very good."

"I'm sorry to hear that."

When I was a kid, instead of solving a problem for me, my dad gave me the tools to solve it myself. Just as I'm wondering what might help Lilah get through this, a memory pops into my mind: Bella leading the Boomerangs in a brainstorming session.

I scan the rapidly emptying store. "Hey, do you guys have a blackboard in here? Or maybe some big sheets of paper?"

Lilah's brow furrows. "Do you want to draw?"

"Not exactly."

"Um, Grandma has a bulletin board in her office."

"I need something we can write on."

She sighs. "I don't know."

Seeing her this way is breaking my heart, so I jump to my feet. "I'll be right back." Thinking that maybe we could use a broken-down box, I head to the storage area at the back of the store, where I find a stack of old event posters and a mug full of markers. Stopping to ask Doris if I can use both, she waves me on. "I need to clean out that room anyway."

Back in the children's section, I clear a space on the floor, turn over the poster, and write "IDEAS" at the top in purple. Holding out the mug of markers to Lilah, I ask, "What color do you want?"

"What for?" she asks.

"I was thinking we could brainstorm ideas for what to do with these books and maybe what you can do instead of reading stories to kids here."

"Brainstorm?"

"Yeah, your mom calls it a 'yes session.' She did it at work. I think you just say 'yes' to every idea, write it down, and then read over what you wrote. There's usually a good one in there somewhere. So, where are other places that people read books?"

She shrugs.

"Come on, sweetheart. I know this is sad, but—"

"I'm not sad. I'm mad."

"That's understandable."

"I don't want the yarn lady here. This is our bookstore."

"I get that. Sometimes, though, when things change in ways you don't like, something even better happens."

"Like what?"

"Well, that's the tricky part. Usually, you don't know what that thing is until you get to it—and getting there can be scary or make you angry or sad. But that's when I like to make a plan because then I have things I can at least try out."

I'm not sure if this is the right way to talk to an almost six-year-old, but it's the best I've got.

She takes a green marker from the mug and flips it in the air a few times.

"So… if you could give these books to anyone," I ask, "who would that be?"

"But I don't want to give them to anyone."

My eyes scan the shop as I wonder how on earth I'll ever get her to shift her thinking. When the antique cash register catches my eye, it gives me an idea. "Do you get upset when someone buys a book that you love?"

"No, because Grandma orders another one."

"Hmm. But what if you could give books to some kids who don't have any books at home?"

"What kids are those?"

"Unfortunately, there are a lot of people who don't have a lot of books in their houses."

"Why not?" Her expression is so full of horror that I have to stifle a laugh.

"Well, maybe they don't have room. Or they don't have enough money to buy books."

"That's terrible."

"I know."

She frowns, probably trying to picture what a house without

books would even look like. "But if we gave them books, they couldn't keep them anyway if they don't have room."

"Do you ever go to the library?"

She shakes her head.

"Well, anybody can borrow a book from the library. Then they keep it at home for a couple of weeks, before bringing it back so someone else can read it. That way they can read lots of books, but they won't take up too much space in their house."

She picks up a book. "So, if we gave these books to the library, then kids who don't have books at home could read them?"

I nod, hoping that my mom's offer to buy up the children's section is still good.

She stands up. "Let's do that."

"Right now?"

She nods.

"Oh, uh"—I check my watch—"I don't know if it's open, but we could try. Why don't we call?"

Lilah helps me find the phone book behind the counter, and we search the blue pages for the Newton library. When I call, I get a recording that gives me the library's hours. "They're closed. But they are open on Saturday. What do you say we go this Saturday morning and bring some books with us?"

"Then I could still visit them, right?"

"Exactly. You could read them at the library, or you could check them out a few at a time. And you'd know that lots of other kids were getting to read them too."

She sighs, but then she nods. "Can we get Chinese food now?"

Holding out my hand, I say, "That sounds like a very good idea."

■

LATER THAT EVENING, when my mother and I are driving back to my apartment, a question that I didn't even know was spinning inside my head comes tumbling out of my mouth. "Mama, how did you know that Dad was—that you were in love with him? That he was the person you should spend your whole life with?"

She folds her hands on top of her bag. "Those are two different things, you know."

"Uh, no. I don't know." I glance quickly in her direction. "Weren't you in love with him?"

She nods slowly. "I was. But I loved other men before him."

"But you loved him more."

"I wouldn't say that."

She says this like it's no big deal, while this news pretty much undermines my entire worldview. "But you guys had—you were, like, perfect together."

She pats me on the arm. "Honey, the music didn't swell, and a rainbow didn't suddenly appear in the sky. We had both dated other people through high school and college, but we met at a time when we were both just ready." She looks out the window, and a little laughing sigh, or sighing laugh, falls out of her mouth. "I mean, he made me happy, and he made me mad. He was a good man, I knew that. He came from good people. But really, at some point you just decide that this person is worth it."

"Worth what?"

"Well, you know. Making those little adjustments that allow two people to get through a life together. Bending a bit here, opening up a bit there, letting go of this or that."

"That sounds..." I clear my throat. "Unromantic."

"I don't know," she says, drawing the "oh" of "know" out even more than her accent usually allows. "I think it's very romantic. Caring enough about someone else that you make room for things that are important to them. And accepting them as they are because you can. Romance isn't about chocolate and flowers. It's about... upchuck and the runs."

Choking on an inhale of surprise, it's several moments before I can get enough air in to speak. "Mama, no offense, but you should never write a romance novel."

She shrugs, unmoved. "I'm just practical, I guess. But you know what I still miss about your father?"

I just shake my head, but I think, *I hope it's not something about the runs.*

"I miss the half-filled coffee cups I used to find everywhere." She waves her hand in the air. "In the house, at the shop. I'd find them behind planters and out by the forklift. Drove me crazy at the time, especially when one of my favorite mugs would disappear for weeks. But now," she says, patting her chest, her voice a little wobbly, "I still keep an eye out for them. Even searching for them reminds me of the way he'd take a slow sip of coffee and then lift the cup in my direction to say, 'Here's looking at you, kid.'"

I'm speechless again, but this time it's because of a full-on backlog of emotion.

She just shrugs. "We built a life together moment by moment. It takes work, but it's all worth it because what you get in return is someone who knows every little thing about you and loves you anyway."

As I park the car in front of my apartment building, her words circle my brain like an airplane waiting to land, while my heart thuds heavily down here on the ground. Afraid that leaving the car will end the conversation before I've gotten the advice I'm suddenly desperate for, I leave the keys in the ignition. "But what if I'm not sure that she feels the same way?"

"Well, how is it that *you* feel?"

I search for an answer in the shrubbery still lit by the headlights. "Honestly, I feel raw, like someone has cracked open my chest with a crowbar and exposed everything inside."

"Mm-hmm."

"There are moments when she relaxes and lets go—if I make her laugh or she's excited about an idea and shares it or she's moved by something—that being with her is better than anything. But then she pulls away, and I feel… exposed. And alone."

"Oh dear," she sighs. "Someone hurt her."

"I think a lot of someones did."

She crosses her arms over her narrow chest. "Then you have to be brave. I mean, you could give up," she adds, like I'd better not. "But you do have that little girl to think about." She shifts and reaches for the door handle. "Does she have a drinking problem?"

"Uh… wh—what makes you ask that?"

Tilting her head to the side, she squints into the mid-distance. "You haven't had a beer since I got here, and there's none in the fridge. I wondered why."

"Well, yes. She did. But it's a huge secret because it happened when she was a kid on the soap opera. You can't talk about it to anyone, okay?"

Ignoring that, she asks, "She's a good mom, isn't she?"

"She is," I say, slowly removing the keys from the ignition.

"You might have to be willing to be number two on the priority list for a bit. That usually happens after you've been together a while, you know, when a baby comes. Both of you would take a back seat to the other while you put most of your energy into that little life."

"I've been trying to show her that I can be a good dad," I say, sounding a little too whiny even to myself. Bella's *That tone doesn't work on me, mister* echoes in my mind.

She's not reaching for her door handle either, making me think she appreciates this little bubble as much as I do. "Good," she says, nodding. "But what would happen if you took a chance and told her how you feel?"

"What if she shuts me out?" I ask, my voice barely more than a whisper.

"Then you accept that she's not ready, but you don't give up. Give her time. She'll grow to trust you. You're a good man, Henry, if I do say so myself." She pats me on the shoulder and then busies herself with gathering her things and exiting the car. "You have to trust that. And enjoy the good times. When she pulls away, don't take it personally. That's true for Lilah too. They've lived without you for years. Give them a chance to get used to the idea of you."

Letting all this sink in, I usher my mom into the apartment and get ready for bed.

Alone, but determined that it won't be this way for long.

Chapter 19

Dear Editor:

I'm the official president of the new Mary Tanner Fan Club.
As you know, she portrays Laura on *The Daring & The Divine*.
Anyone interested in joining, please contact JANE DINGUS,
RD#1, Box 145 Elizabeth, PA 15037. Sincerely, Jane Dingus

Dear Readers:

*Before joining any fan clubs, we suggest that you write to the serial
asking for a "proof" letter from the star to ensure that the club is
bona fide. It's possible for there to be more than one club for a
particular actor, but don't pay those dues until you've got confirmation! –Editor, Soap Chat*

BELLA

It's been a long week between getting Lilah through all the changes,
Henry's mother sweeping into our lives, and long shoot days capped
off by performances. What my days are not ending with is sex with
Henry. I'd like to spend as much time together as possible naked and
horizontal—or, what the heck, vertical would work too—but there's
nowhere to do it.

His mom is lovely, if a bit pushy, and Lilah loves her. But she's sleeping at Henry's apartment. It's too soon to have Henry spend the night at my place—I don't want Lilah to assume he's moving in with us since I don't even know if that's something either of us want. Nor am I up for facing Mrs. Smith at breakfast after spending the night with her son. She seems like the no-sex-until-marriage type.

So Friday lunchtime, when he buzzes me from his office and asks me to meet him to work out "a few kinks in the schedule," I don't care that we're in a building with hundreds of other people, including a bunch of impressionable preteens. Maybe he's found some secluded, unused office where we can have a lunchtime quickie. To make things easier, I stop by the bathroom on the way, step into a stall, and step out of my panties. After stowing them in my purse and touching up my lipstick, I'm ready.

Unfortunately, when I get to his office, James is there too.

With a calendar.

To work out kinks in the schedule.

Just like Henry said.

When James finally leaves, I close Henry's office door and shove him up against it. "I thought working out kinks meant that you found some secret place to have sex, *Hal.*"

He doesn't drop eye contact as he reaches back to lock the door behind him. "I do have a couch. And I don't have a meeting for half an hour, *Bel.*"

"Neither do I. And if you check under my skirt, you'll find that I came prepared."

"Did you now?" Sliding his big hands up the backs of my thighs, he palms my butt cheeks, picks me up, and carries me onto the couch. Grinding into his ready-to-go erection, I scrape my finger-nails through his beard and drag my lips over his, teasing them apart with my tongue. When he growls, I wriggle out of his hold and push him onto the couch.

"Whip it out, mister. We ain't got all day."

"You can't talk in that accent. You make me think of my mother."

"Oh, we can't have that," I croon, dropping to my knees and unhooking his belt. Moving quickly, I ease his cock out of his boxers and stroke up its length. Within moments, my lips, tongue, and hands have him biting his own fist in an attempt to stifle a groan.

"I want to make you come," I say before taking him deeper into my mouth.

"Fuuuuck," is all he seems able to say in reply.

Since time is precious, I go for it, stroking and sucking until his entire body goes rigid and he keens softly in what I'm pretty sure is ecstasy. The hot liquid pumping into my mouth seals the deal.

After I grab a box of tissues to clean up, he pulls me close and groans into my crotch. "Damn. We don't have time for anything else. You took off those panties for nothing."

"I don't know. That was pretty hot."

"I need you in my bed," he growls.

"When does your mom leave?"

"Tomorrow, late afternoon."

"I have a show tomorrow evening."

Talk about kinks in the schedule.

"Are you off Sunday?"

"Yeah."

"Then you are mine both Saturday and Sunday nights. Think we can work that out? If I take Lilah tonight and all day tomorrow?"

My answer pulses low in my body as he pulls me onto his lap. "I think we can."

Taking my face in his, he whispers, "I love you, Bel."

A smile so wide it feels like it might crack me in two spreads across my face, but I can't help but make light. He is riding a blow job high, after all. "You don't have to say that to get laid, you know."

"I know," he says, all serious. "But it's the truth, and I need to tell you. I would like to be your partner in everything." He takes my hand and presses it over his heart. "You've had a piece of me since—well, probably since I watched you do that back walkover on TV. Every other moment I spend with you, you steal a little bit more."

I'm speechless, both in my head and outside of it. I don't think I can say the words back, so I kiss him, hoping that he'll feel all the unnamable things I'm feeling.

And be patient enough to let me catch up.

HENRY

She didn't say it back.

I let that thought linger in my mind and prick my heart for precisely thirty seconds. Then I set it aside and move on because I'm hauling around a lot less baggage than she is. Plus, I have a list longer than my arm to get through if I want to take the weekend off and spend my days with Lilah and my nights with her mother.

My mother has been unbelievable. In her uniquely bossy way, she's got everyone in love with her, from Carol to Doris to the mailman. And of course, Lilah.

Friday night, when Bella has a show, I take my other girls to the movies. We feast on popcorn and soda while watching a goofy comedy called *Honey, I Shrunk the Kids*, then go out for pizza afterward.

Saturday morning before my mom has to go to the airport, she, Lilah, and I take the books to the library, where the sleuthing I made time for yesterday pays off. I didn't say anything to Lilah, but I called and found out that the library has a story hour at ten. I also found out from Doris that more than one mom has complained about said story hour, saying that the librarian who does it is unenthusiastic at best, hostile at worst.

The moment one child recognizes Lilah as she passes through the arch that leads into the children's section, I feel for the librarian. Within seconds, every single kid in the room has wiggled off a lap or lurched up from the floor to toddle-run at Lilah, mobbing her like she's a miniature rock star. Which she is.

Thankfully, a couple of moms take charge of the situation. I overhear one say to the librarian, "Poor little thing, she loves to read to the younger kids, but they're closing the bookstore." Another takes Lilah by the hand and steers her past her groupies to meet the librarian, who gives up her throne willingly, if not downright joyfully.

Lilah looks over the books the librarian had been preparing to read, shakes her head, and runs over to me. "I need that box."

After I set it on the floor, she rifles through it and pulls several titles before skipping back. My mom's smile is as proud as mine as we watch Lilah do her magic. The kids are silent, enthralled by her engaging reading style. When she asks questions afterward, the older ones shout out answers. The librarian frowns but doesn't shush them. By book number three, she's settled on the floor too, clapping along with the kids when Lilah finishes the last book.

I lean over and whisper to my mom, "I think Lilah just got herself a new gig."

BELLA

Comedy of Errors is a blast Saturday night. We play to a packed house under a moonlit sky, and I feel freer onstage than I have since… well, I don't think I've ever felt this way. Adriana has cracked something open in me the way no character ever has. Playing Helena last summer was a success, but she ended up being far too similar to Quinn. Her machinations only created pain, primarily for herself. A good life lesson, but no fun.

On the other end of the spectrum, performing Speed last fall was easy. It was awesome to let out my inner goofball with Ben and his dog Puck, but in the role of Adriana… it's like I'm getting to practice laying it all out there and damn the consequences. Demanding love and attention and giving it too. She doesn't get everything she wants, but since it's a comedy, she gets a happy ending of sorts. At least the way Nick has interpreted it.

Which is giving me the tiniest bit of hope that I can have that too.

When Henry told me that he loved me, my first instinct was to retreat. I want to believe him, and his actions support his words. I can literally feel the waves of desire washing between us when we make love.

It just feels like I still have too much in my debit column to pay off before I get to have my own happy ending.

"I wish you would come out with us," Jess says, breaking into my thoughts. Cal is working a concert, so Jess is going out with "the boys," meaning Will, Mikey, and Randall.

After stowing my costume in the laundry bag, I meet her gaze head-on. I officially can't tell her that I'm an alcoholic, but I think she has an inkling. "You know that's not my scene. But let's do something this week, just you and me."

"Alright," she says, pushing her lower lip out. But then she waggles her eyebrows. "You go get some good sex."

I see her waggle and raise it with a full body shimmy. "I think I will."

Less than an hour later, I'm panting at Henry's side, having just gotten some good sex. "I could get addicted to you," I say with a sigh.

I'm only half kidding, and he must sense that because he traces a finger over my brow and asks softly, "You keep saying that. I want to know: What does that mean to you?"

I shrug, trying to keep things light. "Pretty much what I said. If I give in, I won't be able to give you up."

"Is that a bad thing?"

"It's bad to be dependent on you."

"What if you depend*ed on* me instead?"

I roll onto my back. "This isn't a linguistics debate, Henry."

He nudges my shoulder. "I'm just trying to understand. Or see the positive side."

"Okay, Mr. Pollyanna. What's the positive here?"

"Well, I get that if I were propping you up somehow, that wouldn't be good, but—" He sits up and leans against the headboard. "Let's look at it another way. Is there anything that's pleasurable that you're not afraid of being addicted to?"

I do my best to accept that he's just trying to be helpful. "Sugar, sort of. I mean, sometimes I overdo it."

"What happens when you overdo it?"

"I feel sick to my stomach. And just… yucky."

"What do you do if that happens?"

"I lay off for a while."

"And then what?"

"After a week or so, I can have it in moderation again."

He shifts, folding one knee so he can face me. "But you couldn't do that with alcohol or drugs?"

My every instinct tells me this is dangerous territory, but I make myself take a mental step back and think about what he's saying. "Well, I never tried. They pretty much say you can't if you're an addict. I never tried to give it up until I got sent to rehab." I'm not exactly sure where he's going with this, but I need him to understand that there is a difference between a sugar high and a cocaine binge. "I don't really want to find out. It's too dangerous."

"I get that. But still, you *can* control your appetite with sugar?"

I shrug. "So far."

"What about me?"

"What do you mean?"

"I mean, if you felt addicted to me in a way that was detrimental, what would happen?"

Pinching the bridge of my nose with my thumb and index finger, I do my best to take his questions seriously, even as my speedy heart tells me that it's not a good idea. "Well… spending time in bed with you while neglecting responsibilities. Or even forgetting that they exist."

"Okay." Taking my other hand in his, he massages my palm with his thumb. "What if you share some of your responsibilities with me so that you can enjoy time with me? Like, you could depend on me to take care of Lilah when you can't, which is only right since I am her other parent. But you could also depend on me to… I don't know, go to the grocery store or feed the cats if you have other things to do."

"What about you?"

"You'd help me with whatever I need. It's a give-and-take instead of a giving-over."

"Again with the semantics."

"Don't you think words are powerful, Ms. Shakespeare actress?"

This conversation is literally making me feel itchy. As I run my nails up and down my calves I grumble, "I thought you didn't know how to do this."

"Do what?"

"Do…" I roll a hand in the air between us while I work up the courage to say the damn word. "Relationships."

"I don't know what I'm doing." He laughs, and his hands go up in the air like he's surrendering, but not necessarily in a bad way. "I'm just trying to figure things out because it's important to me. Lilah's important to me. You're important to me. This thing between us?" He scoots closer and gently touches my brow and my chest as he says, "Here and here"—he scoops me up and settles me onto his lap, his seemingly ever-present erection pressing into my center—"and here? It all feels real and powerful but also tender and vulnerable."

He pulls me in even closer until there's nothing between us but breath. "Tell me how to show you that I love you, Bel. Because that's what this is. For me, at least."

Chapter 20

"WHERE ARE THEY NOW? Isabelle York, who had quite the run playing inveterate troublemaker Quinn Carter on *As the Earth Revolves,* has surfaced after a long hiatus. Thankfully, unlike her character, the actress's cancer was kicked in real life. Now, she's back in TV Land, this time on the other side of the camera. Ms. York, as we'll call her now, returns as a producer on the show where she debuted in the first place: children's TV show *Boom.* We can't wait to hear more…"
Daytime TV News, August 1989

BELLA

Monday morning when I pull up to GBH at the same time as Henry, having said goodbye to him just a few hours before when I finally made myself leave his bed and drive home, even exhaustion can't wipe the smile off my face. I don't think I've ever felt this combination of giddiness and hope. This man has lightened my load and my heart—as well as lit up all my parts like the body in that old Operation game.

"What are you laughing at?" he asks, as he opens my door for me.

"Nothing I can share at the moment," I singsong.

"I really want to kiss you right now," he whispers.

"I know. Me too."

"Can we tell everybody soon?" he asks.

The idea has my heart racing and not with desire. But then I remind myself that I'm not alone in this. I have a partner, and I want to trust that he'll have my back.

"How about I tell Carol and see what she says?"

He takes my hand and gives it a squeeze. "Sounds like a plan."

Five minutes later, I find a While You Were Out message on my desk with a request to see Carol ASAP. Thinking that perhaps the universe is giving me a little nudge toward full disclosure, I head to her office.

"Hey, Carol, what's up?"

The set of her jaw tells me that whatever it is, it isn't good. "Close the door behind you, please."

I do so, and when she gestures for me to sit, I do that too. "Is something the matter?"

She runs a hand through her perfectly coiffed hair, mussing it. "I really don't know where to begin."

My breakfast churns in my belly as she slides a piece of paper over the desk.

"This was in the mail this morning, addressed to 'Producer, *Boom*.' Thankfully, the mailroom didn't give it to the volunteer screeners."

My hand shakes as I pick it up, so much so that I can't read the typed words. Setting it back down on her desk, I pin my hands between my knees as I read.

To Whom It May Concern;
Isabelle York is a drug fiend and a lush and shouldn't be working with children.
If you don't fire her, I will leak PROOF to the press.
Signed,
A Concerned Citizen

"Is there any truth to this?" Carol asks.

Fighting tears of rage and a swell of despair, I nod. "Yes."

"Are you—do you use drugs—"

"No," Hand up, I interrupt her. "Oh, no. I've been clean for more than seven years." I meet her gaze. "I swear."

A line forms between her brows. "We did the usual background check when we hired you."

"Nothing would've shown up. I was never arrested, and anything else in my background was scrubbed clean."

She drags two fingers across her forehead, but the crease of concern remains. "I guess it's not surprising that you didn't tell me if it happened that long ago, but I wish you had."

"Because you wouldn't have hired me?"

She opens her mouth and then closes it again. "I don't… I don't know, honestly. It is a concern. I mean, because you are working so directly with the children."

I nod. "Do you want me to quit?"

"I have to think about it."

I nod again. "For what it's worth, I couldn't have told you."

"What do you mean?"

"I guess since you already know, I can fill in the details." Heart pounding, I make an attempt to slow it by taking in a deep breath, but my voice still wobbles. "When I was on the soap, I was abusing alcohol and a whole slew of drugs." Rushing to clarify, I add, "I went through rehab, and I'm clean now—I haven't had a drop of anything since."

After a beat, she asks, "You're sure the pressures of working on TV again won't be a trigger?"

"I was never self-medicating back then. It was an unfortunate case of an unsupervised teenager in too many adult situations, like a kid in a candy store, but instead of getting a stomachache, I got into a world of trouble." I'm not going to lie, but that doesn't mean that I have to spell out each and every predicament I ever found myself in. "I got away with it for a surprisingly long time. The soap did a good job of keeping it quiet, didn't want to be blamed for aiding and abetting the corruption of a minor."

"Is that what happened?"

"Yes and no. Some of my, uh, usage was recreational, but there were also people on the set happy to supply whatever was needed to get me through the day. You know, a little hit of this or bump of that to keep you perky."

"How old were you?"

"Sixteen when it started. Twenty-two when I got clean."

"My god."

"Anyway, the reason I can't talk about it is that in return for paying for the rehab stint at a secluded treatment center and scrubbing my reputation, I had to sign a non-disclosure agreement. Maybe it wasn't the smartest move, but I wanted to leave it all behind. I'm not allowed to talk about it at all. After I had Lilah, I was kind of glad because I never want it all to boomerang back on her." A dry laugh coughs out of me. "No pun intended."

Carol sighs and shifts back in her chair. "I really don't know what to do about this. I think I have to talk to our legal department."

"I understand." I get up, averting my gaze from the letter. "Do you want me to go home?"

She shakes her head firmly. "No. I don't want to cave to blackmail unless we have no other choice." She stands and comes around her desk to take my hand. "I wish I'd known, but I understand why you couldn't tell me. I'm sorry this happened to you."

"Thanks, Carol."

I give her hand a squeeze. Before I make it out the door, she asks, "Do you have any idea who might have written this?"

I shake my head and make my exit. But as I walk back to my office, the name of the one person who recently learned this story echoes in my mind.

Henry.

He wouldn't do that, Izzy says.

Would he? I guess Quinn's back too.

Why would he want you to be fired? Izzy asks.

I don't know, so he could have her to himself? Quinn lobs. *Or so he could have a reason to take Lilah. Or so she'd be dependent on him. Any or all of those things.*

Shutting them both down, I change directions and walk to Henry's office. He's on the phone when I get there but motions for me to come in.

Digging through a pile of papers on the credenza under the office window, he says, "I told you not to use that."

What did I tell you? Quinn hisses. *He told someone, and they used the info.*

Oh my god, Izzy gasps.

Probably thought he was doing her a favor, Quinn says. *Men are idiots.*

This is Lilah's father! Izzy scolds.

Still a man, Quinn says. *Only good for one thing.*

Henry turns toward me and mouths, "Sorry."

My butt lands on the chair by his desk. *Is* it possible that he let my secret slip somehow? Or told someone on purpose? After all, it's not like I really know him. He could've been conning me this entire time. He could be trying to take Lilah away.

"Well, there could be some serious blowback, but I'll see what I can do to fix it. Yeah. Bye." After hanging up the phone, he skirts the desk to perch on its edge. "Sorry about that."

My worry must be all over my face because his frown deepens. "What happened? Is Lilah okay?"

I shake my head. "Nothing happened to Lilah. She's fine, as far as I know."

"Then what's the matter?"

Meeting his gaze, I ask, "What was that phone call about?"

He shakes his head. "Ugh. I let Tim do the rough edit with Sam on the latest episode because I wanted to get ahead on the fine-tuning of the earlier ones. But I just checked their work, and they used the overhead shot in the cooking segment, which totally looks down the front of Amy's shirt. I'd told him to delete all that footage, but they forgot. I can't imagine what would happen if Carol saw that."

"Oh," I say, my voice shaky.

He pulls up a chair next to me. "Bella, what's the matter?"

I shake my head. "Carol got an anonymous letter threatening to publicize my addiction problems if they don't fire me. Blackmail, basically."

"Oh my god." After a few moments where he seems to take in the news, he sits back abruptly. "Wait. Did you think it was me?"

Wincing, I nod. "I mean, you're the only person I've told about it, so…"

"Seriously?" On his feet, he paces to the window. "You think after… after everything we've talked about, after I've worked so hard to show you how much I want to be there for you and Lilah, that I'd do that?"

"I'm sorry. I don't have the best judgement about men, so—"

"I can't believe you think I'd do that."

My face drops into my hands, and I drag my nails over my scalp. "Everyone in my life who I think is on my side has proven that they're really just out for themselves. My dad gave up on me, and even my mom, she's moving in with a friend, so Lilah and I are really on our own now."

Hearing his intake of breath, I throw out one last defensive line. "I may have trust issues, but I come by them honestly."

"Well, I have issues with not being trusted."

I don't know what to say in response to that or what I can do to fix it. Except leave. So I get to my feet and move toward the door. "Okay. Well, this was just awesome. I guess we can work out a schedule for when you'll see Lilah. I won't be here for much longer, so you won't have to worry about that."

Before I can escape, he grabs my hand. "Bella. What are you doing?"

Sliding my hand out of his, I shove it into my pocket. "Getting out of your hair."

"For good?"

"I'm obviously broken," I say to the door. "It'll be easier for everybody if I just leave."

"You're just giving up?"

When I risk a glance back at him, the ferocity in his eyes makes my heart skip a beat. "I don't know what else to do. I can't fight back against some anonymous letter writer because if I say anything, my old network will sue me. I don't want to be responsible for bringing bad press to the show, so it's obviously best if I quit. And I don't know how to do"—I flail a hand in his direction—"this without fucking it up, so let's just end it before we do or say something worse to each other. And before Lilah gets the idea that we could actually be a family."

Like I have.

Bracing one hand on the door, Henry places the other on the side of my face. His touch is gentle but firm as he turns my head until I meet his still fierce gaze. "You might be ready to give up. On us, on your job, on your life. But I won't."

If only I could believe this fairy tale. All I can do is shake my head.

"It's okay. And it's all going to be okay," he murmurs.

"I wish I had your confidence." Clunking my head against the door behind me, I moan, "I don't know what to do. I am so tired of hiding."

"Are you? Because I think I might be able to take care of that."

"What do you mean?"

After pressing a soft kiss to my forehead, he crosses behind his desk and flips through his Rolodex. When he finds what he's looking for, he picks up the phone.

"Henry, what are you doing?"

Eyes on the card in his hand, he punches in numbers. "Fixing the problem."

Crossing the short distance between the door and his desk, I press the switch hook button before he can finish dialing. "Henry, this is complicated. You can't just jump in and call people."

He drops the receiver back onto the cradle. "Well, I can't do nothing." He sweeps a hand around his office. "I fix things. It's my job."

"I am not your job," I grit out.

He crosses around the desk to take my hand. "But if I can do something to make this go away, don't you want me to?"

"Maybe we could discuss what you plan to do first?"

"Right. Sorry." Running a hand through his hair, he winces. "Now that I think about it, I'm afraid this might actually be my fault."

I take a step back. "Did you tell someone about my addictions?"

Hand up between us in that defensive gesture I haven't seen for weeks, he says, "I didn't, but my mom guessed. She noticed I wasn't drinking and just put two and two together."

"But why would she blackmail me?"

"She wouldn't." He shakes his head. "But she is a blabbermouth. Who the hell knows what she said on her plane trip home or to any of her friends?" He runs a hand over his face, and when he drops it, his expression is pained. "I'm so sorry, Bel."

My own hands are shaking as I make my way to the couch, the place where he told me he loved me just days ago. Wishing we could go back to that day, wishing we could just stay there, I collapse onto it and close my eyes.

An arm drapes over my shoulders. "We're a good team. We can figure this out together. I promise I won't do anything without talking to you first, but this is what I have in mind."

I keep my eyes closed as I listen. By the time he's finished, I have a few ideas of my own. When I open my eyes again, the world has stopped spinning.

After kissing my cheek and my forehead, he whispers, "You might have to remind me to slow down at times, but I'm here, Bel. I'm on team Dabba Dabba Do for the long haul."

■

HENRY

A quick call to my mom where she swears up and down that she didn't let Bella's alcoholism slip is a relief and takes her out of the running, but by the time we've sat down with Carol and talked through the possibilities, the list of potential blackmailers includes way too many suspects.

"Before we go any further, you should see this. It came in with the packages after you left my office." She upends an envelope and a stack of photos falls onto her desk.

Picking up a faded Polaroid, I squint at it. "Is that you?" I ask.

Bella picks up another. "This one sure is."

Flipping through the pile makes me nauseous. Shot after shot of the girl I think of as Izzy, half of them with a guy or two groping her. If these got out, *Boom* would most assuredly take a hit.

"These could help us narrow down the list," I say, my voice shaking slightly with suppressed rage. "If Bella can tell where they were taken or with whom, we might be able to figure out who took them."

"Good luck with that. It's bad enough when people tell you about the crazy things you did during a blackout," she mutters. "It's worse to actually see the evidence."

Carol shakes her head. "It's still so disturbing to me that so many crew members and other cast members—people who should've been mentors to you—would be supplying you with illegal drugs."

Bella gathers the photos into a stack before setting them carefully onto Carol's desk. "Not to excuse anyone's behavior, but it was the climate back then. Our shoot days were so long, and the pressure was high. Coke to keep you going, Valium or a shot of whiskey to calm you down… it was a vicious cycle."

I scan the list again, which includes pretty much every line on a production call sheet. "What about your agent?"

Bella folds her arms across her chest, hugging herself like I'd like to right now. "She was a little upset when I ended up pregnant and decided to retire, but I really don't see what she could gain from this. Anyway, she's pretty direct. If she wanted something from me, she'd just pick up the phone."

"I guess the question is why now?" Carol asks. "Why not years ago?"

"Maybe someone saw my name in a press release about the new *Boom* and..."

"Decided that you didn't deserve to have a career?" I finish, stuffing my hands in my armpits to keep myself from touching her.

"It would make sense." She tips her head to the side. "You know, I wasn't aware of anyone losing their job because of me, but that doesn't mean it didn't happen. If it did, they might still be angry."

"Lost their job because they gave drugs to a minor. Not because of you," Carol says sternly. "I want you to know that I don't blame you or think less of you. This was not your fault. You were a child."

Bella nods. "I appreciate that. But I'm not going to let *Boom* take the fall for me. If you feel like you need to fire me, at least publicly, do it."

"That might help, actually," I say.

Bella's focus ticks over to me. "How?"

"If the person thinks they've won, then they might be easier to find."

Carol taps her chin. "We could announce that you'll be taking a leave of absence due to a family matter. That might buy us some time. We wouldn't necessarily be giving in to the threat, but it might make them feel like we're taking it seriously."

"That makes sense," I say.

Bella scoops the photos up. "Whatever you decide to do, I need to take a trip down to New York. Talking to some people in person will get us answers faster."

I stand and set a hand on Bella's shoulder. "If it's okay with you, Carol, I'd like to join her."

To Carol's credit, she just raises a single brow. We haven't yet told her our entire story, and maybe it's not really her business. But at this point I don't give a shit because I need to be by Bella's side. I do add, "I have a contact in the legal department at NBS who might be able to help."

Carol checks the large calendar on the wall by her desk. "Since we wrapped up shooting Friday, I suppose that means you can take a day." Eyes on me she clarifies, "*One* day."

By the time Carol and I finish tying up a few other loose ends, the color is back in Bella's face and she's got a page full of notes.

"Thanks for your help," she says to Carol, her voice steady. "Hopefully, we'll be back quickly with some answers."

"Keep me posted." Carol's gaze flicks to the hand I've placed on Bella's shoulder, but she just says, "And let me know if there's anything else I can do. You're an integral part of the team. Both of you."

Chapter 21

"The effect on viewers of this touchy story line has been utterly dynamic. People have been writing in by the hundreds! But I'm all for controversial subjects on daytime TV. Aren't you?" *TV Today*, August 1989

BELLA

An hour later, we've packed a couple of bags, dropped Ribsy at the kennel, explained everything to my mom, and are on the way to the Big Apple.

After passing through the toll plaza and accelerating to merge onto the Mass Pike, Henry reaches over to massage the back of my neck. "I couldn't help but notice that 'Dad' was at the top of your list."

"Yeah, well, he went from being my hero to my teacher to my roommate to a stranger."

"That must feel pretty shitty," he says, after a quick glance in my direction.

An unwelcome lump forms in my throat, but I just swallow around it. The man doesn't deserve any sentimentality. "I have no idea what he'd be capable of. He already cleaned out my trust. He may need more money. And he did have a Polaroid camera."

"Probably half the people you knew had one."

"True, but there were specific departments that always used them. Props, hair and makeup, the script supervisor." As I list the departments, I put an asterisk next to names corresponding to those departments. I add an extra star by the people who actually supplied me with drugs, as opposed to just partying with me. At least as far as I remember.

Dropping my head back against the car seat, I shudder. "That girl? The one in the Polaroids? I just don't feel like she is me."

Henry rests his hand on my thigh. "For what it's worth, I don't either."

"But it *was* me. I can't forget that. I may have been underage at first, but I was old enough to know better by the time my mom got me into rehab."

He doesn't say anything, which I appreciate. Nothing would make me feel better right now. Except perhaps doing exactly what we're doing.

HENRY

Bella suggests taking the Merritt Parkway instead of I-95, and not only is the route a bit more scenic, we're able to find an old-fashioned diner to get lunch. Even though she insists that she doesn't have an appetite, she manages to eat half my fries as well as her own cup of chowder.

Sitting back in the padded booth, she rubs her stomach. "I guess I was hungrier than I thought."

Raising my hand to catch the attention of the waitress, I lift my coffee cup in the air with a hopeful smile. Moments later, she's refilling our cups as she lists the pie varieties on offer. When I ask if she'll bring us her favorite, she nods approvingly and returns moments later with a large slice of blueberry pie, obviously home-made, topped with vanilla ice cream.

As we dig in, Bella sighs. "Pie always makes things better."

"Agreed." Studying her, I'm relieved to note that she's relaxed considerably over the past couple of hours. I haven't pressed her for more details about her father or any of the other suspects on her list. When she came to my office this morning, everything about her was hollowed out, like she'd been literally gutted by the letter Carol showed her. Even though it hurt that she'd suspected me, the panic in her eyes made it clear she wasn't thinking straight

The thing is, even if we figure out who is trying to blackmail her —and I really hope it isn't her father—the list of people who enabled her drug use and partied alongside her is long. Unless she can get ahead of the narrative and tell her own story, this could happen again.

I wait until we're back in the privacy of the car and heading south again to say, "You take life by the horns and ride it, Bella. That's who you've always been."

She shakes her head. "That's who I *was*. And look where it got me."

"That's who you *are*. You could've hidden your light under a bushel and never let it out again when you left New York."

"That is what I did."

"You didn't have to have Lilah. You could've had an abortion or given her up for adoption, but you chose to raise her. By yourself. That was pretty fearless—which is different than being reckless, which doesn't take other people into account."

Her brow creases. "I've done everything I could to keep her safe."

"There's a difference between keeping your child safe and living in fear."

"Is there, though? Can you be fearless when you know how cruel people can be?"

"I think you have to be. You've survived by facing your situations head on. Taking the job at GBH must've been scary, especially when you saw me in that lobby."

She half laughs, half sighs. "I did wish the earth would open up and swallow me in that moment."

"But you came back anyway."

She shrugs. "I had to."

"What I'm saying is, you could've given up. But you didn't. Every time life has put an obstacle in your path, you've found a way."

"Over, under, or through," she mutters. "That's what my mom always said about me."

"I think it's a pretty amazing example you've set for our daughter. I think that's a big part of why she's dealing with all the changes so well."

She shifts in the seat, gaze skimming the trees flying by outside. "Why are you saying all this?"

"Well, I'm wondering, if we can get NBS to let you out of that non-disclosure agreement, would you consider going public about being an addict?"

She stiffens in her seat. "Why would I do that?"

Keeping my eyes on the road, I take her hand, which has gone clammy.

"If you do it, if you tell your story, then you're in control." Pulling her hand to my lips and giving it a kiss, I add, "And you're setting yet another example. For Lilah, for the Boomerang kids, for all the kids out there."

"An example of how to fuck up your life?"

"You can paint a realistic picture of the dangers a young actor faces. If more people know, they'll be more likely to intercede before things get out of control." A quick glance in her direction tells me that I shouldn't push. The pink has left her cheeks again. "Just something to think about."

BELLA

As we get onto the Henry Hudson from the Saw Mill Parkway, Henry says, "I've never come into the city from the north. It's not quite as dramatic as the view across the Hudson."

Keeping an eye out for the George Washington Bridge, which will tell us that we're almost to Manhattan, I ask, "Have you been back to New York?"

He glances over at me. "Since the last time I saw you there? No."

"Not even to move out?"

He shakes his head. "My roommates sent me my belongings and divvied up my furniture. None of it was worth anything."

It doesn't seem like he wants to get into why, but just as I'm wondering if his relationship with his father was more complicated than I'd thought, he turns the question back on me. "What about you?"

"Did I give away my furniture?"

"No, have you been back?"

I shake my head. "Not since I found out I was pregnant. I didn't have any reason to."

"What about your things?"

"My father sent me my clothes, and I left the rest. Kind of like you and your roommates, I guess."

"But he wasn't just a roommate. He's your dad."

"He was just a roommate at that point. And he was barely home, anyway. I don't know who he was sleeping with, but it wasn't my mom."

Traffic thickens, and the knot behind my solar plexus tightens the closer we get to Manhattan. Henry's quiet as he navigates through the congestion, but when I reach across to place a hand behind his neck, he flinches.

"You okay?" I ask.

"Yeah. Sorry. Just thinking."

"About your dad?"

He nods, and a muscle in his jaw twitches.

"You want to talk about it?"

"I don't know if you'd want to hear it."

"Why wouldn't I?"

"Well, because… if I could have the chance to make things right with my dad before he died, I'd do whatever it takes."

"What do you mean? I thought he was your biggest supporter."

"He was. At first. But then when I'd been there a couple of years and was still only making enough money to share a crappy apartment in Hoboken with a bunch of other guys, he didn't get why I wouldn't just come home." He blows out a breath. "Our last conversation got kind of ugly."

Before I can argue that his dad didn't steal money from him, I catch the expression on Henry's face. Whatever happened, it haunts him still. "I'm sorry."

He squeezes my thigh briefly. "Not your fault."

"I'm still sorry that happened to you."

A large blast from the horn of an eighteen-wheeler trying to make an exit by changing lanes cuts off whatever reply he was going to make. The George Washington Bridge looms, and as we pass under it, I make a decision. Taking Henry's hand, I ask, "Can you take the exit at 95th Street?"

FIFTEEN MINUTES LATER, after I give Henry a lingering kiss goodbye, he takes my cheeks in his hands and says, "You sure about this?"

I nod. "No. But yeah. It'll be okay. I'll be okay."

"Well, leave me a message at the hotel if your plans change. Otherwise, I'll see you there in a couple of hours."

We've decided to split up. While Henry meets with an old friend who is now in the legal department at the National Broadcasting Service—often referred to as No Bull Shit by its employees—I'm going to talk to my dad.

I'm halfway out of the car when something occurs to me. "Thanks, Henry. For doing this."

He grabs my hand and kisses it. "Just hope I can be of help."

"You are already, you know."

"That makes me very happy."

"Okay. Wish me luck."

"Good luck. Remember, he probably loves you more than anything."

I almost argue, but he needs to get going, so I just wave goodbye and force my body to go through the revolving doors into the building where I lived from 1974 to 1982. Once I'm inside, the familiar scents and sounds bring back a rush of memories that wake Izzy and Quinn. They've been silent for what feels like weeks, but they waste no time making their voices heard now.

Remember when we saw these marble walls and gold lighting fixtures and thought we'd hit the big time? Quinn asks, her voice more reverent and less cynical than usual.

I remember coming in after a snowball fight with Dad in Riverside Park and rushing upstairs to make hot cocoa, Izzy says.

How we'd go to the market together and make gourmet dinners Sunday nights in our fancy kitchen, Quinn remembers.

Oh, and the lady next door with all the cats! Izzy says.

Blinded by the memories, I don't even see the doorman as I head for the elevators.

"Excuse me? Miss? Can I help you?"

Startled, I turn back to find an unfamiliar face. "Oh, I'm sorry. I'm here to see George York."

The man gives me a stern look. "Wait right there. I'll call up."

The doormen who worked in the building when I lived here were all like surrogate uncles to me. I'm sure they helped drunk and high me get into the elevator and head for the right floor more than once.

"You can go on up," the man says after hanging up the phone. "Do you know where you're going?"

"I do. I used to live here."

"Well," he says, his tone softening. "Welcome home."

A quick elevator ride and a few short strides down the hall, and I'm in front of our door. Before I can knock, it opens.

I blink for a few seconds before speaking. The man standing in front of me is my dad but isn't. Sunken cheeks and thinning, graying hair make him look much older than Mom. "Dad. Um, hi. Sorry for just showing up."

"Izz." He shakes his head. "I can't believe it."

"It's Bella now, actually."

He nods. "Bella. I like that. More grown-up." Stepping back into the apartment, he gestures inside. "Come in." He looks down the hall. "You're alone?"

"Yeah, I came down to the city with my…" What to call Henry is a whole story in and of itself, and I'm not ready to spill the reason I'm in town. "With a friend. He has a meeting, and I thought I'd stop in."

Though it's been seven years since we've spoken in person, he doesn't skip a beat. "Well, I'm glad you did."

As he ushers me into the kitchen, he asks, "Do you want something to drink?"

Before I can say I don't drink anymore, he says, "I was just making some iced tea. The heat is crazy."

"Sure, that'd be great."

He takes his time, cutting lemon slices and a couple sprigs of mint before filling two tall glasses with ice and pouring tea from a large carafe. After handing me one, he lifts his glass to clink mine. "Cheers."

He gestures toward the living room. "You know where everything is."

In fact, I do because everything is almost exactly the same. The layout, anyway. What's new are the posters on the walls and the signs stacked in a corner and the printed leaflets in boxes everywhere.

"What is all this?" I ask as I sit on the couch.

My dad sits on a chair opposite and sets his glass on a ceramic coaster on the coffee table. Then he moves a stack of papers and slides another coaster my way.

After taking another sip of his tea and clearing his throat, he asks, "Have you heard of Act Up?"

"I think so. It has something to do with AIDS?"

"It does. We work to make lives better for people with AIDS and to demand more money for research, better access to drugs, things like that."

I take in the large volume of leaflets and signs and posters. "You're part of the group?"

"I am. Do you remember Larry Kramer?"

"The playwright?"

"That's him. We've been friends for a long time. He was responsible for getting things going. I do things mostly behind the scenes." He takes another sip of his tea. "Anyway, what brings you to New York?"

He asks this like it's something I do once a month, which refuels the anger that waves of nostalgia had doused the moment I stepped inside this building. Now, it comes roaring back.

"Well, let's see. I guess I'm wondering if cleaning out my savings —your granddaughter's college fund—wasn't enough to pay for whatever lifestyle you've got going on here. Did you have to resort to blackmail too?"

His hand shakes as he sets down his glass. "I'm so sorry about borrowing that money, Izz—uh, Bella. I fully intend to pay it back, but"—he gestures at the piles of posters and leaflets—"I'm still working on that."

"And the blackmail?"

When tired eyes meet mine, they look genuinely confused. "That I don't know anything about. Someone is blackmailing you?"

"Someone sent a letter and some old Polaroids of me to WGBH, where I'm now working, threatening to expose my issues with addiction if they didn't fire me."

He shakes his head. "I'm sorry that's happened, but it wasn't me."

Sitting back, I cross my arms over my chest, not quite ready to let him off the hook. "Are you sure you're not still angry at me for destroying your marriage?"

"Oh, Izz—sweetheart." A half laugh escapes past his lips, and when he shakes his head, his expression is one of disbelief. "Have you not talked to your mom about this?"

"Not really. But I know I drove a wedge between you. I practically demanded to move to New York."

"You were a kid."

"An obnoxious kid."

"A persuasive kid."

"Exactly. A kid that could only see what she wanted."

"Ambition isn't a terrible thing. You had a gift. People loved to watch you perform." Eyes on his folded hands, he pauses, seeming to consider his next words. "They still do."

"What do you mean?"

Meeting my gaze, his is clear as he says, "I've seen your plays."

"What?"

"Your mom told me you were acting again."

"When?"

"She and I talk." He shrugs. "I came up with my partner, and we saw *All's Well* and *Two Gents.* We hope to get up to see *Comedy of Errors.*"

"Your partner? Did you... start a business?"

"No, I'm a dialect coach now. But my partner is my... Alex. We've been together for almost five years."

"Alex like Alexandra?"

"Bella." He sighs like I'm being incredibly dense. "I'm gay. That's why your mom and I split up. I can't believe she never told you."

I'm speechless for a few moments, finally getting what she meant about him having his reasons. "I... I was so angry at you for a long time and didn't want to hear anything about you. And then recently —" I break off. "I just never guessed."

He moves to sit next to me on the couch. "Sweetheart, you have every right to be angry with me. I was less than useless to you back then. I was selfish, high on the whole lifestyle... I didn't even know you were in trouble until it was too late. I don't know how we both survived. I'm sorry, for all of it."

"Oh," is all I have to say to this, still running all of my dad's behavior through this new lens. "Why didn't you tell me? That you're... that you prefer men?"

He shakes his head slowly. "Ironically, I didn't want you to hate me. But I have a feeling that happened anyway."

"I was *hurt,* Dad. I felt like you gave up on me and abandoned me, and… when I found out you took the money—" Suddenly my dad's appearance, his involvement with Act Up, and the money all add up in my head. "Oh my god. Are you sick?"

He blows out a breath. "Both Alex and I are HIV-positive, but we are lucky enough to have access to AZT, which has kept us healthy so far. Most people can't afford it, which is why we protest."

"Did you use my money to pay for that?"

"That was to help friends." A fierceness replaces his habitually gentle manner, and he gets up from the couch to pace. "There are so many men who have died in pain or alone because they don't have health insurance. I needed to help the ones I could. I'll pay it back eventually, but the high cost of the meds is making that more challenging than I'd expected."

Before I can tell him that I don't care about the money, he takes both of my hands in his. "I'm sorry, baby. I'm sorry about all of it. It took me a long time to let go of the shame. The self-hatred, really. I thought what I wanted was perverted, and I was in a bad cycle. But that doesn't excuse my neglect." When he raises his head, the love in his tear-filled eyes is undeniable. "I loved you. So much. Still do."

"I love you too, Daddy." A sob hiccups out of me. "I miss you."

And then he's nestled next to me on the couch, arms around me while I sob onto his shirt.

Chapter 22

"AT HOME WITH... Nathan Reed. All stars have fans, and over the years this fetching actor (Bruce on *Ryan's Wish*) has received a multitude of letters from admirers. It's still hard to believe that one woman would write to Nathan regularly over a ten-year period! I read the most recent missive, and it's purely and completely devoted, but unsigned... Does she want nothing in return for her dedication? No pictures, no answers, no recognition?" *TV Tattler*, August 1989

BELLA

By the time I make it downtown to the hotel where Henry and I are staying, my mind is so full and my heart so wrung out that all I want to do is fall into bed. So that's what I do. After calling to check in with my mom and Lilah, brushing my teeth, and running a washcloth over my face, I strip out of my clothes and crawl into bed.

I don't fall asleep, however. Talking to my dad and being in our old apartment was like opening a Pandora's box. As a slideshow of memories flash through my mind, all I want to do is give the girl I see a big hug. She was trying so very hard to fill herself up with what she thought was love but was really just attention.

Surprisingly, not all of the memories are negative. He did take care of me in little ways. Made sure the refrigerator was full, made me wear a coat when I didn't want to, coached me for auditions. Away at rehab, I shoved everything that happened in New York into one big closet of evil, never to be reopened, but now I realize that life wasn't all bad, even after I started using and he disappeared into what I now know was a search for connection with other men.

"Oh, what a tangled web we weave," I whisper to the empty room. The lady Scot got that right.

When the hotel door opens, I've retreated so far into memories I've almost forgotten where I am and the reason we came down here in the first place, but the smile on Henry's face is exactly the thing I need right now.

That smile fades when he sees me huddled under the covers. "Oh no. Did it not go well?"

Sitting up, I just hold out my arms. After he shucks off his sport coat and shoes, he crawls into bed and pulls me into his side. We just sit there for a long time, and the role this man should play—is already playing—in my life is suddenly crystal clear.

"I need you, Henry Cornelius Smith."

HENRY

When I enter the hotel room, I've got plenty of news to share and I'm guessing she does too. But when she tells me she needs me, I know it's a huge step for her, and I'm struck dumb.

But only momentarily. Hugging her even closer, I whisper, "I'm here for you. Whatever you need."

"Thank you. That means so much to me right now." She nestles her cheek into my chest, arms still around me. "I wish we could stay here forever."

"I agree about the forever part, but I think I'd rather it be somewhere else."

"Like where?" she asks, her tone uncharacteristically tentative.

Wanting to reassure her that I'm not planning on going anywhere, I say, "The location doesn't really matter—Boston, New York, North Carolina, or the moon, I don't care about that. I just want to snuggle with you in a bed big enough that a little one could join us here."

"Like Ribsy?"

The tease in her voice makes me ridiculously happy. "Ribsy, yep. Maybe even those cats of yours."

"That'd be interesting."

"Then there's Lilah and…"

"And?"

"You know, the six or seven other babies we could make."

She pulls back to narrow her eyes at me. "That'd be an awfully big bed."

I stroke a hand down her back to palm her butt. "Big beds are good for other things too."

Chin on my chest, she grins. "I'd suggest we try some of those things, but"—with a groan, she pulls away and sits up—"I think we need to talk before that can happen."

After grabbing a shirt from the floor and putting it on, she sits cross-legged on the bed to face me. "I'm not going to get any rest until I start solving these problems." She squeezes my knee. "Then we give the bed a workout."

"Well, in that case," I say, swinging off the bed and grabbing my briefcase, "put some pants on too, girl, or I won't be able to concentrate."

We meet at the tiny table in the corner. Bella shuffles through the stack of Polaroids we brought with us as I open my briefcase and pull out a few documents.

"You first," she says, as I set my briefcase on the floor.

"Your wish is my command." I'm dying to know what happened with her dad, but this is her show, so I flip through the photocopies of the agreement Bella's family signed until I get to the highlighted sections. "Basically, Joe and I went over the non-disclosure, and long story short, he's not going to fight you on this. He wants you to feel comfortable living your life and telling whoever you need to about your history. At the same time, he said that if push came to shove and you tried to drag the network's name through the mud over it, they do have a very well-funded legal department."

Her brow furrows. "So, what does that mean in terms of dealing with this blackmail and *Boom?*"

"If it goes public, they want to be on top of it. He offered to deal directly with the WGBH legal team."

She's churning through way too much in her head, so I draw a finger across her brow. "We're on your side, Bella. You didn't do anything wrong."

She takes this in, nodding slowly. "My dad and I had a big talk." Her smile is fragile but hopeful as she continues. "We still have a lot to work through, but I'm glad we got the ball rolling. The letter wasn't from him, but after we went through the Polaroids together, we're pretty sure we know who it is."

Setting one of the photos on the table between us, she points to the blurry image of a woman in a mirror, the camera flash obscuring part of her face. "That's the photographer. She always had a Polaroid camera with her on set to keep track of things, but my dad remembered that she'd whip it out to catch what she called 'memories' too. I never thought anything about it until now." Bella taps the image, in which she's wearing a colorful, sparkly dress that I can't even imagine her in now. "I remembered her taking this. It was my seventeenth birthday."

"We need to find her."

She leans off the bed to grab her purse. "It just so happens that my dad's a bit of a pack rat. He kept our old call sheets filed away with other paperwork." She pulls a faded mimeograph from her purse. "So I have her address from 1981."

I check the clock on the bedside table. "Too late to head there now. But we could do it first thing in the morning."

"Actually, my dad wants to go with me." She leans back against the headboard and takes my hand, a relaxed smile on her face that I hope to see more often. "I appreciate everything you're doing, but he knows her. We hope that together we can get her to stop whatever it is she's got planned."

Taking her hand and bringing it to my lips, I say, "Whatever you need. We should get back on the road by late morning, though."

"Agreed," she says over a yawn.

"I had dinner with Joe. Did you eat?"

"I had something with my dad. I think I just want to go to bed now, if that's okay." She drags herself out of her chair, strips again on the way to the bed, and crawls under the covers. "I wish I had the energy to…" The end of her sentence is engulfed by another yawn.

"Go to sleep, sweetheart. I'll join you in a couple minutes."

After putting everything back in my briefcase, brushing my teeth, and hanging up my slacks and coat, I get into the bed and wrap my limbs around her, spooning her.

"Thank you, Hal."

Kissing her softly on the shoulder, I answer, "Anytime, Bel."

BELLA

The next morning, after sleeping like the dead, I wake up with more hope for the future than I've had in a long time. Even though I still have to face Nancy Billingsley and whatever grudge she's got against me, it makes a huge difference to know that I've got not only Hal but also my dad in my corner.

After scarfing down a bagel and a schmear like you can only get in this city—and admitting to myself that I do miss some things about New York—I give Henry a quick kiss goodbye. The plan is to try and surprise our suspect before she leaves for the day, which will only work if she's no longer working in television and has taken on a job with normal business hours.

"You've got Joe's office info, right?" Henry asks.

After I talk to Nancy, we plan to meet at the network, where I'll sign a new agreement. "I've got quarters, too, in case I need to call. Hopefully, she hasn't moved."

"I'll ask around, see if they have a forwarding address, just in case."

I give him another kiss and grab a cab downtown. Half an hour later, I've met up with my dad, and I'm pressing a doorbell marked with Nancy's name. When she answers, my father takes over—we decided that he might be less of a threat—and she buzzes us in. When she opens the door to her third-floor walkup, she's obviously surprised to see me, but she ushers us into her tiny living room.

"I suppose I know why you're here," Nancy says as she points to a loveseat. As we settle onto it, she perches on the only other chair. "I have to be at work at eight forty-five, so you might as well go ahead and yell at me now." Holding up a finger, she adds, "But I will say this. I got fired for having drugs at work, so it wasn't fair that you didn't get punished."

Meeting like with like I jump right in, doing my best to keep my voice calm. "I wonder if you could put yourself in my shoes. I was working a full-time job from the age of fourteen." I point to my chest. "That part was my choice. But when adults I worked with offered me drugs and alcohol, I lost my childhood. I thought if people I looked up to said it was okay, it would be. Unfortunately, it wasn't."

My dad leans forward, putting his elbows on his knees and clasping his hands together. "I'm partially to blame here, but it was still wrong that people offered Izzy those things."

Mirroring his posture, I add, "I was in situations I never should have been in, making decisions I shouldn't have had to make. When I was older, in my early twenties, it was on me, but by then it was too late. I was an addict. I had to get away from it all to save my life."

Shifting in her chair, she toys with her watch strap. "It's just unfair that I had to pay the price."

"It is unfair if you were the only one, but believe me, I'd trade places with you."

Her head jerks up. "But you have a job in TV again."

"I do," I say, struggling to stay on an even keel, frustrated at the childishness in this woman's tone. "But I've worked hard to stay clean, and I'm working hard to keep this job."

Nancy glances at the clock, and my dad jostles my knee with his. Just as I'm starting to worry that she'll kick us out before we work this out, something occurs to me. "Did they actually tell you that you were fired for giving me drugs?"

"Well, yes and no." Gaze lowered, she picks at a cuticle. "You see, I was always losing track of things. They'd get so mad when I lost my keys—claimed they were so expensive to replace. One day, these men came in with a big German shepherd and told me to stand up and step away from my desk. The dog found a stash of some kind of drugs in a drawer. It wasn't mine, but I knew that whoever they belonged to must've had a set of my keys. I thought it'd be safer to claim the contraband than to admit that I'd lost them again. I mean, directors and producers did lines of cocaine right in front of everyone on the set, so I figured it wasn't that big of a deal.

"That time it was, though," she says, her tone souring. "They said they were cracking down, and since there was a 'zero tolerance policy' in place, I had to go. After I left, a friend told me that the new rules were because of you getting hooked on drugs, so I always... blamed it on you."

She gets up abruptly, crosses to her kitchen counter, and pulls several tissues out of a Kleenex box.

When she doesn't sit back down, my dad asks, "Are you happy, Nancy?"

"I don't know," she says before blowing her nose. After she throws the tissue in the trash, she flings a hand in the air. "I wasn't happy then, I suppose. I was so scared of screwing up that I did. A lot."

"That sounds like an unfortunate self-fulfilling prophecy," my dad offers with more generosity than I can manage at the moment. "What are you doing for work now?"

Still standing by the counter, she says, "I'm a receptionist at my cousin's dental practice. I try to stay away from those magazines, but one of the other girls showed me an article about your new position because she knows I worked on *As the Earth Revolves* and wondered if I knew you."

I want to ask why she did it, but when my dad places a gentle hand on my knee, I keep my mouth shut.

She blows her nose again and then sighs. "I'm sorry I sent that letter. I read that notice, and I got mad all over again." Hugging herself, she adds, "And I'm sorry that all happened to you. I didn't know you'd started so young. All I saw was this beautiful young woman who had everything she wanted."

"I wish that were true," I say softly.

She nods, and then meets my gaze, a puzzled expression on her face. "How did you know it was me?"

"You were in one of the photos, your reflection in the mirror as you took the picture."

"I never was good at keeping track of the little details," she says, sighing. "But you remembered me?"

"Of course I did."

"Well, that makes me a little happier—that I'm memorable." She smiles, but her eyes are a bit watery as she says, "Sometimes I feel invisible."

My heart squeezes at the pain in her voice, but before I can say anything in response, she asks, "Can I have my Polaroids back?"

          ■

OUTSIDE ON THE STOOP, after Nancy troops off to her job at the dentist's office, I'm still feeling a bit off kilter. "So many twists and turns."

"She's a bit of a kook," my dad says.

"Yeah. Thanks for coming up with that bit about the Polaroids being with lawyers."

"I thought that would get her to back down." Wincing, he adds, "She could go off again, though."

"Which is why I'm going to tell my story," I say, as we head in the opposite direction from Nancy. I hadn't decided for sure until right this moment, but something about the way this woman bent my tale to fit her own makes my choice clear. "If I'm not hiding anything, no one can hold anything against me."

My dad puts an arm around my shoulders to give me a quick side hug. "That sounds like a very wise decision."

"What about you?" I ask. "Will you do the same?"

He hesitates, withdrawing his arm and sliding his hands into his pockets. "Unfortunately, the world doesn't see my situation in the same light."

"What do you mean?"

"Well, while people are starting to get that being an addict is not a moral failure, they don't see being gay in the same light."

"Is that why you wouldn't let mom tell me? Even though it meant that I thought you didn't care about me anymore?"

He stops in the middle of the sidewalk, looking up and down the quiet street before continuing. "If I'm in certain circles, especially here in New York, I feel safe. But there are parts of this country where my sex life is still illegal, where people think I'm mentally deranged and a danger to their children." When I take his hand, he gives it a squeeze. "But we're working on that."

My heart hurts with his, and I'm suddenly full of grief for all the time we've lost due to my stubbornness and his fears. Stopping on the corner, I say, "Henry and I have to get back today, but I'd love to meet Alex sometime soon. And will you come up and meet Lilah?"

"We'd love to," he says, his eyes filling, as mine are.

"I've missed you, Dad," I whisper.

"I've missed you too, sweetheart."

Chapter 23

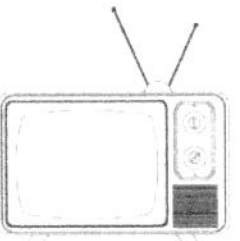

"WHAT DOES DON REALLY WANT—LOVE? SUCCESS?
Tune in this week to find out on *All His Children!*" *TV Today,*
August 1989

HENRY

Bella and her father set off to confront the blackmailer long before
business hours, so Joe isn't in yet when I show up at the NBS offices.
I don't want to leave Bella hanging in case she calls in, but there are
too many memories in this building for me to just sit and wait.
Instead, I head up 8th Avenue to kill time and do some thinking while
I walk.

Interestingly, meeting Joe yesterday didn't leave me with regrets
about my career trajectory. On the contrary, if I'd followed the path I
was on, I'd be stuck in an office making phone calls and taking meetings. I'd be making a hell of a lot more money, but I wouldn't be
hands-on and I wouldn't have the creative opportunities that GBH
promises.

What I do still regret, and what keeps running through my mind,
is the last conversation I had with my dad. The last time I saw him
face-to-face, neither of us were smiling. It was the Saturday after

Thanksgiving. He found me in my childhood bedroom packing up to fly back to New York. He knew when my flight was. He'd offered to drive me to the airport, but he wouldn't stop needling me about my choices.

"Seems like you just got here and now you're going back," he said.

"I have to work, Dad." I was hungover from going out with high school buddies the night before and antsy to get back. At least one of my rivals had been working through the holiday, so my voice was chock full of condescension.

"Life's not just about work."

My dad's irritatingly patronizing tone poked the bear that was my big fat ego. Yet I couldn't look at him as I lit into him. "*You* work all the time—all of you do. You people don't talk about anything else. I don't even know who or what you're talking about half the time. It's like I'm not a part of the family anymore."

"You're the one who left." The accusation made me wonder if it was how he'd always felt, if he'd just been humoring me. If his so-called support had a time limit. "You can come back anytime, join the family business."

"I can't if I want to have a career in television." My eyeroll was probably epic, and I'm sure I huffed out a ridiculously superior sigh. But then he spat out the thing that pierced my heart.

"I regret the day I gave you that camera."

And he just kept twisting it.

"You're living in an apartment with I don't know how many other guys when you could work for us and have your own house down here. You could make commercials for us. Start your own family. Be a part of this family. You've been gone so long people forget we have a youngest son, and I'm wondering too."

I couldn't speak.

"I'm sorry if what we built isn't enough for you."

"Well, I'm sorry if what I've worked so hard for isn't enough for you," I finally said.

"But what has it gotten you? You're nowhere near doing what you want. You're just spinning your wheels up there, wasting time and money."

I was done. "You know what, you don't have to drive me to the airport. I'll just take a cab."

The last words I ever said to my dad were "I don't need anything from you."

BELLA

I'm high on hope by the time I reconnect with Henry in midtown and sign new documents proffered by his friend Joe, which, miraculously, both free and protect me.

"Something that should've happened the first time around," Joe says with a rueful nod.

As I shake his hand, I say, "Good to know that Shakespeare wasn't right about all the lawyers." It's clear that he doesn't get the reference, so I add, "In one of the *Henry* plays, ironically, a character declares, 'The first thing we do, let's kill all the lawyers.'"

Thankfully, Joe laughs and wishes us well.

As promised, Henry has checked out of the hotel and loaded up the car, so we're on the road to Boston in time to make it back to GBH before the end of the day. My voice fills the car as I catch him up on what happened this morning, both with Nancy and my dad. It's not until we cross into Connecticut that I notice Henry hasn't contributed much to the conversation.

"Did something happen this morning?"

A pained expression crosses his face. When he doesn't answer, I ask, "Did you run into an old colleague at the studio?" My heart thuds in panic. "Did they offer you a job? Are you going back there?"

Half surprised, half angry, he demands, "Do you really think I'd do that?"

I sink into my seat. "Well, I don't know. I mean, it could be tempting."

"You think I'd just up and leave Lilah, right when we've begun to connect? Do you really think that little of my ability to be a father?"

My hand reaches for him, even as my body shrinks away. My voice, thankfully, has the sense to apologize. "I'm sorry. It's a bad habit... to assume that I'll—we'll—get abandoned."

He doesn't shrug off my hand. Nodding, he says, "I know. I'm just... I can't stop thinking about my dad."

Rubbing my hand up and down his upper arm, I keep my mouth shut to give him space to continue.

"I just miss him," he says, his voice ragged. "And I wish I had the chance to make things right. Like you did."

"I'm sorry," I whisper. "That must feel terrible."

When he glances over at me briefly, he's tortured but determined. "I need you to have faith in me. I need you to believe that I won't do the same to Lilah."

Stroking the side of his face from his cheekbone to his soft beard, I whisper, "I'm going to fuck up, Hal. Parents do. But we'll work together, and we'll do our best. That's all we can hope for."

Leaning into my palm, he just nods. My heart breaks for him.

And falls even further for him.

⁙

WHEN WE STOP to get gas halfway back to Boston, I need to pee no matter how disgusting the bathroom. It's not as bad as it could be, but I get through the process as quickly as possible anyway.

After I wash my hands, I pause to fix my ponytail, and my gaze is caught by my reflection in the wavy metallic surface of this restroom's excuse for a mirror. Before we left Nancy's this morning, she'd flipped through a file box and pulled out two photos. It seemed to pain her to give them up, especially since I'd refused to return the others, but when she handed them over, she said, "It's important to hang on to your memories."

I've been staring at those photos for the past half hour. One is from my first day on the set of *As the Earth Revolves*. In it, I'm still

Izzy, braids and all, ready to conquer the world. The other was taken right after they cut my hair for the role of Quinn. I loved that Stevie Nicks-style shag.

Now, even if I squint in the smeared mirror, Izzy and Quinn don't magically appear to give me sage advice or even terrible advice. But when I turn my head from side to side, I can see them both in my profile. Maybe it's time that I follow Jess's example and find a therapist to help me integrate my past with my present. I could also stand to work through some of my fears around being an addict.

Meanwhile, the voices in my head may have faded over the past weeks, but I can still meet life with Izzy's drive and optimism, even while Quinn's world-weary cynicism keeps it all real. I can be silly—even if there's no way I can still do a back walkover—but I can also have sex with the man I love that's hotter than anything any soap writer could even imagine.

This trip to New York closed the book on two major storylines in my life, either of which could've ended tragically. But my dad didn't abandon me; he was just doing his best to deal with the shitty hand he was dealt in life. And because of Henry and his friend Joe, I'm free to own, and maybe even share, my biggest secret.

Well, not the biggest. I'm grateful that Nancy never found out about Lilah—or maybe just wasn't interested. I guess that's the other thread that's no longer hanging. My secret baby has a dad. He loves me.

And I think that maybe it's time I own up to loving him, too.

HENRY

As Bella slips back into the passenger seat and clicks the seatbelt, she's subdued, but not like she's upset. Without planning to, I take her hand and kiss her knuckles.

"I love you, you know," I say, even as the skin around her eyes tightens.

"You don't have to keep saying it."

"Can't help it." After giving her hand another kiss, I put the truck in gear.

She's quiet for a bit, and my mind drifts to Lilah and Ribsy and the work we have to get back to. When she eventually says something, she's so quiet I don't quite hear her. "Sorry, what?"

She shifts in her seat to face me. "I said, when you got on the phone to Joe—back in your office at GBH—were you calling him because you wanted to prove to me that you love me?"

"Nope." This I am clear on. "I did it *because* I love you. If I can help the people I love in any way, why not do it?" I take her hand again and give it a squeeze. "I know I should ask first. I can work on that." I shoot her a smile. "But you might have to remind me."

She takes my hand in both of hers and holds on tight. "Okay, then. Well, this is kind of the same."

When she doesn't go on, I ask, "The same as…?"

"Well, saying the L-word isn't easy for me. I know my parents love me, but it's not something they ever said aloud. I know what I feel for Lilah is one kind of love, and what I feel for my friend Jess is another kind of love. I'm starting to get that what I feel for you might be yet another kind of love."

I'm afraid if I look at her I'll either run us off the road or shut her down, so I hold my breath and nod.

"It's a connection that we've had since the moment we met, but it's more than that," she says softly, almost to herself. "Every new thing I learn about you makes me want to know more. I admire your work ethic and your smarts, your willingness to put it all out there, to take risks. Most important, I think, is that I trust you. Trust you enough to rely on you, depend on you, without feeling… I don't know, obsessed or overwhelmed by these feelings. I used to think that love was supposed to feel like a drug that I couldn't stop, and that scared me."

She shifts in her seat before continuing. "After you left, the night we met?"

I nod, and when I glance at her briefly and see her fingers

clenched tightly in her lap, I have to hang on tight to the steering wheel to keep from reaching out to her.

"I thought I was fine with it—with you just taking off. But when I got back to Boston, I couldn't focus. I couldn't stop thinking about you, fantasizing about a life with you." She shakes her head. "I'd never felt that way before. But when I figured out I was pregnant, I convinced myself that what I felt for you was all about hormones, like some elemental need to be with the baby's father."

She takes in a deep breath, then lets it out again before continuing. "Since I couldn't find you, I made myself forget about you, which worked just fine. Until you came back."

When she holds out her hand, I don't hesitate, I grab it like it's a lifeline. Because it sure does feel like one. "Like you said a while ago, what I feel when I'm with you is just... like I'm home. So," she says, pausing to take another deep breath, "would you like to move in with Lilah and me? In a house that we find together?"

The smile stretching my lips is almost too big for my face, and there's a lump in my throat that may make me sound like a sap, but I don't care. "Yes. Yes, Bella, I would love to move in with you and Lilah."

When I risk a glance in her direction, I'm overjoyed to see that her smile mirrors mine. Still, I have to ask, "Ribsy too?"

She laughs. "Ribsy too. And the cats. I guess we'll just have to find a place big enough for us all."

Chapter 24

"Veteran daytime star Layla Robins reflects on her career shift to independent films: 'When I started out, I was just too interested in pleasing other people, in trying to be everything they wanted me to be. It's a common problem with people who start on camera as youngsters! For the first time in my life, I'm faced with growing up. There's more to life than work!'" *Soap Chat*, August 1989

BELLA

It's been a long time since I've sat in a chair bathed in the hot lights of a television studio, but it's been even longer since I appeared on this side of the camera as myself. It's slightly terrifying to be here without the armor of a character to play and someone else's words to speak, but it's exhilarating too.

When we returned from New York, I met with Carol and told her that I wanted—needed—to share my story. She was hesitant at first, but after we went over the pros and cons, she agreed that if a story about me being an addict were to come out, it'd be better for me to tell it. We followed that up with a meeting with the *Boom* cast parents and then with the executive producer of WGBH's news programs, and the plan for this evening's taped interview was quickly put in place.

I did a pre-interview with the show's host, so I'm prepared for her first question. "What made you want to tell your story, Ms. York?"

"Well, it wasn't an easy decision." I'm sweating like crazy under the light cardigan I'm wearing, and I'm really hoping that it doesn't show on camera. Or maybe it should. Maybe it should be clear how difficult this is. "I lived a little too much of my life in the public eye as a teen and young adult. Back here in Boston, I've done the opposite, keeping a very low profile, because until recently I was kept from speaking about my experiences working as a child actor due to an agreement my parents and I signed. Now that I've been freed from that, I want to tell my story in the hope that others might avoid the pitfalls I blundered into, whether they are a performer or not."

The host nods, thanking me, and then speaks directly to the camera. "We're taking a different approach for this in-depth interview." Standing, she gestures off-stage. "I'd like to introduce the investigators who will take my place tonight."

Jared and Tara look a little nervous as they join us on the set. After introducing them, the host leaves us, and the kids take her place. When the producers pitched this idea, I was concerned that it'd seem like a blatant plug for *Boom*, which premieres next week. It may end up being that, but I'm now convinced that answering these teens' questions directly is the best way to address my mistakes in a way that could prevent others from following in my footsteps.

Still, when Tara asks her first question, my mouth's suddenly so dry that I'm not sure I can get the next words out. I've never had stage fright, but this is different. I take a sip of water, and then surreptitiously seek out Henry, who promised to stand stage left of Camera A. Just a glance at him helps me get back on track.

"Shortly after my first season as a cast member on *Boom*, I signed with an agent and worked as an actor in New York. This was unusual among my peers, and in fact, the next year WGBH included language in the contracts that prevented cast members from pursuing a career on camera for at least two years, which I believe was a smart move."

"Why do you think that?" Jared asks.

"As I said, after I left *Boom*, a few agents approached my parents about representing me as an actor. They said no at first, but I pushed until my parents relented. My father and I moved to New York. I was extremely lucky, but to be honest, I also worked hard. I took acting classes, and I did a correspondence course to graduate high school."

"What was the problem, then?" Tara asks.

"Well, when I booked the soap, I thought I'd achieved my dream. But with that success came pressure and an entrée into an adult world that I wasn't ready for. I attended events and parties where I was treated like an adult when I was still a teenager. As a result, I began drinking alcohol well before it was legal for me to. This became habitual. When I'd show up to the set tired after a long night out, there always seemed to be someone around with a pill that'd help me get through the day."

"Why did you take the pills? Didn't you know they were bad for you?" Jared asks.

"I saw other people taking them and because I trusted the adults who gave them to me, I didn't think they'd hurt me. I didn't know any better."

I hold up a hand. "I want to be clear. I'm not blaming anyone but myself. At every step of the way, every drink I took, every pill I popped, I made the choice myself."

"Did you get in trouble?" Tara asks.

"I got away with it for a long time, but when I lost weight to the point that it showed, people noticed. My agent and my parents met with the executives at the network, and they decided that I'd go away and get clean but we'd keep it all hush-hush. They didn't want to look bad because they'd let things go so far with a minor under their wing. Meanwhile, since my character was fighting cancer, they'd float rumors and let everyone believe that I was fighting cancer."

"You lied?" Tara asks, scandalized.

I nod. "I did. And I feel terrible about that, but that's one reason why I wanted to tell my story today."

I make myself look directly at the camera. Picturing the piles of cards and presents I received, my face burns with shame. "To each and every person that sent me get well wishes or even worried about my health, I apologize. I regret going along with that deception almost more than anything."

Turning back to Jared and Tara, I continue. "At the same time, I want people to understand that I was fighting a deadly disease. It wasn't leukemia; it was addiction. It took many months in rehab, but I did finally beat it. I came home and, thankfully, have been healthy ever since."

"Do you wish that you hadn't gone to New York and acted on TV?" Jared asks.

"That's a good question. I want to say yes, but that's not very useful."

"Why not?" Tara asks.

"Partly because I can't change the past, but also because I wouldn't be who I am or have the people in my life that I do today." I catch Henry's eye again, hoping that he knows I'm talking about him —and Lilah. "What I'll say is I'm glad that actor unions are more careful with children on sets these days. Still, there may be people who will offer you drugs and alcohol, no matter where you are. No matter how fun or harmless it may seem to take a drink or a pill, it's a dangerous path. It can be deadly. I was lucky, but I did have to fight for my life."

As planned, I wrap it up by speaking directly to the camera. "If you're already on that path—no matter what your age—and you feel out of control or like you have nowhere to turn or no one to help you, I hope you'll take advantage of the services listed on the screen. There are professionals who won't judge you, who understand that addiction is a terrible disease, and who will help save your life too."

HENRY

The day after Bella does the interview, she and I drive into work together for the first time. We're still looking for an apartment to move into, so for now we're not getting to spend the night together as much as I'd like. I do go over and have breakfast with my girls every morning, though.

As we pull into a parking space, Bella says, "I think it's time we tell everyone."

"Tell everyone?" I'm not sure which of the many secrets she's talking about at this point. "You laid your soul bare on national TV last night."

She takes my hand, and her palm is damp. "At the production meeting, I think we should just give everyone the Cliff's Notes version of our history together. I don't want to hide anything anymore."

"If you're sure, then, sure." I kiss her knuckles. "You get the ball rolling, and I fill in the details?"

That gets a smile out of her. "Seems to work for us."

Half an hour later, we walk into the conference room hand in hand. Carol raises a brow but doesn't comment. James doesn't notice, but the girls do. We're the last to arrive, so after I pull out a chair for Bella, she sits and clears her throat.

"May I make an announcement before the meeting begins?"

"There's more?" Tim asks.

"Shut up, Tim," Keeley says. "Bella's been through a lot."

"It's okay," Bella says. "I don't want to take up any more work time than necessary, but we also wanted to make a couple of things clear so our relationship won't be a distraction."

This gets James's brows up.

I catch Bella's eye, and when she nods, I jump in. "Let me tell you a story—"

When Carol interjects, "We do have an agenda to get through," I add, "A short story."

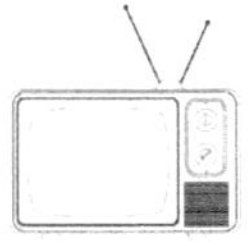

Chapter 25

"Ginger East (Luellen on *Weeks of our Lives*) is doing the steady scene with a ruggedly handsome gentleman named Warren Hall. Sources tell us they're making all kinds of plans together. Ginger may even be buying a weekend cottage in the country with her beau. Can the pair be thinking about middle-aisling it?" *Soap Chat*, September 1989

HENRY

The Friday night of Labor Day weekend, I'm in my favorite place in the world surrounded by my favorite people in the world—toes in the sand, kicking back in a beach chair, Tarheel baseball cap on my head, and an RC Cola in my hand. On my right, the woman I'm meant to spend my life with. On my left, my twin sister. In front of us, my little girl plays in the sand with her cousins. The kids range from three to ten, but they all get along. I'm sure it didn't hurt that the first thing everyone did was throw her a belated birthday party, showering her with presents and serving her favorite flavor of cake. And Chinese food. (My mom knows how to do her research.) Ribsy's even relaxing on a blanket under an umbrella, helping to keep an eye on the children.

My family has been going to Carolina Beach for Labor Day weekend since we were kids. My aunts and uncles and my parents would rent houses next to each other, and we'd spend the long weekend swimming, sunning, eating, and playing games. It's tricky to find enough houses now that the family has expanded, but somehow, we managed to squeeze in last minute. We're resting up for pre-dinner bocce after a rousing game of Nerf football. I was a little worried that a bookish girl like Lilah would shrink away from sports, but she's jumped in on everything.

When my mom asks Bella for a book recommendation and the two scoot their chairs together for the discussion, my sister pokes me in the arm. "Ow."

She rolls her eyes. "Don't be a wuss."

"Don't poke me. Just say my name like a normal person if you want my attention."

She sticks her tongue out at me, but then she grins. Pointing at Bella, she whispers, "I approve."

My brows go up, but I just waiting for the punchline.

"I mean it, Corny." She jostles my knee. "She brought my brother back."

I think I know what she means, but that doesn't mean I'm going to stop messing with her. "We're not moving to North Carolina, you know. We're just here on vacation."

Shaking her head, her expression shifts to mock pity. "So sad they dropped you on your head when you were born in the effort to get the best baby out." Leaning closer, she whispers, "What I meant was you're yourself again. I haven't seen you laugh this much since…"

"Since dad died?" I finish the sentence when she doesn't.

She takes in a breath but pauses for a moment to think before continuing. "No, since you moved to New York. You got all intense those two years, like you were trying to be someone you're not. Whatever you're doing now suits you."

When I waggle my brows, she rolls her eyes. Again. "I didn't say *who* you're doing, you horndog. I mean your work." She lifts a finger.

"But speaking of that, when are you guys going to get pregnant again? Because this time I want our kids' ages to line up."

Before I can respond to this, a tussle breaks out between a couple of the bigger boys. I'm on my feet, ready to wring their necks before they hurt my little girl, but Bella gets there first. She says something to the boys and then the rest of the kids, and they all follow her down the beach a bit, where she huddles with them for a few minutes. Then, she breaks away, moving in a wavy pattern across the sand. The kids follow, but they aren't in a straight line, more of a clump. Suddenly, one of the kids is leading instead of Bella. She doesn't seem upset about it. Instead, the look on her face is one of childlike delight. Another takes over, and the group zigs and zags over the sand, through the surf, and even around a couple of teens sunning on a blanket.

It's almost a piece of performance art: oddly beautiful, even moving, and I reach for my camcorder—not as high-quality as the Super 8 film camera I still own, but more convenient to shoot vacation video with. I line up a shot I like, capturing a random guy joining the group for a few moments before continuing on down the beach with his pals. I stand, intending to get closer to the water to change up the camera's perspective, but something has me hesitating.

For the first time in a long time, my desire to be a part of what's happening is greater than my desire to record it. So I hand the camera off to my sister.

Growling, "Don't drop it in the sand," I jog over to the kids and Bella and slip into the group.

No one objects to grumpy old Uncle Henry joining in. Instead, Bella shoots me a welcoming smile, but I can't linger on it. The bodies around me are sweaty in the hot sun, but the energy doesn't flag and I have to pay attention to follow the shifts of leadership. When one kid challenges the group's connection by breaking off suddenly, my body follows the group's lightning shift in direction before my mind can catch up, and that's when I feel it. Pure joy, like I haven't felt since I was a kid.

When the group mind decides to fling itself into the ocean, the spell breaks. Some kids grab boogie boards, others—including Lilah—head back to the shade under the umbrellas.

Bella laughs when a wave knocks us both in the back, and I grab her hand as we tumble through the surf toward shore. "What was that?" I ask softly.

Her grin wide, she looks like the girl I first fell for so long ago onscreen, in my living room. "That was a game we played on *Boom*."

"Is it called school of fish?"

"It is," she says, her voice high and light. "How did you know?"

I shake my head. "That's just exactly what you all looked like."

Nodding, she adds, "I've played it in acting classes too, but it was never quite like that."

"Magical?" I ask.

"Yeah, like this whole weekend." Turning back to look over the horizon, she lets out a deep sigh that's full of both relief and weariness. "I needed this."

It's been a rollercoaster of a few weeks. We found a great townhouse to rent but moving out of the apartment was still tough on Lilah. *Boom*'s ratings are great, but the station has received an onslaught of letters in response to Bella's interview, both in protest and support. Thankfully, NBS assigned a PR person to help Bella negotiate the blowback from soap fans, but it's still been a lot for her to deal with.

"We'll get through it," is what I say to her now.

She squeezes my hand and rests her cheek on my shoulder. "Thank you."

"For what?" Putting an arm around her, I revel in the fact that I can do this in public.

"Mostly for sharing your family with me. I've never had this before, so I didn't know what I was missing." She snakes her arm around my waist. "But for everything, really. I couldn't have gotten through this summer without you."

"That's funny. I was about to thank you."

"For what?" When she faces me, there's real confusion in her eyes like she doesn't know how much she's given me.

Taking her other hand, I bring both of them to my lips before whispering, "For bringing me back to life."

Before I can ask an important question, Lilah breaks away from our encampment to run toward the path between the dunes. "Lucy! Ben!"

Shading my eyes with my hand, I find Bella's friends coming down the pathway between the dunes. After my girls hug the newcomers, I shake hands with them. "Nice to see y'all again. I'm so glad you could make it."

When we decided to move in together, Bella called Lucy to book some training time since we had no idea how to make peace between my dog and the bookstore cats. I suggested that maybe the cats would want to stay at the store, but not only did my girls shoot that down, they pointed out that cats in a yarn store would be disastrous. I thought it'd be pretty funny myself, but I knew better than to argue.

Lucy was a pro, and Ribsy is doing a pretty good job of controlling his impulse to chase the cats. I will point out that Desdemona has not once controlled her impulse to scratch my poor guy on the nose, but I guess he'll survive. When we were scheduling our last training session, we discovered that we'd all be on the Carolina coast at the same time. Ben is shooting a new TV show just a few miles away, so we invited the couple to join us for dinner.

"It's so beautiful here," Lucy says, her eyes sweeping the horizon.

"Do you have your suit on?" Bella asks. "The water's super warm. We still have time to swim before dinner, don't we?"

Before I can answer, my mom does. "Always time for another swim."

Moments later, Ben and Lucy have stripped down to their bathing suits and we're all bobbing in salty water that's just a hair cooler than the air temperature—meaning *perfect*. As Bella chats with Ben about some guy named Jay who is down here from Boston too, I play jump-or-dive in the waves with Lilah. My ears prick up, however, when Ben tells Bella that there's a guest-star role that'd be perfect for her. I don't hear what she says in response, but after Lilah jumps on a raft my brother is anchoring for the kids, I swim closer to my other best girl.

When Ben turns to speak to Lucy, I sneak a kiss to Bella's newly freckled shoulder and pull her close so we can float over the waves together. "I couldn't help hearing what Ben said about the role you'd be good for. You know I'd do whatever I could to make it work if you wanted to go for it."

She doesn't reply for a few moments, her gaze over the water. "I don't think I'm interested in returning to that hamster wheel, but I am happy that I could. Not just because you'd help out with Lilah."

A big wave's about to break over us, so after a quick glance to make sure Lilah's okay, I dive under it. After Bella and I pop up together and swipe the water out of our eyes, she adds, "I feel grounded enough to go for a job like that, but I'm just not interested."

We've drifted away from the group, and I decide to seize the opportunity. "Which role would you most like to play next? Sexy young mom, hot TV producer, or"—swimming around so that we're eye to eye, I do my best to keep my voice steady as I ask—"best wife a man could ever have?"

There's a flicker of surprise in her eyes, but she doesn't hesitate to drape her arms around my neck. After she pulls me close until our foreheads touch, she whispers, "All of them. Because I love you, Henry Cornelius Smith."

My lips find hers, and my hands stroke down her sunscreen-slick skin beneath the water. I can't show her exactly how happy she's made me right this second, but I pour all the feeling I can into the kiss.

"Eww! They're smooching!" one of my nephews calls out.

My sister chants that rhyme about kissing and a tree.

I take a breather to yell, "Shush. I'm trying to propose over here!"

That silences Jill, but before I can get back to business, Lilah calls out, "It's okay. Kissing is how they made me."

My childhood crush, my long lost one-night stand, the mama of the best little girl in the world, and my bride-to-be shakes her head.

Laughter dancing in eyes that match the color of the sea surrounding us, she whispers, "Guess it's time to get her some new books."

And then, dear reader, *she* kisses *me*.

Afterword

If you're not quite ready to say goodbye to Bella and Henry, you'll want to get the novella that tells the story of their wedding night and introduces all five characters in my new Carolina Classics series, *I'll Stand By You*. It'll take you from the neon, big-haired 1980's into the boho, laidback 1990's.

You can also get bonus scenes from this, or any of my books, by joining my VIP club at karengrey.com.

If you loved this Boston Classics novel, leaving a review is the absolute best way to support an author. You can leave one wherever you downloaded the book, or on Goodreads or Bookbub.

Also by Karen Grey

What I'm Looking For: *The course of true love never did run smooth*, but in this smart and sexy retro rom-com with a finance-nerd heroine and a drama-geek hero, returns on love can't be measured on the S&P 500.

Forget About Me: An underwear model, a best friend's little sister, and a dog who steals the show make for an unforgettable mix in this bittersweet romantic comedy.

You Spin Me: If two lonely people fall in love over late-night phone calls, will meeting face-to-face make them, or break them? In this heartfelt, slow-burn retro romcom, it may be the end of a decade, but it's the beginning of a love story.

You Get What You Give: When a fiery redhead and the guy she thought was a one night stand turn out to be rivals, his family feud causes shockwaves bigger than the surf stirred up by the latest hurricane.

Hold On To Me: In this slow-burn, boss-assistant, entertainment biz romance, a bad cop movie production chief takes on a sexy assistant who challenges her every assumption.

I Want It That Way: She's a driver to the stars who just wants to get her tubes tied. He's a former child actor who needs to get back behind the wheel. A fake relationship seems like the perfect solution.

When I Come Around: When two besties work together on a movie out of town, a secret friends-with-benefits deal seems like a good idea. Until their friends weigh in.

For Fork's Sake: Grumpy, nerdy soil scientist Sam finds passionate, idealist Diane interviewing his grandma for her YouTube channel. Feathers fly between these farm business rivals!

The Single Dad's Guide to Recreation: He's the new-in-town single dad tasked with cutting costs at Climax Parks & Rec. She's the program director with classes on the chopping block. It should be easier for them to keep their hands off each other.

Acknowledgments

As always, it takes a village to raise a book.

Sarah Pesce of Lopt 'n Cropt again served as my editor and Jax Warren was back to proofread. The book would not exist without their professional services. I had the volunteer assistance from five beta readers for the first time, so I'd like to recognize Anni, Christie, Victoria, Jodi and Liz for taking the time to read the book early. Your encouragement and criticisms were invaluable. (Special brownie points to Liz Taylor for her generous donation to Romancelandia Loves Louisiana, and her name for the bookstore cat, Desdemona.)

Research! Many articles on the history of television were consumed, as well as a multitude of TV and soap opera magazines from the late 70's and early 80's, but a handful of people took the time to share their experiences working on the real life PBS show, *Zoom*. I so appreciate them for letting me steal their memories. Much gratitude goes to cast members Donna Moore, Bernadette Yao and director/producer James "Don't Call Me Jim" Fields.

I am so grateful for all my friends (new and old, ones I see in person and ones I only see virtually) for their support of me personally and of my writing process. Finally, having my husband in my corner and around to ask random questions about TV production was inestimably helpful.

About the Author

KAREN GREY is a *USA Today* bestselling and award-winning author of vintage romantic comedies with smart heroines and hunky heroes. Drawing on a long career as a performer, her retro 80's and 90's romances are populated with characters working both on- and off-stage in theater, TV and film. When not reading or writing, she's lounging at the beach or hiking in the mountains. Or dreaming about both with an IPA in hand and a dog or a cat nearby.

(Author photo: Celestial Studios)

For the latest news and bonus materials, join her free VIP club at:
followkarengrey.com

facebook.com/karengreyauthor

instagram.com/karengreyauthor

goodreads.com/karen_grey

bookbub.com/profile/karen-grey

tiktok.com/@karengreyauthor